Багряна —
'89

CLARA

Thirteen Short Stories and a Novel

CLARA

Thirteen Short Stories and a Novel
by LUISA VALENZUELA
Translated by Hortense Carpentier and J. Jorge Castello

Harcourt   Brace   Jovanovich   **HBJ**   *New York and London*

Printed in the United States of America

Library of Congress Cataloging in Publication Data

Valenzuela, Luisa, 1938-
    Clara: thirteen short stories and a novel.

    CONTENTS: The heretics: Nihil obstat. The door.
Trial of the Virgin. City of the unknown.
The minstrels. The son of Kermaria. [etc.]
    I. Title.
PZ4.V155Cl   [PQ7798.32.A48]   863   75–42311
ISBN 0–15–118095–4

BCDE

Contents

THE HERETICS

Nihil Obstat

As you can imagine, I'm seeking total absolution of my sins. That's not something new. No, it's been that way with me since I was a boy, since I was eleven and robbed a cap full of coins from a blind beggar. I did it so I could buy myself a medal, and of course I had figured things out very carefully: the medal had the Sacred Heart on one side, and on the other an inscription offering nine hundred days of indulgence to anyone who said an Our Father before the image. If my calculations were right, four Our Fathers was enough to get Heaven to forgive me for the theft. The time left over turned out to be clear profit: nine hundred days in itself isn't an eternity, but a series of nine hundred days, one after another, adds up to a holiday in Paradise. Now, that's a pleasure worth contemplating.

As for having a good time after death—don't tell me it's a joke to have to walk through this God's earth burdened with gnawing sins and guilt hanging over you, weighing you down if they can be absolved so easily.

Also, I thought about the wafers, which were terrific while they lasted. Let me tell you that I, Juan Lucas, named after two evangelists, as is proper, attended Mass at six o'clock every morning to take Communion. By making a little effort to behave myself, more or less, and by going to a different church each time, I could make one confession last me all week. Seven days of getting up at dawn left me with a crop of six sacred wafers that I could keep in reserve against hard times. I stored them in a carved wooden box on which I had pasted an image of Saint Inez and which I purified with holy water from one of the several bottles I keep around. The most critical moment came when I had to slip the wafer out of my mouth after Communion, but if I settled in the darkest corner in the church, it was easy. Even the pious old women were half asleep at that hour. They didn't realize that, a few feet away, they had a saint, and that

3

I was that saint, denying myself the responsibility for even the least offensive of my most delicious sins.

Generally, my stock of sacred wafers was used up during summer vacation, what with the temptation at the beaches with girls in bathing suits and the wafers I sold to friends who wanted to redeem themselves once and for all. As you can see, I've spread the light among my friends, even though some of them may not have deserved it.

My self-Communion was a simple, but devout, ceremony. At night, after a wild spree, I would bless the wafer again and administer it to myself, celebrating my own purity. It was the perfect absolution, without all the church rigmarole that makes you lose so many good hours at the beach. Besides, going to sleep with a bad conscience upset me a lot, as if I hadn't brushed my teeth. Understand what I mean?

Last year I met Matías. Frankly, I'm a healthy, happy boy, as you can see, at peace with the Creator at all times. Matías, on the other hand, is a tragic one: gloomy, always dressed in black, always frowning. At first I thought that perhaps that kind of behavior led to salvation, and I began to imitate him; I dressed in black and I stopped laughing. At night we walked the dark streets and he would talk to me.

"The path to God is for the chosen. Torturing yourself won't amount to anything if you're not one of us. Kneel down, you despicable worm, and pray."

My manner of praying, of kneeling, and of being a despicable worm, persuaded him that I was indeed one of them.

"Tomorrow the grand penitence begins," he said to me one day. "We will fast for three days, we will live only on bread and water, in absolute silence and in deepest darkness."

The whole thing was beginning to look ugly to me, but I took heart and asked him, "How many days of indulgence do you think you'll earn with all that sacrifice?"

Nihil Obstat

"You're a worm, no doubt about it. I knew it. A perfect mercenary, selfish. And to make matters worse, you're not seeking the benefits of this world, but of the other, which is more serious. You know how God punishes the greedy and the arrogant."

He stared at me with loathing for a long time, and then added, "But I will save your soul. Save it simply for your own good, and not to find my salvation in you, as you would do in my place."

He rolled up the sleeves of the habit he wore when he was sure he wouldn't be seen by anyone who knew him as a bank clerk, and he shouted, "I'm going to tear that lust out of you for all eternity, even if it means tearing your skin into shreds!"

He grabbed the whip he had hanging in what he called his "gaucho corner" and began to whip me furiously. I suppose he did it for my own good, as he said, but I assure you I was happy he hadn't decided to use spurs or a branding iron instead. My back turned all purple, but he didn't stop until his arm grew tired. I can't see why my penitence has to be in direct ratio with the endurance of his biceps. It's unfair: there are days when he isn't so strict and I scarcely have to atone for anything. And the blows, as you can well imagine, don't add up like wafers.

The fasting? Oh, yes, of course we did that. As far as the darkness was concerned, it was deep and total only from dusk to dawn, from the time the bright neon signs outside the window were turned off until the first rays of sunlight filtered through the blinds. You know how these modern apartments are, everything comes in: noise, smells, lights. The flashing reds and greens from the neon sign gave Matías a devil's face that puffed up and shrank as he ate the dry bread. Personally, I wasn't too excited; I don't believe that's any way to achieve saintliness. I prefer simpler things. Deeper. Blessed things. At least with the whippings there was pain, and I could believe something was happening. But not eating, and sitting in the dark, and hardly speaking. That can't redeem anyone. It's too boring.

"We have to sleep in one cot to make sure we suffer from discomfort even in our sleep," said Matías.

In reply, I suggested that we sleep on the floor. "It's hard and very uncomfortable and at least we won't have to squeeze together in this heat."

"No. We must be up against each other, pressed tightly together so our vital force doesn't escape us. We must unite our souls. We must conserve the spirit that eludes us so easily when it is weak. Embrace me, brother."

As far as I'm concerned, no one will ever get me with that story again. Matías did what he could, of course, even to the point where he wanted to kiss me on the mouth to infuse a little of his saintliness into me. It didn't do anything for me, though, all that sacrificing on his part. In the book where I keep an account of the pardon time earned, I could only record three years, one for each day we spent penned up together. And, as you know, three years of Paradise in the sum of eternity isn't very much.

It was at that time that Adela came along, a splendid girl but very earthy, very different from Matías. She never wanted to go to Mass with me, not even to confession. I tried to persuade her to swallow one of my wafers, but she laughed at me. She came to my house often, stayed a little while, and *whack!* we would commit the sin of the flesh. She had soft skin. And it was warm, always warm and vibrant. I tried to explain it to Matías: I told him that when I had her in my bed, so blond, such clear eyes, I imagined she was an angel. Nevertheless, Matías answered: "An angel? She's a devil! You must leave this woman who is Satan incarnate, this serpent who puts the apple in your hands and will not stop until she sees you dragging yourself through every hell."

Nihil Obstat

"No," I said, defending her. "Adela is a good girl. You can't talk that way about her. She doesn't hurt anyone, and she makes me happy."

"Lust!" he roared, until at last I realized that he was right. But I can't do anything else, even though at times I think it's wrong. It seems most wrong when Adela comes to knock at Matías's door and calls after me like a lunatic. At those times, Matías fiercely defends me; he throws her out, clawing at her, and then comes into the bedroom to quiet me and to tell me not to worry.

But I am worried, Father, and that's why I want you to tell me: how much time in Paradise can I add in the book for having given up Adela so much against my wishes?

The Door

The first days of July brought cold winds and the ominous threat of a harsh winter to Santiago del Estero. A mass of gray dust floated in the air, and each gust seemed to bend the withered trees to the breaking point. Only the tall cactuses maintained their spiny, uniform profiles erect against the hurricane, until they also fell, just to demonstrate how hollow they were inside, how empty was their show of strength. The white dust had bleached the landscape. The cold that slid through the skeletons of dead animals was made more unbearable by the sound of splitting canvas and the crackling thorny bushes.

Inside the hut, the wind raced mercilessly, as if across an open field. It didn't help to shut the carved door. The straw roof, the walls of tin and canvas, were poor protection. Huddled around a dying fire, Orosmán, Belisaria, the eight children, and the grandmother sought warmth from each other rather than from the smoldering coals. The fourteen-month-old baby cried in the crate that served as a crib, and Belisaria asked herself what they would do with the newborn when it arrived. From the depths of the silence, she heard the voice of her oldest child, Orestes:

"We can't go on like this, Papa. Let's go to Tucumán. . . ."

"To Tucumán, to Tucumán," the children chorused.

"They say there are lights in the city. And the houses are tall and strong; no wind runs through them."

And Orestes again:

"Don Zoilo says we'll find work there. They need many hands for the sugar. He says there's a lot of money."

"Papa, Don Zoilo went to the sugar harvest last year. He says that now he's too old to go back and that he'll sell you his cart."

"Orestes says we can exchange it for the goats and the two sheep. We won't need them there."

Orosmán protested, "How are we going to go, with Mama the way she is, eh?"

Belisaria paid no attention. "I'll go just the same."

"But Grandmother is old now."

"I also want to get warm, I want to be comfortable in my old age."

That night sleep came much easier to the family in the hut, with hope covering them like a shawl.

The following morning they were bursting with activity. First the discussion with Don Zoilo, who, in addition to the goats and the two sheep, wanted their door as well, an impossible demand. To part with the door was to betray all tradition. The door had five devils carved on it, and an angel above to frighten them. Actually, the angel looked more devilish than the devil himself. But that was the fault of Orosmán's grandfather, who had made the door back in the mission without knowing how to carve in wood. Nevertheless, the priests had told him that the door was very beautiful, and they had said, "Let's use it in the chapel." Instead of feeling proud, the grandfather had made off for the country that same night, leading his horse with the door loaded on its back, because he did not want the door to be for God, but for himself and his kin. Among his kin it had remained, and Orosmán would not be the one to exchange it for a miserable roofless cart made from thick tree trunks, not even if it were the best cart in Santiago.

Finally, with the delivery of the animals, the deal was concluded and the cart changed owners. The horses neighed happily under the weight of harnesses that had lain unused in a corner of the hut for five years. The long rawhide laces stroked their flanks to brush away flies, and they felt a new vigor.

Orosmán and the children loaded the sacks of corn, along with everything they could find in the hut. Little by little the cart filled up, until the entire hut was piled there. The burlap walls were used to wrap belongings, and the straw from the roof was stuffed in to fill gaps and to make mattresses. Finally, only two posts remained standing, like a cross above the tomb of the little hut to which they would never return.

Don Zoilo, squatting on the ground and sipping maté, said to them, "Take my advice, go directly to the city. They'll take better care of you there. You'll get better pay. Don't take work in the country, go to the city."

Such were his words of farewell. Orosmán, mounted on the middle horse, cracked the whip, and they were off. On the open road, a cold night caught them by surprise and forced them to halt. They warmed some food on the fire made wispy by the wind, and then slept buried in the cart between bundles and straw. The following morning brought them a little sun, like a promise, and led them to the road that went directly to the city. Behind them was the thorny and dry slope, but the landscape, at each step more arid, refused to change. As the afternoon slipped away, the sky began to take on ugly tones of gray until landscape and sky merged in a haze at the horizon. Night returned to cover them, their hunger, and their cold.

When they began moving again, they could see green at the sides of the road, planted fields: the city was near now. Suddenly a roar jolted them out of their weariness. Another followed, then still another.

"Cannons," said Orestes in a hushed voice. "That's how they told me cannons sound: they make everything tremble."

"Don't talk nonsense, my son. It must be the noise of the big city," and he whipped the horses to quicken the pace.

The road into the city was lined with houses and gardens, and there were swarms of people hurrying toward the center of town. The cart followed the crowd, circled a plaza, then plunged straight ahead through a narrow street. Suddenly, as they turned a corner, they caught sight of a platoon of soldiers and heard a commanding voice give the order to march.

They continued moving ahead. The tall buildings were covered with flags, sky blue and white, and the crowd was getting larger, multiplying itself into all the people in the world who couldn't stop shouting and singing. Cars and surreys pushed the cart toward the main plaza, and Orosmán and his family, bewildered, let themselves be carried along. The tanks advancing toward them only made their frightened eyes grow larger, and to top it off, there was a policeman who shouted, "Keep moving, keep moving, you can't stop here."

The drums of the band were striking an ever faster beat, and the cart was being dragged into the current. A mounted sergeant approached them, shouting, "You can't go through there, don't you see it's forbidden?"

The horses were no longer responding to the reins, the smaller children were crying, buried in the straw. They passed several large posters with a difficult word, SESQUICENTENNIAL, which they couldn't read, and Belisaria began to cry in silence because this was hell and she had to pray to the Little Virgin to get them away from there.

Finally, they found a street that led them away from the plaza, although they had to force their way through the crowd. They passed before a whitewashed house that was at the center of the commotion, with its two windows covered by green grates at either side of the door.

"Look, a door almost as pretty as ours!" shouted one of the children, but nothing could get their attention, not even that flare of lights and the contours of the cathedral that hung in the night like an admonition. In the sky, evil fires were exploding, red and green, and in the brightness their faces seemed to be those of souls in pain.

Like a lost soul, the cart was being dragged through that cyclone of shouts and colors, through the pitching and rolling of the city.

The guns thundered again, the clamor was deafening, and as soon as the horses found themselves in a street free of the encircling hordes of people, they burst into a gallop.

Orosmán couldn't get the horses under control until they reached the open country, where the city was no more than a red stain in the sky, like a sunset. From then on the long, tiring journey went slower, but it never halted. Finally they arrived at the two crossed posts that stood over the place where the hut had been. The cold was crouched there, as if waiting for them. The need for a fire was great, especially after that long hard trip that had lasted a night, a day, and part of another night. A fire was also needed to scare off the souls of the dead, and one of the children groaned, "Burn the door." He had been trying to light some twigs, but got hardly a spark.

"Not the door, no!" Belisaria protested. "It's the only thing we have, it watches over us. If we burn it, for sure a curse will fall on us."

The silence was long and painful.

"A worse curse would be for Grandmother to die of cold," Orosmán concluded.

They took leave of the door with piety and devotion, but the flames grew rapidly, and the devils' faces twisted into grimaces that mocked them, all of them, including the angel.

But they did have the heat, and when Don Zoilo passed by in the morning, the coals were still burning. He was enormously surprised to find that Orosmán, with his wife, his mother, and his children, had returned, and that all were praying at the foot of the wooden cross, the only sign of the hut that remained.

"How come you're back?" he asked them without dismounting. "You're going to have to begin again."

The Door

"Yes," Orosmán answered. "And now we don't even have the door to protect us. But we had to return, even though we may die of cold."

And looking at his hands, he added, "Because when we arrived there, Tucumán was at war."

Trial of the Virgin

to Arturo Cuodrado

"Very pretty and all that, but what has She done for us? Not even a minor miracle. We're fed up, I tell you."

Over his head hung a bloated starfish, its eyes staring out from a tangle of net. His face was ravaged by wind and salt, his hands shapeless from years of tugging at nets.

"A dog's life, I tell you. And that *Temerario* sinking at the entrance to the harbor. We could practically see them drowning, but we couldn't do a thing about it. Of course, it was the boss's fault that Luque went out again. With a storm like that, you can't go out, the *Siempre Lista* crew told him. But Luque wasn't one to lose a good catch of salmon when he'd found it. He thought he was in Her good graces. He kept a picture of the Virgin alongside the helm. But Virgin of Miracles or no Virgin of Miracles, I personally don't think She ever heard Luque.

"She had been brought from Spain, a gift of fishermen of other seas. A pretty statuette, a little sad, with layers of lace that looked like foam. A pretty statuette, and better still, miraculous; anyway, that's what they said. That's why She never lacked a carefully lighted candle, or two, or three. At Her feet She had votive candles in tin cans, more to tempt Her to grant wishes than in gratitude for some cure She hadn't performed—a little like those plaster eggs left in nests to encourage hens to lay more eggs. But this, clearly, wasn't a miracle-laying statuette, although those who brought Her swear to the contrary, and you can't ignore that kind of faith."

At first, the fishermen thought the image would have to be allowed to get used to the place. Ironically, some said that She should be tempted with better bait, but the fishermen shook their heads: the ways of Heaven had nothing to do with the secrets of good fishing.

While they prepared hooks on the long line to catch salmon, or mended the seines, they never stopped thinking of Her, hoping for some miracle. When they returned, their ships loaded to the gunnels, they knew very well that their catch was no miracle at all, but a fulfillment of the law of the sea, in effect long before She had appeared in the village. On the dock, as they flung the salmon through the air onto the truck, they thought to themselves, A true miracle would be finding a good concrete dock under our feet one morning instead of those rotting boards, where any one of us could break a leg on a moonless night.

The women had a more fanciful, although no less selfish, idea of the Virgin's obligations. When the boats were out of port, they gathered around Her, more to envy her fine velvet cloak, the lace trim, and the silver necklaces than to pray for the safe return of their men.

Galloping across the vast desert, the wind came to the melancholy little town and found it empty, the men on the high seas and the women in church: work and faith, the perfect combination to let the wind run unchecked toward the beach and whirl about wildly and play with María, who found it pleasing to amuse herself with the wind, to let it pass between her legs or tangle in her hair or tickle her skin, making her laugh.

"Look at that mad creature, making a fool of herself. She's too old to spend her days collecting shells and running around barefoot."

María never looked enviously at the Virgin's silver necklaces, because she had a long necklace of her own, of snail shells. She never went to church either, and she ignored the women who tried to turn the Virgin against her with stories of María as a new Eve sent to seduce their men or, even worse, a venomous serpent with the body of a woman, ready to spring on the village and cause sin to flow through the village like rich wine. But why would that matter if the women were the beneficiaries of this sin, and if it was their virtue that slipped away through their husbands' splendid nets? Free on the beach, María was the threat that someday would break the long-established order, leaving them out in the cold.

"Little Virgin, saintly figure, give me blue cloth so I can make myself a new dress. Or María will take my Ramón away."

"Oh, Little Virgin, to think that she carries your name! She is the devil itself! Yesterday I saw my husband looking at her. His eyes were shining as they have never shone for me. She has bewitched him!"

The Virgin had a face that seemed to understand everything. And yet, month after month, María continued to run, free and wild, and so did the desire of the men. But why should María want men, when the caresses of the wind were so much softer and asked nothing of her?

As they drank their wine in the café across from the wharfs, the fishermen didn't look at the mouth of the river or keep vigil for the high tide that would permit them to go out. Their eyes were fixed on the spot where, sooner or later, María would pass by, her hair tangled with seaweed.

One day the summer came at last, the sun appeared, the sea paused to take a breath, and the cold wasteland beyond the houses glistened with unexpected tones. The fishermen did not leave port, they stayed in the café, their glasses before them, waiting to see María pass by. The air shimmered, radiant, an omen of important events. As the sun was setting, herding a flock of rosy clouds, María appeared. Her soaked dress outlined her body: she had made friends with the sea in defiance of the wind that had abandoned her. Many pairs of eyes followed her as she walked home, many potential friends who thought they could give her more satisfaction than the wind or the sea. It was a moment of silence, of muted sighs, of unuttered calls. Then they continued drinking as if nothing had happened, and went home with the desire for María pounding in their hearts.

Felipe, who was recently married, found the only flower in the village where it grew, hidden between some rotted boards a few feet from his house. He plucked it for his wife but, after judicious reflection, turned around and went to church to place it at the feet of the Virgin.

"I bring you the only wild flower that has grown in this port. I have never asked you for anything, but now I want María. Give me María, just this once, and I will bring you flowers from the most distant corners."

Felipe was not the only one that night to have the brilliant idea of asking the Virgin for help in getting the virgin. Among the others was Hernán Cavarrubias, carrying his heavy bronze lantern, his treasured possession, under his right arm (his left having been torn off by a winch) to give to the Virgin when he asked Her to make María his. After all, he argued, if we're dealing in miracles, there is no reason a one-armed man should have less luck with a woman than a whole man.

The following morning, the boats left at dawn, filled with hope. When they reached the sand bar, the point of real danger, the fishermen neglected their helms and gazed back at the beach, where the sun had risen and María was bathing naked.

The women went to church a little later that day, carrying gifts along with fervent prayers for the Virgin of Miracles. But they found the altar already covered with offerings. At first they felt hatred and jealousy. The Virgin was monopolizing the generosity of their men. But it didn't take long for them to understand that it couldn't be a mere statue that the men loved so much. The shells, the flower, the ring, and even Hernán Cavarrubias's lantern represented something more: the smell of a female.

They held a long secret meeting in the church, and decided to consult old Raquel and bring her the gifts intended for the Virgin: the old woman was a famous witch, and she could be impartial, for she had no man to lose.

Old Raquel well knew the depth of the human soul. "That woman has addled their brains because she's out of reach. They know that with all their pleas and offerings they'll never have her. They think of nothing else. Dreaming costs nothing, and the grass is always greener in the next man's yard. Wait till she's caught; as soon as one man touches her, the rest won't want her."

"But they don't want to touch her, or by now they would've grabbed her some dark night. The way they've grabbed us. They prefer her the way she is."

"Why do they want to defile her? She doesn't try to tempt them, and she doesn't go after them."

The old woman was thoughtful, her head sunken between her shoulders, hard and black and bulging as an owl's. Finally she spoke.

"It all depends on how hard you work at it. Today is the Day of the Virgin, exactly three years since She came to us. Go make a big celebration, with plenty of wine. We can even have a procession, put the Virgin on an altar at the wharf. Father Antonio never refuses these things. Then choose a man. Point him out to me, and I'll see that he goes after María."

Silently, the women went home and began frying fish cakes and shrimp for the fiesta. Bent over their stoves, they laughed to themselves as they thought about the night, the wine, and the humiliation of María.

In the afternoon they set up tables and benches facing the wharf. They framed the altar with paper flowers and set huge jugs of wine all around. At sunset the boats crossed the sand bar, one behind the other. Farther down the shore, María was playing in the cold waves again, her hair streaming like Medusa's. Not one of them could decide to stop his boat, and they entered the mouth of the harbor in single file. As they sailed in they heard the sounds of Olimpio's accordion. Drawing closer to port, they could see the tables, the oil lamps, the jugs of wine, and the altar. "It's the Day of Our Virgin, the Day of Our Virgin," the inflamed women shouted from the land.

There was a certain tension at the fiesta. The men were thinking about María, who was swimming in the sea bloodied by the setting sun. But with the wine and the pungent smell of salmon roasting on the hot coals, they relaxed. Father Antonio decided the time had come to lead his parishioners to the church.

The Virgin was taken from Her canopy to ride through the village. Dust hardened the lace borders of her gown, while the fishermen intoned songs that they believed were psalms but which sounded more like the woeful ballads of drunken sailors. The procession ended when She was placed in front of the improvised altar.

They lit candles to Her and stood there gazing at Her, as if waiting for the miracle. The women took advantage of the confusion to serve more wine. They began to dance around the tables and on top of the tables, their petticoats whirling furiously. The sober wharfs had never witnessed anything like it, but who could care about traditions when the honor of the village was at stake? Only old Raquel remained at the altar, as if submerged in prayers. Finally she spoke to the women.

"The time has come. Choose your man and I'll do the rest."

"Not my husband," one woman said.

"Not mine either. Nor my father. Nor my brother. Nor my son."

The old woman was angry. "So you made the fiesta in order to throw it away? You must make a sacrifice to the Virgin, and then you'll live in peace."

But the women were stubborn. Raquel walked away mumbling.

"Call Hernán Cavarrubias, who has no wife or mother or daughter. He deserves María," a woman shouted after her. For a brief moment old Raquel was silent. Finally she went looking for Cavarrubias. She told him that she had had a vision: María loved him and was calling him, she was hiding somewhere in the village because her desire made her shy. He must take her by force because that was what she liked.

"It's a miracle. The Virgin has listened to me because I offered Her my lantern," he said. The wine gave him courage, and he ran off to find María and make her his.

With each glass they served, the women spread the news. There was not a man on the wharf who didn't know about Hernán Cavarrubias and who was not consumed by envy. Cavarrubias returned much sooner than expected, defeated.

"María's gone. She isn't at home or on the streets or at the store or on the beach. The earth has swallowed her up."

The men thought that perhaps the sea had swallowed her; it was better that way, because now they could continue to desire her as before. Meanwhile, Cavarrubias was bitterly lamenting his fate, trying to extract some consolation from the Virgin. Suddenly he realized that that it was all Her fault.

"The Virgin is to blame," he shouted. "In spite of the lantern, She made me look bad. She never loved us. We have never gotten anything from Her, have we?"

At the other end of the wharf, the women were whispering, reproaching themselves for having sent the one-armed man instead of one of their own to end the myth of María. Finally one of them lifted her head above the group and spoke out.

"It's not our fault. We asked the Virgin for help and this is what She does. We were only after what was ours, our men wanting us. Nothing that could have offended Her. If She didn't do us the favor, it's because She wanted to humiliate us."

Little by little, a crowd had gathered in front of the Virgin, with the full measure of accumulated grudges and prayers. Someone lowered Her from the altar, and the reproaches were hurled at Her with fury. A judgment was quickly reached, and the penalty executed. Hernán Cavarrubias hurled the first stone.

City of the Unknown

to Juan Goyanarte

When I first heard him sing, I told myself, This man has a voice that could raise the dead, and that one time words didn't fail me.

My life doesn't have much to do with fantasy, not even science fiction. It's made of little things that the gods offer me when I am deserving and which I recognize as different from a million other things. Take pebbles, for example. I know that pebbles are my friends. One day when I was feeling especially clearheaded, I found a pebble shaped like a hen. A while later, I found one that was like a woman with only one breast and a hole for a navel. Unimportant things, of course, compared with my city. I first discovered the city in my dreams; later I looked for it where I had dreamed it, on the other side of the Andes, overlooking the Pacific. It's a city of pointed arches and hard red walls that I thought the mountains had created for me.

He has a voice that could raise the dead, I kept telling myself as I listened to him sing. I knew that, in order to reach him, I had to descend many steps, the same steps as those I descended when I was moved by a dark purpose, like the force that had driven me to that neighborhood of longshoremen and sly prostitutes.

I didn't like looking for him, knowing of his existence, unmasking him. His was the voice of another race, torn from his guts after the third glass of brandy, and only I knew it, although there were other people there, pale and ghostly next to his black animal skin, who listened in an almost reverent silence. I returned twice, three times, always at the fifth stroke of twelve, as he began to sing. I came in time to witness the ritual of patrons putting aside cards and dice and licking their lips in anticipation of his singing. On the third day I decided: I will take him to my city that hangs over the sea. His voice could raise the dead, and my city is full of spirits that dance around me and tell me things each time I arrive from across the mountains.

Only he could raise the dead of my city and enable me to understand that contour of nature which, helped by the wind, imitates the work of men. Those who died there already knew the mystery that hung from the highest peaks, the mystery that kept me awake those lonely nights among the rocks. Year after year, every summer, almost religiously, I'd leave the volcanoes of Copahue to try and solve the secret of my city. Seated at the table in the corner, listening to him sing, I realized that I couldn't do anything without his help.

Why should I let daylight rub out his existence, I thought. And the following morning I returned to the seedy club to ask where I could find him. But there he was, in the same spot as the night before, only with a changed expression. His empty bottle rolled across the floor. Cautiously, I went down the steps and brought a chair to his table. I tried to explain. I talked for an hour, and I didn't succeed in getting so much as a glance from him.

"No one can help but you," I pleaded. "I'm leaving in two weeks. Come with me." All my pleading, and still he didn't lift his eyes, so I left, dragging my feet in despair. As I went out to the street, it occurred to me that perhaps he didn't understand ordinary words and that he could only be reached through some obscure, cabalistic signals. I ran back to see if something could still be done, and I pushed open the swinging door. He looked up, his eyes showing a flicker of understanding, enough to feed my determination. Night after night I got there just as he was beginning to sing. Gradually, I moved out of my corner and into the sad light that encircled him, but he gave no sign of recognition.

The night before my departure I decided to play my last card. I sat at the table in front of him, put my knapsack on the floor beside me, and waited. He seemed asleep. Only when he began to sing did his eyes brighten up.

I need him to revive my dead so I can understand, I kept repeating to myself for strength. Finally, I took the tickets to

Copahue out of my pocket and put them right before his eyes. He looked down and stopped his song abruptly. His silence stirred the quiet. The audience recovered its composure. A man drew his chair close to mine and tried to embrace me. But I only had eyes for the singer. I could see his muscles tense up until his arm shot out like a spring and hit the man's jaw. The man fell, dragging the chair down with him. My singer picked up the tickets and the knapsack with one hand and with the other pushed me across the room and up the stairs.

In the miserable hotel at El Bajo, I discovered that his body had the exact shape I wished for, but he didn't want to have anything to do with mine. Or with my gratitude. The next morning our clumsy trip began, along dusty pampa roads, through mountain paths, nights and days with interminable delays. He traveled silent and erect, seeing nothing, never complaining or showing surprise. He needs liquor, I thought. I'll buy him a few bottles so he'll sing with all his might when we arrive at my city.

As daylight was fading, we arrived at Copahue, the valley of volcanoes, with its hot springs from the bowels of the earth that turned the mountain into hell. We arrived to the smell of sulphur and the sight of eternal snows.

In the hotel it was our custom to sleep in the same bed but not to touch each other. However, that night the temperature fell below zero and he began to shiver under the blankets. I didn't want him to suffer next to me, and almost instinctively I gave him a little of my warmth. Suddenly his arm came alive, each cell in his body came alive, and there was nothing I could do but remain as I was and let the rites be fulfilled.

I woke up late that morning and wanted to feel him close. I reached out across the covers, but I didn't find him. I felt that he had left me forever. Intentions and laws had been violated by an offense to purity, by a yielding to desire, just as we were approaching my city. I dressed as quickly as I could and ran out, heedlessly bucking the wind that pushed me back and made me fall, impervious to the tiny mounds of lava that spurted in my path, burning my feet. The farther I ran, the more he faded from my mind, his arms, his black body. "My dead souls," I screamed, "I am losing my dead."

I was sure I would never see him again, that he had vanished like my breath. But at last I saw him by a lagoon of boiling mud. He was looking at the giant bubbles that swelled and ruptured in deafening bursts. He was cold and shivering, and he seemed mesmerized.

I seized him by the hand like a child and took him across to the other side of the valley, to the Indian market. I bought him a thick poncho, and I laughed to see him so solemn, looking so much like a gaucho. He smiled, and suddenly his face took on the same expression he had when he sang.

We bought food, we hired horses for the following morning, we raced from place to place, hand in hand, arranging the details of our great adventure. I didn't forget the brandy either, but as I was paying for it, I realized I wouldn't have enough money left for the return trip. But at that moment the return trip was unimportant.

At the break of dawn, we left the stone houses and the muddy, red-hot lagoons behind us. We let ourselves be carried through the barren mountain paths, through roads hanging over precipices, onto narrow tree trunks lying across turbulent streams. Only the horses knew the secret of how not to topple over the edge, and they had to be allowed to move ahead unbridled.

At Chanchoco, a small Chilean village of flat-roofed huts and silent Indians, we broke our long journey. But we couldn't rest in that sea of hostile glances. We stayed there only long enough to eat something hot and change horses; then we were on our way again, through the mountains, toward my city, to bring my dead back to life.

City of the Unknown

Up there in the mountains, where the landscape is dreary and oppressive, there is a feeling of lightheadedness, but he felt cold and shook under his poncho. I was beginning to feel sorry that I had brought this man, accustomed to heat and languor, to this climate. But the prospect of unveiling the mystery of my city made me cruel, and I kept moving ahead without looking at him. Every so often I would hand him the bottle, and after a long swig he would seem to revive. In that way we finally reached the large rock corral where I always let the horses free.

We climbed the rugged mountain by foot. He must have known intuitively that we were close, for he began to sing in a low voice, breathless, until at last we reached the caves and high walls of bright earth colors that formed my city over the sea. As always, I was overcome by the strange peace of the place, and I sat next to him on the edge of the precipice, our backs to the waters roaring below. I had to restrain myself to keep from running through the labyrinths, and I remained quiet while he contemplated my city, as if to penetrate its meaning.

He began to sing again, his voice vibrating against the rocks. While the sun was sinking behind the mountains, his song lofted and swelled, invading the dark reaches of the caves. I tried hard not to hear his voice; I wanted to get the message that would come from the dead. His song entered the tunnels, whirled around, and echoed back changed. Suddenly, where the whirlwind should have been, I saw a ghostly light that rose from the earth, a wavering white vapor. In that strange light the mystery would be unraveled, and I held my breath in order not to frighten it away.

I didn't want to look at him, but I prayed for him not to stop singing, because his song would bring me the truth. He kept on singing, louder, deeper, and the ghostly light assumed the shapes that were separating out from the shadows, striving to reach the light of the violet-colored sunset.

At first the shapes seemed nebulous, but then, little by little, they grew more defined, until my expectation turned into terror and I wanted to scream. But I couldn't. I wanted to draw back. But I couldn't. The forms were in front of me, closing in. I expected their souls, but their bodies appeared before me instead, bones with flesh hanging from them, sinister smiles without lips.

"Shut up!" I screamed at him when I recovered my voice, but he didn't hear me and he continued singing while the dead came closer, implacable, swaying to the twisting rhythm of his song.

"Be quiet, be quiet!"

In desperation I covered my eyes, but nothing could stop the forms, and the images slipped through my fingers as they advanced. Only he had the power to make them disappear, if he would stop singing, but he intended to go on. One push would silence him eternally. There was no other choice, and it was so simple. The rocks under him gave way, and he fell into the abyss without a whimper.

The corpses had been snuffed out with the last note of his song. It took me a long time to get over the visceral sensation of horror and loathing they produced in me. But then I realized how alone I was in the night and in the world, and I began to feel all the pain that had been his, the breaking of his dark body. At some time that dark body will soar back up into the mountains—that is, if someone like him, with a voice capable of raising the dead, comes to my city.

I am still waiting.

The Minstrels

"Why do you keep asking what they are called? You already know. I've told you twenty times, letter by letter, syllable by syllable. Why do you ask me again?"

The boy didn't realize that he was torturing her, and he lowered his head, hurt, biting his lips. The pitch-black hair fell over his forehead. He frowned. He didn't want to anger her; their name was not what mattered. What did matter was the word from his mother's lips. When she said it, a small bell-like sound broke loose in her voice, the voice that was sometimes sad but at other times resonated with deep pleasure. Of course, he wasn't going to insist, that wasn't a man's way. Rather it was to pretend indifference. He reached over to pick up a pebble that lay on the ground between the hind legs of the cow, a perfect pebble, the kind that shatters when it is thrown against the hard barn wall. As the boy bent over, the docile cow's tail swatted him in the face, and his mother laughed.

"They were called the Minstrels." The name had burst out of her.

The boy raised his head as soon as she spoke, but it was too late. He could only catch the last notes of her laugh, in which there was neither the pain nor the anguish that he liked to hear behind the gaiety.

There was no one like his mother in the entire village of Bignon. Even though she was poor, people respected her and addressed her as they would any local woman, calling her Jeanne, a peasant's name. He was called Ariel. Ariel loved and hated his name. He repeated it at night when he was alone in his high bed, buried in the thick woolen mattress that swallowed up sounds, or when he walked through the fields during threshing time and saw the men at work in the distance, or when he romped in the fresh sweet-smelling hay. Ariel . . . But when he had to say it in school, when the bigger children taunted him and asked, "What's your name, pretty boy?" and patted his head, expecting his hair to be soft and silky rather than hard and wild as in fact it was, all he could do was turn around and run. From afar he would shout, "Ariel, Ariel," regretting his cowardice.

On those afternoons of flight, he would return to the farm burning with shame. The three miles on foot from the small town of Meslay to Les Maladières were not enough to cool his cheeks. He left the asphalt road reluctantly, and he took no pleasure in slipping down into the muddy path or kicking the fragile pebbles or leaning against the withered apple tree. On those days of shame (shame at not having had the courage to say his name) he didn't greet the neighbors or bend over the duck pond to find the goldfish that lived at the bottom of the grayish-green water. And, finally, when he pushed open the rickety wooden gate at Les Maladières, he did not run to the small barn where his mother usually was milking the cow at that hour of dusk.

On those days she would call him.

"Ariel!"

That call had a dry and special sound; he felt relieved and ran to take refuge in her warm skirt, between her open legs and under the cow's udder. She would hand him his bowl of warm milk, and Ariel was purified as he listened to her sweet voice.

"You have Yves's eyes, blue and deep. Yves was the one who sang happy songs loudly. He shouted them, almost, and I trembled with fear: the Germans might hear him and take all of them away from me. You have the same eyes as Yves. . . . I looked at them a great deal and I wanted to keep him with me."

Mother and son sat silent, surrounded by the warm smell of the barn, buried in their thoughts of Yves, while the cow lowed with impatience.

On other occasions, Jeanne the Strong One (as they called her in the village where she grew up) would tell her son, "You have Antoine's hands . . . long and slender, not pudgy like mine, and he played the mandolin like an angel playing the harp."

Or else, "Your hair is as bristly as those thickets out there, just like Joseph's. . . ."

And Ariel would leap up and shake her arm until it hurt. "No, Mama, no! You told me it was Alexis's hair. Have you forgotten already?"

And Jeanne the Strong One laughed with that delicate and sad laugh he loved so much.

"How could I forget? You're right; Joseph's hair was black too, but soft to the touch. But Alexis's was hard, like yours. I used to laugh because he couldn't comb it. I'll never forget that."

It had all begun on a very clear May morning. Georges Le Gouarnec, her husband, had just gone off to the war. "I see they need drunkards now," Jeanne had said to him in farewell. He walked away and then came back, not to kiss his wife but to put the last two bottles of homemade brandy in his knapsack. He had left her alone on the farm. She did what she could, but the old tractor stayed idle in the shed, she had to hire men to sow and harvest her small farm, and most of the apples rotted on the ground because she couldn't make cider, nor did it interest her. When spring came, and the farm work made too many demands on her, she began to miss her Georges.

Nevertheless, on those May mornings she felt lighthearted and almost ran as she drove the flock of geese to the feeding trough. She would have liked to toss her long-handled pick into the air and dance with her skirts swinging above her rubber boots. The geese cackled as usual, with their beaks pointing to the sky, seemingly in ill humor. She screamed at the men until she saw them coming, singing softly as they walked down the dirt road that went past the duck farm and the neighboring farmhouses.

She could barely hear their song, but Jeanne knew that something sweet was being sung by the way they swayed together, like the poplars in front of the church in the breeze of autumn dusks.

She closed her eyes and counted them as if they were engraved in her memory: there were nine. Impossible. You can't have nine identical human beings. Maybe two, or three at the most; her loneliness had played a nasty trick on her and multiplied the men. She opened her eyes and saw them clearly against the rough wall of the farmhouse. They had stopped singing and stood in a row facing the geese. There were nine, truly, each one different although each back was curved in the same way under the weight of a knapsack.

Jeanne wanted to go closer to them; she felt the heat of the goose feathers against her legs and the heat of the men's stares on her face. It had cost her dearly to walk between the flock of geese, and she didn't dare to look directly into the faces of the strangers as she dried her hands on the kitchen towel that hung from her waist.

At that moment Ariel raised his head. "Is it something new you're remembering, Mama?"

She set aside her memories to return to her son.

"No, not something new. I've told you everything. There's nothing more for me to remember, only to begin again."

"You were thinking about the day they came. . . ."

"That's true."

"And where was I?"

"Still in Heaven. You came down many months later."

"That's why I didn't see them. But are you sure you've told me everything?"

"Very sure."

Not everything. There are things a child of eight cannot be told, even if he has Alexis's hair and Antoine's hands and a voice that promises to be Michel's voice.

Michel was the first, and she had chosen him because he sang better than the rest; he was the soloist, with the deep voice, and when he opened his mouth, everyone else fell silent. Ariel, the voice of Michel. "Someday you will have Michel's voice, my son."

They were fleeing from the war, and they had not come upon a better place to hide than this isolated farm in the middle of the poor and wild land of Brittany. Only one barrel of cider was left in the cellar, and Jeanne the Strong One wanted to cry because Georges Le Gouarnec had gone away without preparing more. On the other hand, when he was there and the whole house was filled with the smell of apples, there was that other smell that came from the loft where he kept the still, that other smell that she hated but which she longed to smell again. Brandy, hundreds of bottles, all of which Georges Le Gouarnec had drunk throughout his life from morning to night, and which Jeanne would have liked to recover now in order to keep with her the nine men who sang songs and told sad stories.

To keep them. The first night was for Michel, she had decided, and for the first time since her husband's departure she returned to the bedroom and to the high, deep bed where she sank in Michel's company. The others installed themselves in two cots and on the dining-room floor.

"What were they called, Mama?"

This time she was caught off guard, and she answered simply, "The Minstrels."

She had already taken the two pails of milk into the house and she was feeding the sow that was about to have piglets. She ordered Ariel to collect the eggs from the henhouse. "Don't break any, like Robert, who always came back with the basket dripping."

Robert had turned out to be the worst of all. He never wanted to pluck the geese or check the motor of the tractor, even though he had been a mechanic at some time in his life. He knew how to tell marvelous stories, though, and he sat at the table with a large bowl of cider cradled in his hands and talked for hours. The others were much more helpful; they helped her kill the hog and make blood sausages and other meats, which later they took with them when they left. Yet, it was Robert's laziness that made Jeanne place all her hopes in him. When he took his turn with her, on the fifth night, she carried the washbowl out to the water pump, where she scrubbed herself in the moonlight. In bed, between the soft quilts, she murmured unfamiliar words to him and lavished new caresses on him, invented for him.

When she got up early the following morning, she looked at his eyes to see if he was going to stay, but he turned over and went back to sleep. When night came, Marcel replaced him in the big bed, and the wheel continued turning.

Jeanne always left her bed in the early hours of morning, and as she gently stepped over the sleeping bodies on the dining-room floor, she wanted to shout at them to stay. Later, she would prepare breakfast; the good smell of onion soup woke them, and she no longer worried whether or not they would leave her, for their voices, their smiles, their jokes were filling her life. And when she served them the soup as they sat at the table on the long, narrow benches, she counted them again to be sure of the figure of her happiness. It was nine.

Now it is one, a young one, huddled next to the fireplace on winter nights. Jeanne would have liked to share her warmth with him, but she, too, feels cold, cold inside. She says to him, "Ariel, sing me a song. . . ."

And Ariel, obedient, sings a song he has learned in school:

Sur le pont d'Avignon
L'on y passe, l'on y danse. . . .

The Minstrels

"No Ariel, not that one; a serious song."

With the best intentions, Ariel changes the rhythm and intones *The Marseillaise*.

At other times, Jeanne the Strong One, dispirited, doesn't want songs. "Ariel, my son, tell me a story," she will say.

Ariel will then tell stories he has learned at school, about bad boys and good boys who come to blows, or stories about dogs and cats and horses. These are the only stories he knows. Sometimes he feels encouraged to talk about the goldfish that live at the bottom of the duck pond with the grayish-green water, the shiny fish that only let themselves be seen by people with good hearts. But he prefers not to think about them too much, since he has never actually seen them himself.

One day each year his mother sits him on her knee and tells him the stories she likes to hear. On that day there is no work except for feeding the animals. Ariel doesn't go to school. It is February twenty-first, his birthday. Jeanne the Strong One sits in her low chair, peeling potatoes, tirelessly recounting the stories that the Minstrels had once told her, cheerful stories of princes and shepherdesses. Sometimes the stories are about orgies with women and wine. She can tell these stories to Ariel in spite of his age because they are so ancient that Ariel will not understand them.

What she cannot tell about are the true nights with the Minstrels, nights changed into words that burn her mouth, words that she would like to spit out. But she must keep them to herself: Ariel is her son, only nine years old today, and a son cannot be told these things.

"Mama, how are children born? Like calves? Do they have a father, like the bull we hired last spring?"

"For children it takes nine months, and they all have a father. No one can be born without a father."

Ariel knew that already, but he wanted to be sure: nine months and nine fathers. When he went to bed, he didn't think about Jeanne's stories. He thought that he was the richest little boy in the world, because in order to have him, his mother had hired nine fathers. Alexis's hair; Antoine's hands; Michel's voice; Yves's eyes . . .

Lying on the cot in the dining room, Jeanne the Strong One was also thinking about Henri. He was the leader, and he was the first one to talk to her when they arrived at Les Maladières.

"We are the Minstrels," he had said by way of introduction. "The government has given us rifles, but we only want to wield our mandolins. We prefer the ring of our own voices to the sound of bullets. If you, dear madame, would be good enough to give us shelter for a few days, we will try not to compromise you. We will head south as soon as the danger has passed."

They stayed nine days and nine nights, and then they left for the south, singing.

"Ariel! You never pay attention. Repeat what I said. Show me where south is." In the middle of the geography class, and without apparent reason, Ariel would begin to cry.

Jeanne no longer cried. Perhaps she had never cried. She did all she could to keep them, but they had gone. The one who returned, finally, was Georges Le Gouarnec, her legitimate husband.

It seems he came back merely to get a double ration of brandy and to insult her because the whole village knew about her secret guests, even though no one had ever seen them. Nine pairs of horns didn't weigh heavily on his alcohol-filled head, but what the inhabitants of Bignon might say, the chance that they might mock him; that he couldn't endure. He mumbled filthy words and spat on his wife's bare feet as she walked in front of him carrying the tub of dirty clothes to the water pump. But Le Gouarnec's hatred brought to life her memories of the other men, and she stood in front of the pump without pumping, her arms at her sides and her eyes full of dreams.

Georges Le Gouarnec allowed the four seasons of the year to pass, one by one, without tending the wheat that was rotting in the fields. He was only biding his time until the apple juice fermented and he could lock himself up in the loft and tangle himself in the pipes of the still. Exactly one year after his return he left again, a little before Ariel's birth. By this time Jeanne no longer needed the stimulus of his hatred to evoke the men who had brought joy into her dull life.

"Mama, which one of them loved dogs?"

Jeanne shook her head. Right now she didn't want to think any more, she didn't want to answer. She would have preferred going to sleep, but she had promised Ariel that she would make plum jam. He watched her, uneasy.

"You've forgotten already, see? I told you that one day you'd forget them and we'd be left without anything. Without them we won't be able to go on living."

Jeanne made a face, but she answered him. "Me, forget? No, it's just that I'm tired."

"Tired of them?"

"Of them, no, my love. Come, let's look at the table where they carved their names."

She passed her hand gently over the table where the names were. Ariel imitated the caress.

The years passed, until one morning Jeanne awoke knowing it was an important day. Ariel was thirteen. Finally she could pour out her heart to him, tell him of her great love for the Minstrels and satisfy the old thirst she had to share the story with someone.

When she walked into the kitchen to light the fire, she found she had to lock her heart away once more: Georges Le Gouarnec had returned after thirteen years of absence, more puffy and red-faced than ever, and he stood facing the oven. When Ariel ran into the kitchen to kiss her, she could only murmur: "Ariel, say hello to your father. . . ." She felt her cheeks burn with shame, sure that Ariel had closed his eyes because he didn't want to see the man.

Georges Le Gouarnec shook him by the shoulders.

"Say hello to your father, stupid!"

Ariel slipped away from the large hand that was clutching him and fled to the fields, burying himself among the thickets.

"I know it isn't him. I know it isn't. The Nine Minstrels are my father, not a fat mean man who smells bad."

Ariel threw himself to the ground, face down, next to the hare's nest he had discovered the day before, and he shut his ears against the old man's shouts. When the stars began to pale in the sky, long after Le Gouarnec had fallen asleep on the thick mattress under the feather quilt, Jeanne the Strong One went to look for her son.

"Mama, Mama, it isn't him, is it?"

"No."

"And you'll never forget them, will you?"

"Never, never."

"Mama," he cried, and his voice rose hoarsely.

She realized that the time had come for Ariel to be like them, to follow his own path now that her bed, the one she had shared with them, was creaking under another weight, ordinary, unpleasant.

At sunrise on the following day, on his way to the farm where he had been hired to do the milking, Ariel threw nine stones into the duck pond, giving each one a name.

While her husband's redundant snoring rocked the house, Jeanne the Strong One leaned over the names on the table and decided to trace the letters and write Ariel the stories the Minstrels had told.

The Minstrels

Ariel wrote her, in turn, that the owner's daughter had gone to Mass in her white dress and that later the dress changed into a pair of wings, taking the owner's daughter to the kingdom of the wild ducks.

Ariel was now telling stories of his own, but Jeanne the Strong One never let him forget the Minstrels; she mentioned them in each of her letters. He didn't realize that the fields grew green, dried and froze, over and over again. He didn't realize that time passed, that three years is almost a lifetime for a boy who had turned thirteen when he left home.

He didn't realize it until that other, hostile letter arrived in a brown envelope reeking of incense. It was from the priest of Bignon. On the envelope it said Ariel Le Gouarnec, not simply Ariel, and he knew it was bad news.

Jeanne the Strong One was dying. Ariel couldn't do anything to stop it, only try to make her say the word that would help her recover part of her strength.

She lay in bed, her hand suddenly fragile, lost in the feather quilt. Ariel squeezed the hand he had known when it was hard and alive.

"Mama, tell me what they were called. . . ."

From the dining room came Le Gouarnec's voice, cracking the silence like a whip. "I never get a greeting or a look from you. Me, your own father. You're a son of a bitch, that's for sure, but I am your father, after all, your poor old father . . ." And the syllables ran together like the brandy spilling over the names on the table.

In the bedroom Ariel tired to control himself, but he shook her hand more furiously each time; he shook her arms, her shoulders.

"Mama, tell me about them. What are they called?"

For an instant he saw a flash of pain in her eyes. He wanted to leave her in peace, he didn't want to shake her hand any more, to demand anything from her. From the dining room came the grunts, the shouts, the laughter; above all, the laughter.

"He thinks he's the son of God! He thinks he's the son of gods and tumblers, but I spit on all of them and their progeny, because it was this stinking jackass, I, who made you, for glory, peace, and tranquillity in my bitter old age. Amen."

Ariel pressed the other hand, unable to control himself any longer.

"Tell me their names. Don't leave me without them."

Jeanne the Strong One turned her face toward the wall, but she forced herself to speak in a thread of a voice.

"I don't remember any more . . . but go, go find them . . ." and her eyes closed on that small dream.

The curses that Georges Le Gouarnec never stopped mumbling during the three days of the wake were the funeral prayer for Jeanne the Strong One, but so were Ariel's hopes when he left, running toward the south, toward the sun, to find the Minstrels.

The Son of Kermaria

The children's laughter echoed from the main road, and three old women dressed in black made the sign of the cross. It was the bitter laughter of tired men, of demons, and the old women, who no longer trembled before anything, did tremble when they heard that shrill, discordant laughter.

"I'm the doctor. . . ."

"I'm Death. . . ."

"I'm a rich man. . . ."

"I'm Death. . . ."

"I'm Death. . . ."

"Dummy! You can't have two Deaths, one after the other. You have to be a pauper, or the butcher, or anything, but you know you can't be Death, not if it isn't your turn."

"I can if I want to," Joseph said. "After all, I'm the one who invented this game, I'm the one who showed all of you the painting in the chapel, I'm . . ."

Needless to say, they didn't let him finish. They had a very personal idea of justice, and they were quick to act with their fists. Shouting "No favorites," they jumped on poor Joseph. He ran away as fast as his eleven-year-old legs would carry him. As if he hadn't been the one who proposed the game of imitating the circle of living and dead that was painted in the Kermaria chapel. On those oppressive summer days when everyone else slept all afternoon, Joseph's grandfather took him to see the seven-hundred-year-old painting. In the silence of the gray chapel, the boy would describe the flaking contours of the macabre dance to the blind old man.

"There's a skeleton," he would tell him, "taking the hand of a man in a long cape and a flat black hat. The man is a lawyer, and he goes hand in hand with Death. Everyone has his own private Death, no one can escape Her, and She makes you dance and dance and won't let you go for anything."

The grandfather would get enthusiastic at this point. "Go on, keep telling me," he'd say, and he would break into a dance on the worn tile floor, bumping against the straw chairs and the prayer desks. The old man certainly knew how to imitate the figures in the fresco and dance like them; for he was closer to death than anyone was, and he must have felt that bony hand firmly clutching his own.

Joseph admired his grandfather, even if he did spend the entire day swaying back and forth in his rocking chair in the middle of the patio, facing the chicken coop, humming unintelligible songs to himself. And because he admired him, Joseph went to him whenever he needed consolation after a humiliating skirmish with the other children. Often, the old man, deep in his daydreams, wouldn't hear him arrive.

"They must be washing Her. I hear the splashing of water on Her flanks; She must be fresh, taut, and rosy. I'd like to undress myself and roll around on the cold stone slabs and wash these damned eyes of mine, which must be renewed and blessed, with the water that has run off Her body."

"Grandfather!" Joseph grabbed him by the arm and shook him. "Grandfather!"

The rocking chair stopped.

"Joseph, is it you? Go see if they're washing Her, I want to know. Now I hear the brush running over Her rosy flesh. . . ."

"Yes, they're washing Her, all right. Last night Constantine the hunchback climbed in through a window and slept under the altar tapestry. Son of a bitch! He must have left the poor thing full of fleas."

"Constantine the hunchback, Constantine the hunchback, and they don't let me get near Her because those damned old women scream to high Heaven when they see me. They don't even let me touch Her. All because I once buried my face in the basin of holy water and cooled my lips on the lips of the Virgin. In the chapel of Kermaria, of all places, as if She weren't at home there, and I with Her, in the house that belongs to everyone."

"Those old women are witches," Joseph said to comfort him, caressing the little bag of rock salt that hung from his neck to protect him from evil. Then the old man laughed as he remembered the time the children took the polychromed apostles, gigantic Romanesque wood carvings, out of the niches in the Kermaria atrium, then installed themselves in the niches—twelve children with dirty faces, dressed in rags, standing absolutely still and waiting eagerly to frighten the old women who would come at dawn to first Mass.

"Of course they're witches," the grandfather echoed. "I know that better than anybody; I could see it when I was a boy. Always the same, skinny and black. They never change, they never die. They cast the spells that made me blind because I was the only man who went to the chapel and saw them kneeling there, jumbling up their prayers in front of the Virgin and the Child, the Child who didn't know what to do with that big round breast the Virgin offered Him. There they were, praying for the milk in the breasts of every mother to turn sour, so that at night all the children would turn into owls or wolves." The old man fell silent.

"They're witches," Joseph insisted, to get him to go on talking. He didn't want to hear the silence, because at that moment he caught sight of his mother sneaking out through the back gate, and he was afraid to hear her steps going off toward a fate that could only be terrible and mysterious. She wasn't like other women, though; she was still young and beautiful and she had only begun to wear black when her husband died, a few years ago.

"All of them are witches, that's right, and they made me blind. But what they don't know is that I can now lick the rough walls of Kermaria and feel those walls inside me more than ever, even if the stone tears my skin."

Seated on the pressed-earth floor of the patio, Joseph dug his nails into the palm of his hand and wondered where his mother had gone. But nothing could hold him like the old man's words, and he chose to stay rather than run off to find out the truth; to stay and store up warm memories for the cold nights at boarding school, when his imagination would take him back to Kermaria chapel and he would lick its rough, ridged walls or roll on the floor or purify himself by drinking all the holy water. And yet, when vacation time came, his tongue would be cut by the granite, the floor would feel too hard, the holy water taste too stale. He was lucky Father Medard didn't shoo him out with a broom.

"In a few days the pilgrimage will begin," the grandfather said, interrupting Joseph's thoughts.

The pilgrimage was the most important event of the year for the parish of Kermaria in Ifkuit, forgotten in the middle of the Breton underbrush, far from the sea, from the mountain air, simply clinging to the earth with its poor isolated mud houses with blackened thatched roofs. But the group of wild children who hung around the chapel didn't share the pilgrims' joy; they felt dispossessed by the people who came from the most distant corners of Brittany to ask for the good health and physical strength that none of the cathedrals with delicate steeples could offer. So, well ahead of time, the children made elaborate preparations to make their presence felt and to uphold the honor of the village with troublemaking while their mothers stayed away from the chapel.

The women who came were fishermen's wives, from the coast, and they brought with them the memory of an ancient myth, the antiquity of a race, and the smell of the sea. The women of Kermaria inhaled deeply to fill their lungs with the salty odor.

The children, however, were insensitive to the smell of salt air. All they wanted was to get close to Father Medard during Mass

The Son of Kermaria

so they could make themselves dizzy with the smell of the incense that was lavished only during the pilgrimage.

Joseph was the only one who knew something about the sea and the mystery of its foam. During the past summer, his mother, more silent than ever, had taught him to weave as they sat around the family table after supper. At the head of the table, the old man hummed and enjoyed his glass of brandy. He usually chided a bit before being taken to bed.

"Weave, my children. Make socks for my feet that must be warm in winter," he would say, or, "A scarf, I want it long. Don't skimp on the wool—this is going to be a very cold winter, and this poor old man needs warmth."

Mother and son worked silently, not listening to the grandfather's words, not bothering to answer him. Everything was peaceful until one night when the old man reached out and touched the soft wool. His fingers slipped through the open weave, and he thought that all the cold in the world would slip through, too. He didn't realize that his daughter-in-law and grandson were weaving nets.

Joseph had fun weaving nets. What's more, he had his mother next to him, and that helped him forget the days when she disappeared at midday and didn't return until dusk.

The preparations for the pilgrimage were also fun. Little by little, the chapel of Kermaria would take on a halo of cleanliness, and the sky set free a soft, steady rain to wash its sides. The children worshiped the grandfather at this time, because they felt they were losing the chapel and they thought he was the only person who could bring it back. Covered with mud, they would sit on the wet floor on rainy afternoons and listen to him talk, as if he were a prophet of Kermaria, which for them was alive and had a soul.

Father Medard would pace back and forth in front of the shed and never miss an opportunity to scold the children. "Children, go back to your homes. Our Father's eyes are upon you, and He knows what you are up to." He knew what to expect when the parish children got together with the old man, and he was uneasy. But the children only laughed their bitter laughter and spoke in low voices.

At last the day of the pilgrimage arrived. Minutes before evening Mass, the blacksmith's son brought a jar filled with live spiny-finned fish and dumped them into the basin of holy water. The other children filed into the chapel with sullen expressions and sat in the back pews scowling, waiting for the first pilgrims.

Joseph's mother came in with a group of strangers. She dipped her fingers into the holy water cautiously, for she had seen the fish, and her face showed no surprise. With the sad look that had settled in her eyes over the last few years, she caught a fish between her hands and left the chapel, tiptoeing, trying not to be noticed. But Joseph saw her and decided to slip away after her, even if it meant missing the sight of the old women absentmindedly dipping their fingers into the basin of small slippery shapes.

He was going to run after her, but at the threshold a sudden flash of sunlight hurt his eyes, which had become accustomed to the semidarkness of the chapel and the persistent gray drizzle, and he had to stop. When he opened his eyes again, he saw a white form disappearing behind the thorny bushes at the side of the main road, across from the chapel.

Joseph spent an hour within the tangled woodland looking for his mother. The undergrowth stretched toward him like fingers, scratching his legs and tearing his clothes. Each tree, each bush, each crippling plant had its own thorns, long or short, black, white, or orange; he saw them in detail or not at all, so distraught was he in his desperate search. "I have to find her," he told himself. And then, "I hope I never find her." He didn't want his fears confirmed. He didn't know exactly why he was afraid, for he had crossed the circle of demons surrounding the chapel a thousand times. But now something more vital was at stake, something that was part of his flesh and blood. If his mother had wanted to find herself a new husband (at least he was sure of that much), she had betrayed him miserably by not choosing one of the apostles in the church patio or one of the figures in the fresco who were his real friends.

His mother had once told him that to love one has to be mature, wise, and full of piety. He had answered, "When I fall in love, my children will have the face of the wax Child in front of the altar."

The blood from his scratches was streaming down his face, his arms, his legs, and he felt all the heat of the nettles. He finally spotted her at the bottom of the ravine. His eye had been caught by the unusual sight of her splendid white dress. Cautiously he moved a bit closer. In the palm of her hand was the fish, no longer alive.

He sat at the top of a hill behind a thicket and waited. He knew something was going to happen, for his mother had never done anything like this before. Far away, the bell of Kermaria broke the silence, marking the end of evening Mass.

The wait was long, and Joseph grew agitated. Perhaps his mother had not betrayed him, perhaps the man she was waiting for really belonged to the chapel and was none other than Father Medard. But then, on an open path between the thorny bushes, a man appeared—very tall, blond, strong-limbed. Joseph recognized him by his walk as the fisherman who journeyed inland every Friday to sell fish to the parish of Kermaria.

Joseph could only see his mother's back, but by the way her

shoulders quivered, he guessed what the look in her eyes must be —so much her own, deep and sad, fixed on the man approaching her.

The fisherman walked over to the woman and took her by the shoulders with his big open hands, and she began to rise, slowly. Joseph didn't want to witness the meeting of those eager lips, and he cried out, "Mama!"

And then he wanted to roll over and over on the thorns and to be beaten very hard, so the pain he felt inside would go out of him and mingle with the healthy, familiar pain of the flesh. But the blows didn't come, and when he finally opened his eyes, his mother was standing alone in front of him, her hands limp at her sides.

They walked back to the farm in silence, and there mother and son stayed shut in for several days. She spoke only to ask, "What do you know about the sea?" and sometimes she shook him until he cried. Joseph licked his tears, thinking they were the only salt water in the world.

In the meantime, the grandfather wandered about the main road in the rain. When he heard footsteps, he would approach the passers-by and ask for something to eat because he had been forsaken. The neighbors felt sorry for him, but they couldn't forget his affronts to Kermaria, and they shouted obscenities and insults at him.

"Why don't you go to the chapel and swallow wafers and eat candles and get indigestion! Idiot!"

"Time and again you drank the wine that was meant for Mass. Why not do it again instead of begging for the wine from our tables?"

But, like a litany, the grandfather kept on begging: "Pity for a poor blind man . . ."

"It isn't pity you need, but a swat on the behind."

Nevertheless, they let him sleep on the fresh hay in their barns,

The Son of Kermaria

and they painted his walking stick white, and he was a guest at many tables while his daughter-in-law kept herself shut in.

"What do you know about the sea?" she would scream at Joseph at night. And Joseph, his eyes open wide, tried to see her in the dark as he chewed on a bit of stale bread that he had been hiding in his pocket.

Finally, one morning, the sun came out again, the same sun that had shone the afternoon of the pilgrimage and then disappeared behind the gray cloak of the drizzle. His mother packed the sausages that were left in the pantry and made Joseph get dressed quickly and go out.

They arrived at Ploumanac'h at sunset, not because it was a long way off but because they had had a hard time finding someone who would take them there.

"Is this the harbor? It can't be, it can't be," Joseph's mother exclaimed, biting the palm of her hand and looking despairingly at the dry harbor, forsaken by the tide, where the big-bellied fishing boats lay on the rosy sand.

It can't be, but it is, Joseph thought happily. His lips were about to stretch into a timid smile of triumph, when in the distance he saw a man approaching, and he recognized his mother's fisherman. The fisherman had recognized them, too, and was walking right toward them. Without warning, Joseph freed himself from the hand that was holding him and began to run.

"Joseph, Joseph, come back, don't go away," his mother cried, and then, "Ah, Pierre, make my boy come back. Don't let him run away from me."

They began to chase after Joseph. His mother couldn't stop crying. "I wanted to find you again, Pierre, but not to lose him. I came to look for you, I swear it. Catch him, for God's sake, catch him. . . ."

Joseph's hair fell over his eyes. He wanted to escape from that man, yet he didn't want to be parted from his mother. But she was on the man's side, so there was nothing he could do but run with all his might. At moments he felt their voices almost on top of him and he was frightened; but he was even more frightened when the sound of their calling grew distant, and he thought he would never find his way back again.

At last he saw a big door that led to a church courtyard, and he walked in. He knew he was on friendly ground when he had the churchyard stones under his feet, and he stopped to inhale deeply and release a long sigh that echoed in the bell tower. It was beginning to grow dark, and the last violet lights were disappearing behind the stone crucifix and the vault with its fine columns. That would be the best refuge, he thought, nobody would think of looking for him there. Since he was small, he could slip through the narrow opening between columns and sit on the enormous pile of human bones, gray and crumbling, disinterred over a long period of time to make room in the small cemetery for new bones, dead flesh, worms.

All the terror that was floating around finally overcame him, and he shivered. He would have howled like a dog had he not been afraid he might sound like a soul in pain.

To protect himself against ghosts and evil lights, he shut his eyes tight, and he covered his ears with his arms to shut out the moans of the dead. But every so often he cheated and slackened his arms so he could hear if they were still calling his name in the distance, or he peeked through his half-closed eyes to search for some human silhouette.

When the moon came out, he saw the empty eye sockets of skulls fixed on him and, beyond the columns, the crucifix and the bleak profile of the church.

By then fear had become so much a part of his flesh, it almost didn't bother him. He was exhausted by the long trip, the flight, and the fear. He thought that perhaps it wasn't so bad that his mother was going away with a man who was very much alive and who didn't belong to the damned world of the dead. As his head fell on a pile of bones, he thought that the affection he needed and could no longer have from his mother might come from that other woman in his village, so large, so warm, so generous, in the chapel of Kermaria.

Forsaken Woman

I'm letting myself be consumed with jealousy, and that's a bad sign. I think I'll have to stop seeing him for a few days, until I feel better. I recognize this stage, I've been through it before, but never like this. He has green eyes and a tender smile and big wrinkles when he laughs, though he never seems to laugh. My knees have the salty taste of things from the sea; I lick them while I sit huddled on the floor, and I can't stop thinking about him.

When I am calm I run through the long corridors, through the empty rooms, and raise a cloud of dust with my white robe, which drags behind me like a bride's train. But today he won't come. If I have enough will power, he won't come. I don't intend to call on him simply to upset myself and suffer. I'd like to laugh when I'm with him, to be happy and dance, but I can't. I spy on his every gesture, his every word, measure and weigh them, and I don't enjoy the time I spend with him. It's jealousy, of course, I know that feeling well; I've seen it at other times . . . I should make it my friend.

"Mr. Jealousy, the door is open. The house is yours. Do as you will. Come and go, as you will. But leave me alone."

Actually, I am at peace with myself most of the time. I only call on him when I feel lonely, and I only feel lonely at sunset, and even then not every day.

Today the grocer left me the cookies I like, and a box of powdered milk. How can I tell him that I hate powdered milk and that I have no way to heat water? They shut the gas off, they shut it off ages ago. I would have preferred canned peaches to powdered milk. The vase I left for him probably didn't seem like much; nonetheless, it was a Sèvres. But what could a Sèvres possibly mean to that poor man?

I eat the cookies and think about my love. Sunset or not, today I won't make him come. The cookies are filled with the white cream I like so much. No, today I won't make him come; that way I can prove to him that I'm not jealous. After all, when he isn't with me, he simply doesn't exist. There are many things I'm not so sure of, but I'm very sure that he is my creation and no more—like any cruel and true love, the pure invention of the one who loves. No one is loved for what he is, but for what someone else believes him to be.

I picture mine with green eyes, curly hair, and a sad smile; above all, those wrinkles that extend from his mouth and stir me so much. But he's so sad, poor thing. It's not my fault: I'd like him happy and carefree, but he slips through my fingers and becomes sad. But for him to be happy, I'd have to change his face, and his is the only man's face I can remember. For that matter, mine is the only woman's face. It's been a long time since I left the grocer the last mirror I had, the baroque one with the gold frame. It had big angels around it, and the grocer liked it a lot: in exchange he left me five cans of sardines, a large loaf of bread, and two bottles of wine. Everything went well at the time, but the result is I now have to invent a new love for myself, and there are no faces left to choose from.

Some mornings I feel like spying on the grocer, so I can use him as an inspiration. But I run away the minute I hear him coming up the outside staircase, and when he reaches the vestibule, where he leaves the groceries, I'm already at the other end of the house, trembling at the thought that someday he actually might decide to come in and catch me at the end of the corridor.

My knees always have the same salty taste, they're immutable. Luckily, it's never too cold here, or too hot. Once the grocer left me ice cream. I suspected it was a gift, but I waited too long to pick up the groceries, and the ice cream had melted. It made a great big creamy stain on the floor.

My love should arrive at any moment. The worst thing is that I've forgotten his name. Alberto, Mario, Jorge? I have to keep changing his name, because my memory is always failing me, although he's always the same even if I try to change him, even if I try to be deeply unfaithful to him. Besides, I'm a coward —if I weren't, I'd spy on the grocer and have a new face for my love.

My love has gone already. Today his visit was short because I'm tired and I didn't feel like making an effort to keep him. But I did have time to tell him that the essential thing about love is neither to believe nor to love, but to create. I came up with that pretty phrase the other day, and Mario thought it really hit the mark. We decided to do something together. Some people build a home, but we're going to revive this abandoned house and give it a soul.

Just think, I put out the little gold-leaf Boulle chair for the grocer, and in exchange the brute only left me a jumbo can of mackerel in oil, opened, which I'll never be able to finish, and an enormous cheese, round as the world and with all its foul smells. How can you trust the taste of these people? . . . Of course, I don't care about the furniture. I already have seven empty rooms, and they're the ones I sweep with the most enthusiasm, although I don't know where to empty the dust because I've closed the windows forever. The dust looks so pretty piled up, so soft, that it hurts me to leave it for the grocer to throw out with the rest of the garbage.

I believe it's three days since I called my love. The truth is, there are loves that are like drugs, and it's better not to acquire the habit, to leave while the strength to do so is still there. The terrible thing about all this is that one's own individuality is lost, lost forever in the other person. At night I repeat to myself that I don't want to fall in love any more, but then I realize my lack of faith and my cowardice, and I feel like crying.

I took off the white robe to wash it, and now I'm naked. I hope the sun that comes in through the vestibule skylight is strong enough to dry it quickly. I feel very uncomfortable like this;

Forsaken Woman

its long train was already part of me. This noise it made as it dragged across the floor kept me company.

That beast of a grocer doesn't leave soap any more. He's put me in a bad mood. Now he leaves candles for me because he learned, God knows how, that my electricity was turned off. And I was so happy without light—I didn't feel a compulsion to write at night, and I could sleep peacefully.

I told Eduardo, but he doesn't care about these things. He always has that same sad look in his green eyes, and I can't wipe it away by making funny faces. I talk to him about love, and that makes me sick. The other day I insulted him: I told him that he was superficial and insensitive, and I tried to make him admit it. He was hurt, but I needed to see him suffer because of me. Doesn't the egg hurt when its shell is broken? However, the truth of the egg is in the yolk, and I want all his truth. I'll stop at nothing to get to know his truth, even if I have to risk losing him and then suffering.

Silver candlesticks, platters, an old clock, bit by bit everything is going, and I'm glad, because I don't want to be involved with objects. I'm busy enough with love. The trouble is, one morning the grocer left me a bunch of flowers, and now he won't bring me any more food.

The robe is dry but wrinkled. I had to soak it again and put it on wet so I could press it with the heat of my body. Last night, for the first time, I was cold and couldn't sleep. I lay awake thinking for a long time, and I decided that I'm turned inside out like a glove, all tight inside because of a centripetal love.

There are very few things left in the house now. I no longer receive the cream-filled cookies I like so much, and yesterday the stupid grocer left something to entice me back to the outside world that I no longer have anything to do with. I told Fernando to take them away—his hair was as silky as ever, the wrinkles of his mouth more marked, and his eyes so green that the red flowers suited him perfectly. But he didn't take them away, and this morning I found them, wilted, just where I had left them.

The lights went back on—at night, of course, just to annoy me. Suddenly, in the middle of my best Technicolor dream, I woke up because the whole house was ablaze. All that brightness made it seem like a party, but the big rooms were emptier than ever, and I ended up feeling depressed. The one good thing about it all was that it meant the grocer and I were on good terms again, because he must have been the one who paid the overdue electric bill. He must have valued the Capodimonte piece I left for him the other day more than I imagined. It was a beautiful soup tureen decorated with flowers, but in exchange he left me the same things he had left for that plastic piece of junk I dug up in the pantry.

Ricardo asked me not to call him for a while because he has a lot of work to do. I cried after he left, but it didn't take long for me to convince myself that if I went on like that, this whole affair wouldn't end up with love, but with a burial, and that thought calmed me quite a bit.

I wonder if I'll be able to push the piano to the vestibule where the grocer leaves things for me. But I'm afraid it will never occur to him to remove a monstrosity like a grand piano, or the dining-room table that seats twenty, or the English wardrobe in three sections that's in the master bedroom. To think that's all I have left . . . I haven't eaten for two days, and I can't stand it any more. I've just discovered that my knees no longer have that salty taste, and my voice, when I call my love through the long empty corridors, sounds hollow. I've already devoured the entire house, I've eaten it little by little, with the grocer as an intermediary.

I don't want to starve to death, no, certainly not. It would be horrible if my love called on me without warning; he'd find me thin and green, with my robe floating like a ghost's. But I haven't got anything left to give in this house, and I don't have anything to do either, except sit in the vestibule and wait. The grocer will come, I imagine—he's no fool; he'll realize that in exchange for his tin cans I'm giving myself, the only thing I have left to give.

While I wait for him, I call my love and I remember his silky hair, his sad green eyes, and those wrinkles that travel from his nose to his mouth as if he were laughing. I call him desperately, once, twice, while I wait for the grocer, but he doesn't come. Alas, it seems I have infected him with my faults: he is jealous too.

The Teacher

"She's going to be proud of me, yes, she is, when she learns that I faithfully followed the path she once marked out for me."

Mendizábal walked through the neighborhood of neat little houses and carefully groomed gardens, carrying along the memory of his history teacher, a memory as light and sweet as one of those passing loves that scarcely touch reality. With her hair in a bun, and low-heeled, sensible shoes on her feet, she had an austerity that removed her from time. With his diploma under his arm, Mendizábal felt he could at last face her again and discuss the great exploits of history, as he had learned to do, and praise the integrity of a past free of the foulness of more recent events.

At the wooden fence, he extended his hands to examine his perfectly manicured nails, he brushed the dandruff from his shoulders, and he arranged the point of his pale-pink handkerchief that peeked out of his breast pocket.

He opened the gate and entered, but when he got to the backyard, instead of the mother, he found the children.

Jam was dripping from their chins, and judging by the way they were throwing bread at each other, they were angry enough to kill. He didn't realize that this was their usual diversion at teatime and that it always ended in the laughter that he mistook for shrieks of horror.

A hand holding a slice of bread paused in midair when Mendizábal appeared, and a howl was cut short by surprise, but only briefly, for these children couldn't remain still or surprised for very long.

Generously, they thought that the stranger might want to share in their games.

"Come on, come on, play war with us!"

"Let's go, let's go. . . ."

Mendizábal was alarmed and wanted to run away. She had children, of course, she adored children. If his memory wasn't playing tricks, some time back she had talked of twins, Aníbal and Augusta—that's right, pretty names with a historic ring. But, good heavens, the children facing him were animals, they didn't even look like children.

"Have a glass of milk with us. Don't stand there like a dummy."

"Shut up, stupid. He doesn't want that sissy stuff. You offer a man brandy."

"Once I drank half a bottle. . . ."

"Sure, and we had to put you to bed. And you spent the whole night throwing up. It was a joke. Anybody can do crazy things, anybody, especially a person without a brain."

"Do you have a cigarette?"

"Stop that silly talk, or I'll punch you in the eye."

Mendizábal knew nothing of the magic world of children. He wished the ground would open up and swallow him. But a flicker of hope helped him recover his voice.

"Mrs. Ortiz? Is she your mother?"

"You've got the wrong house," he hoped they'd answer him. Or better still, "What mother? We don't know any Mrs. Ortiz. Go away."

But they stared at him with hostile eyes and said nothing. The silence became palpable, unfriendly. The children lowered their heads and nudged each other as if to hide something.

"Where's your mother?" Mendizábal persisted, looking at the oldest child.

They looked at each other out of the corners of their eyes, almost motionless. The youngest took a bread crumb and crushed it between his fingers while the others watched him covertly, stretching the spring of silence until it snapped and they all reacted at the same time. One of the boys kicked the cat that was rubbing against his legs, and the shrieks of the animal mingled with those of the children.

"What mother are you talking about? We don't have a

mother. You're crazy. Get out of here, get out. We're sick and tired of you."

"Get out," they chorused, "get out!"

Mendizábal now understood that he had not been mistaken, for there they stood: identical twins with an identical lock of hair falling over their dark, hard eyes. He stood indecisively amidst that wild howling pack, staring at the shine of his shoes. Suddenly, beyond the noise of the children, he heard the creaking of the gate. The children's expressions altered with the sound, and Mendizábal knew that something was about to happen. The youngest girl jumped from her chair and ran to the house, calling, "Mama!"

The rest of the children reacted as if they shared a single impulse, colliding against the table and upsetting the milk. A few drops splattered Mendizábal's dark trousers. How could he greet her like that? He would have to wipe them clean.

Separating itself from the darkness beyond, a figure appeared in the door, clad in an enormous yellow raincoat, her head crowned by a hideous untidy bun, from which strands of hair fell, yellow and dirty like the raincoat. The figure advanced slowly toward Mendizábal, speaking in a hoarse voice.

"How are you, young man? I am Mrs. Ortiz. You probably don't remember me, which is just as well. It would be better if you didn't remember anything at all. Now you can go. I'm rushed. Forgive me."

It was Augusta, really, and Mendizábal wanted to ask her why she had disguised herself. But Augusta vanished, with the certainty of having fulfilled her duty. Before long, another strange character appeared, this time dressed in a bathrobe, with a tulle hat on her head. Now the voice was subdued.

"I am Mrs. Ortiz, of course, and I come to say good-by. I can't see you today. The truth is, I'll never be able to see you, though you may wish to try us again in a few years. With a bit of luck, you'll find us all dead, rotted, covered with flies. God bless you, my son. And good luck."

Seven Mrs. Ortizes paraded in front of Mendizábal. The last one reached only to his waist and walked entangled in a long muslin curtain. Each said good-by and asked him to leave, but his only thought was to stay long enough to discover the outcome of this madness.

At last, the real Mrs. Ortiz made her appearance. She was more grotesque than all the children's disguises put together. Her hair was short and adolescent-looking; she undulated rather than walked as she approached him with her lips ready. Mrs. Ortiz, teacher, mother, always so majestically out of his reach, how could she appear like that to him?

He thought he heard her say, "You are astonished, my dear Mendizábal. You find me changed, don't you? Well, it's to be expected, with so many young boys around. . . ."

What she really said was, "You are Mendizábal, right? With so many young boys around, I've lost track of the names by now. . . ."

"I think I was always a good student," he mumbled apologetically.

"That's why I remember your name. But now that you're grown up, I can confess to you that good students, bad students, curriculums, all that nonsense bores me."

"I've just received my history degree, like you . . ."

"Poor man. You'll see how arduous it is to live among faceless heroes that become stereotypes."

She smiled at him tenderly, and Mendizábal thought he heard what he once would have liked to hear: ". . . heroes with your face. Sometimes you were Attila, sometimes Alexander the Great. While I was conducting the class I would give their faces a mouth like yours, eyes like yours—following each of my gestures, adoring me. . . ."

But in truth she was saying: ". . . the boys who watched me

with amusement in their eyes, the ones who fought in the back of the classroom, and all the things I had to do to maintain order. Now I'm free of all that, and so happy. I even look younger, right, children? I want to laugh, to have fun."

The children surrounded her, looking at her like puppies, a little afraid of their mistress's quick-changing moods. A spark of admiration escaped from their eyes and made them blush.

"Now go and play; I'll have a chat with Mendizábal, who has been so kind as to come and visit me."

There was a long silence as the sun began to set in all its sweetness, and she saw, in the pensive Mendizábal, still another child. She put her hand on his shoulder.

He jumped back in his chair and decided that he must run away and forget his old teacher, who was damned, possessed by the devil. He opened his mouth several times before he could finally shout, "I have to leave! I'm in a hurry, I have to leave. It's too late, too late."

"You always were a shy boy, but I thought age would cure you. I'll bring you a whisky. That'll calm you down."

"I must go. I must go."

She came closer and took him by the arm. "Don't be so nervous. Those thick glasses are all right in class, but you can take them off here. You look dazed."

She caressed his hair and lowered her hand to remove the glasses, but he slapped her so hard that his glasses flew off and dropped into the grass. Darkness overwhelmed him and he fell down on his knees to look for them. Suddenly, he thought he saw a woman's body moving around on all fours, wanting to rub against him, to coil her legs around his, to plant her hot, painted mouth inside his dry lips. And as he frantically searched in the grass for the glasses, his dim world filled with the shouts of children, who were coming in a group to sink him irretrievably into darkness and the heat of the woman.

The Teacher

He felt a tangle of legs and arms on top of him. With great effort, he extricated himself and crawled to the fence. He managed to get up and walk along the fence until he reached the gate. He opened it, then turned around to close it almost casually. He left the fiendish garden behind and moved toward salvation.

Behind him, the blows and shouts continued, as if in the confusion and anger they hadn't realized that he was far away, or as if they had all been blinded like him and were still fighting among themselves in the bushes and shrubs.

Death must be like the street, emerging from the fog constantly following him. But he was moving slowly, and life was finally able to overtake him. In a fresh uproar, the children were calling his name, destroying his peace.

"Hey, Mendizábal, come here!"

"Come here, we found your glasses."

"Your glasses, here!"

They had climbed up on top of the gate and were pushing one another, stretching out their arms to him.

"Here, here, we found them next to the orange tree."

He went toward them slowly; he felt some hands. When he put on his glasses he came back to life. Suddenly, everything returned to the quiet reality of a blue spring dusk, with no sign of the crisis he had just passed through. Mendizábal cursed the imagination that had played such nasty tricks on him. It had been a bad dream, and he thanked the trees, the clouds, and those seven blond children who were looking at him with pride while they said, "We love you a lot. We're your friends. Call us whenever you need us."

A bad dream, yes, had it not been for the silhouette of the teacher that he thought he saw behind the children's heads and beyond their laughter, trying in vain to get up from the ground.

Irka of the Horses

What could be seen of this universe was feminine, but dry and barren. The three women knitted almost continuously, and the strands of purple wool became entangled, forming shapes that they occasionally tried to identify. The noise of the needles distracted them, and after a week of arduous knitting, they had forgotten the smell of a man.

What they knew well was the smell of the lake, where they spent the long siestas listening to the green flies buzzing over the dead fish. If all the decay of thé world were to be concentrated in one spot, they thought, surely it would be here, where the water was green and had the consistency of rotting plants. At noon, when the sun was at its brightest, the scales of the dead fish glistened, and the flies were iridescent. The smell was overwhelming, pungent and hot. It made one want to inhale deeply, to absorb it and then vomit.

The beach was too narrow for the three of them to stretch out, but the most important thing was to get a sun tan. Behind them rose a cliff of red dirt and bushes shaped like claws.

"It's a malicious landscape," Antonia had said when they first arrived to spend a short vacation, unprepared for what they found. "We have to choose: either we adapt or it will devour us."

Josefina and María Carmela had laughed, and their laughter held echoes of the city, of good breeding, of paved streets. Eventually they adapted, with almost too much ease.

The small house was isolated amid the hills, surrounded by low, bristly woodlands. To get to the lake, the three women had to walk across the open country and through swamps. They enjoyed sinking into mud up to their thighs, immersing themselves in the intimate truth of the earth.

The mares and their foals paced in those same swamps. They were light-footed, but their hooves sank into the mud and left deep, clear tracks. When they ran in fright, their manes and tails flew in the wind, and the hills returned their neighing, distorting the sounds until they seemed more like human cries than echoes. Every sunset, from the top of a cliff, among the thorny bushes, the three women spied on the animals. Especially on the stallion, who stood motionless under an arch opened by the waters that had poured over the red, brittle soil, and watched his herd.

One stormy evening they discovered Irka, the sorceress, an invisible inhabitant of these lands. Her silhouette was outlined on the horizon beyond the mountains; a black and violent cloud drew her profile. The amulet that hung in the kitchen was for Irka: a horseshoe and a green silk bag filled with salt. "To keep the wild horses away," the old hermit had told them, and they had no reason to doubt his word.

That afternoon, they expressed their wishes:

"I'd like to frighten the horses away, make them gallop to the cliffs, and see their shiny hides ripped by the thorns."

"I'd like to drive them to the water, make them leap through the mud over dead tree trunks, and see them swim until they're worn out."

"I prefer that they go on as they are, motionless, until the sky turns green and black; then I want them to run at a furious gallop and crush us. . . ."

But none of the three made a move; the wild horses belonged to Irka, and the sorceress might take revenge if they tried to alter the rhythm of the horses' lives.

On the road back to the house, they discovered the twisted, dry tree with its belly full of serpents. This, undoubtedly, was where Irka lived.

That night they decided to invoke her by lighting green candles in front of the old cracked mirror and eating the red apples of the original sin. They wanted a magic charm from Irka that would give them power and, above all, an inexhaustible avarice that would be always satisfied and always renewed. They invoked her for three nights in a row. Once, with coins under the candles, they asked for a charm that would bring them gold; other times they asked for a love charm in exchange for the fresh heart of a chicken.

In reality, however, they were not waiting for Irka but for Leda, their friend.

"How can the motor of such a small car be so complicated?" Leda asked.

That's life—the right person is never there at the right time. Damn men who know nothing about nuts and bolts! One half of a man's body had disappeared under the hood of her white car. Damn the little white car, too, polished to a high gloss, the latest fashion and all that, but it breaks down on the most deserted highway in all of South America, a thousand million miles from civilization!

And that guy is the only one who passed by in two hours, and what has he done? Stained his shirt with grease from the carburetor, that's what.

Mumbling insults, Leda walked over to the motorcycle parked at the side of the road. A black windbreaker was tossed across the seat. Idiot! He doesn't understand anything. Double idiot! There was a skull printed on the back of the windbreaker. Just like a kid . . .

Leda returned to the car, put on her gloves, then pulled them off again. It was late afternoon, but still hot. She adjusted her big, superchic printed muslin scarf. Made to order for showing off to the cows—great!

The man's head emerged from under the hood.

"I don't know what's wrong here, but you can do one of two

things: walk back alone or come with me. If we're lucky, we'll get to your friends' house before midnight."

María Carmela stepped out onto the porch, and a black beetle hit her on the forehead. Swarms of bugs were dashing themselves to pieces against the light bulb. The nocturnal butterflies, dark and rough, fell at her feet. She looked beyond the porch toward the darkness and the lake and saw the first streaks of lightning.

"We're going to have a storm," she said as she came in, closing the door quickly.

"The spiders are going crazy," one of the women observed.

"We should kill them, quick."

"No! They knit, like us. And they're magic. They are us, walking on the ceiling and the walls. We shouldn't kill the spiders, we should put flies in their webs. Dead flies, but freshly killed, swollen with blood."

The click of the knitting needles mingled with the women's words.

"I know it, I know it," Leda was shouting as they covered long stretches of the road. "You're Death! Death the motorcyclist!"

The man pressed down hard on the gas pedal and listened only to the roar of the motor. Holding him tightly around the waist, Leda tried to shake him and shout, but she only swallowed the wind, the dust, and her anguish. They were riding into the sunset, into the black clouds outlining figures against an unearthly light. And suddenly, very bright, zigzagging, came the lightning, then the thunder, the sky drums growling and reverberating on all sides. She would rather go back toward the darkness than toward that brutal light.

"Stop, stop! You are Death! I don't want to die," Leda shouted, and her answer was the lightning on the horizon, the croaking of frogs on the plain, the mournful lowing of bulls. The live animals don't matter, it's the dead animals that let themselves be invaded by evil. White bones with horns that shine in the night, from the other side of the grave, playthings for the devil.

"I don't want to die!"

As the man turned around, a flash of lightning illuminated his face. He was pale, without eyes, just like the skull on the back of his jacket.

"We'll get there soon," he said in a toneless voice. The wind distorted his words, and Leda knew that Hell was near.

Josefina, Antonia, María Carmela, all three were curled up on the living-room sofa. They didn't dare go out to close the shutters. The lead-colored sky was shining against the windows, intermittently splitting into red streaks.

"We wanted it," Antonia lamented. "We asked for it." She would have liked to say, We provoked the fury of the elements, the unleashing of the forces of evil.

On the mantelpiece, the green candles they had lit to invoke the spirit of Irka were no longer burning, and the flies for the spiders lay limp. The women wanted to forget witches' games. They wanted instead to ask forgiveness, to kneel and pray, but they were unable to do so. They couldn't perform an act of contrition that would make the furies stop, or bring a clear day with the smell of aromatic herbs, free of the devil's laughter, of the lightning's flashing grin.

"Stop, Death, I beg of you. Stop, I don't want to hear the roar of the motor. Get thee behind me, Satan. The wind is inside

Irka of the Horses

me, my hair is swirling around like flies. . . . Son of a bitch, stop!"

"Oh, all this superstition, mystery. What good does it do us to believe in those things now? Let's go to bed. No reason why we should be afraid. It's just a storm like any other."

But the three women trembled.

"No reason why we should believe in magic. We're grown women, educated, civilized. It was an amusing game, that's all. We wanted a charm that would give us power, but that's ridiculous. We're certainly not going to let ourselves be carried away by these jokes."

"Let's get rid of everything—the candles, the mirror, everything. Including this stupid amulet hanging from the ceiling."

The hermit had told them that the amulet was there to ward off the wild horses, to keep them on the lake shore, to prevent them from breaking into a gallop, with the black stallion in the lead, in search of a man to crush under their hooves.

The women had thrown out the amulet. Over the mantel, the hands of the big clock met at twelve. A terrible tremor shook the walls, followed by the dull sound of horses' hooves some distance away. A woman's cry announced the silence.

The storm quieted down and one by one the stars appeared. With the light of the moon, the three women finally fell asleep on the living-room sofa, covered by a red poncho.

"He had gray eyes, didn't he, and a cowlick?"

"I don't know."

"Tell us, Leda. He was strong, wasn't he? And gentle and tender?"

"I don't know."

"He can't be yours if you don't know. Irka's horses killed him. He has a hoofprint on his forehead."

"We made Irka's horses run. They killed him for us. He's ours."

That morning they had found Leda and the dead man in the front yard, under the carob tree. She was weeping, her face close to his. Finally she spoke up: "I didn't leave him all night. I won't leave him now."

But María Carmela, Josefina, and Antonia wanted him for themselves. He was the only man they had, and they preferred him dead, without the power to hurt.

"We unleashed Irka's furies."

"We threw the horseshoe out the window."

"We know about mysteries and spells."

Leda looked at her old friends. They were disheveled, aged. Witches.

Go away, she thought. Stop dancing around my dead man. Your eyes are bulging like owls' eyes, they're going to fall out of their sockets. Your mouths are disfigured. You want to know what's inside him. You want to split him open, disembowel him and poke around. But I won't let you: this dead man is mine. Go away, you loathsome sniffing dogs. This body is mine; my eyes are also bulging. I also want to disembowel him and see what's inside. That's better than possessing their souls when they're alive. That's better than trying to break their will. While they're alive, one can only wound them with words, crack the mask. Now I possess him, dead at my feet, defeated. I can open him with a knife, at last I can have a man, the insides of a man. I want to feel his viscous viscera, warm, slippery. I don't want any woman to look at him, to touch him. I could leave him as he is, in the sun for days, letting him swell up and burst and show off his beautiful colors, letting the flies swallow him, and his own hot smell accompany him like a presence. But these women are here; they want him for themselves, they're devouring him with their eyes, he's making their mouths water.

"He's ours," they cried. "Irka killed him for us. He's ours."

"He's not yours, he's mine. I killed him, and nobody is going to take him away from me. I strangled him with my muslin scarf. I wrapped it around his neck and I tightened it until I couldn't tighten it any more, and he couldn't defend himself. He was Death, that's why I killed him. He stopped the motorcycle in the dark, and told me we had arrived. Everything was black and quiet and filled with murmurs. There was a smell of sulphur. He had taken me to Hell, he wanted to finish me off, and I didn't want to die. Alive he was Death, with his black windbreaker and his hollow eyes, unable to see. Now I've brought him back to life. He's human at last."

"And the horses?" the women shouted at her. "What about the hoofprints on his forehead?"

"I strangled this man myself, with my own scarf. The horses came later, attracted by the smell of agony, by the departing soul. He's mine!"

The three women stepped back. This was no longer a question of magic: they were facing a death that had been premeditated. They thought of the city, the laws, the punishments. Above all, they thought this man must have been beautiful when he was alive, strong and tender.

"Murderer!" they shouted at Leda.

Irka no longer existed; only Leda, who must be punished, who must pay for her crime. Strange, how reality returns in the midst of great conflicts: she must be taken to the nearest town and given to the police. The three of them could control her without force.

The women were whispering their plans, but Leda, absorbed by the corpse, was not listening. A strange gleam appeared in Antonia's eyes.

"She said she strangled him. . . ."

"And," Josefina added, "at the foot of the strangled, they say, a root grows, in the shape of a man. It screeches when it's torn, and it contains magic secrets. . . ."

"It's the mandrake," cried María Carmela. "It's the charm Irka is sending us."

"He's under the carob tree. . . ."

"Let's go look!"

The Legend of the
Self-sufficient Creature

FIRST CHORUS

"No man shuffles cards like that. He's worse than a sissy. He looks like a woman. Disgusting," the peasants say at night, playing at the tables in the tavern.

"She looks at us like a man. Maybe she just dresses like a woman so she can touch us. Let's not go near that devil . . ." the women say in the mornings at the general store.

The place is the same. What about the person?

A man who is a woman, a woman who is a man, or both things at once, interchanging themselves.

Poor little village, so much doubt, so much metaphysical anguish and no way of explaining it. Village? Bah! About twenty scattered houses, flat so as not to offend the plain, and an abandoned church. A few people said that if the priest were alive he would help to solve this mystery, he would protect them. The majority decided to do what they could and to watch the strange being closely. Closely, yes, but they mustn't get too close—not close enough to fall into the black well of contagion.

In the town, as is immediately apparent, there are no Creoles, only Italians and one or two Japanese with names that are never pronounced. (The devil remains, the gaucho has already left.) The gaucho would have known how to decipher the message in his horse's neighing whenever that undefinable being went near the hitching post. The townfolk, on the other hand, understand so little about horses: when they tie them to a post, the poor animals walk out of their lives. But this being has neither horse nor dog, of course: animals recognize the smell of the devil, even if the devil hides behind hormones.

Does this being tear off his manhood first thing in the morning in order to extirpate the devil? And does he put it on again at night for fear of keeping the devil inside a jar?

Or is this carrier of evil of the female sex? Does the devil get inside this creature when it is female and return doubled in its breasts to flow like milk? Or is the perverse creature always running up and down, from breasts to testicles, just for the pleasure of moving back and forth, coming and going on schedule, like the bus that arrives on the dusty road every Tuesday afternoon? But the perverse creature is never late: it becomes male with the first star and wanders around town all night. Sometimes the peasants see him stretched out in the tall grass, sleeping in the cool night breeze. Till dawn, when it returns to the covered wagon—briefly, just long enough for a quick change—to reappear as a female.

These things are discussed at the local tavern while he is there, leaning his elbows on the counter. Under the friendly roof of the tavern and warmed by the brandy, the peasants are united in a brotherhood, and they feel free to discuss sacrilegious things that would make them tremble under the pampa sky. Only the proprietor doesn't get involved in their conjectures; he knows that one customer who is double is worth two single ones. Two customers come out of that strange covered wagon, and that's all that matters to him. The devil doesn't enter into his bookkeeping.

As far as the covered wagon is concerned, that's still another matter. Early one morning the farm workers found it there, on state lands; they didn't know how it got there. A wagon like that isn't something you find every day, and this one was so humble, light brown like the earth in the thistle-covered plain under the blue sky. It had a heraldic air about it that stirred the farmers' ancestral pride. No one objected to the wagon until the other problem came to light and fear enveloped the village streets. At the same time, it was good to feel that something was happening. Mistrust ran alongside the fear, but mistrust was an old acquaintance, and it didn't bother anyone.

The Legend of the Self-sufficient Creature

SECOND CHORUS

Not even lucid minstrels can handle this story with the simplicity it merits, without pretensions.

She is María José and he is José María—two people in each, if names matter. But names have nothing to do with what others may have imagined of the amalgam of two in one being: something very religious, something unspeakable.

There are two, I repeat: José María and María José, born of the same womb and on the same morning, perhaps somewhat enmeshed.

Years passed before a large assortment of impossibilities began to weigh on them—on their desire to fulfill their own wishes. They cannot take a step forward, they are stuck in the mud, helpless. They cannot be apart, because the pain of separation is unbearable. They cannot sleep together for fear of becoming badly entangled, for, as everyone knows, the taboo of the race is sometimes stronger than the race itself.

He goes out by night and makes the darkness his own. She goes out by day while day lasts, but neither cuts the cord or goes too far from the covered wagon, the mother's womb. And to think that they had been so close, so tight, when life started, and now they don't touch, they never even look into each other's eyes out of a visceral fear of temptation.

(In prenatal times, was it yours, the arm that encircled my body; whose, that enveloping pleasure, that placenta?)

Now, without knowing it, he steals that feline aspect that is hers, and she makes her gestures more assertive and, perhaps, who would deny it, looks with desire at the women, the only human beings that cross her path during the day, when the men are in the fields with tractors or tending the cattle (natural tasks of this continent that has its feet and hands and even its soul in the soil). And he, perhaps, longs by night to stretch out his soft hand and touch a calloused peasant hand that knows the knife and raw flesh.

And each time the hand grows more distant and the town closes tighter, forbidding them to explain or be explained.

In any situation, it's such a convenience to establish a guilty party. Our scapegoat is the priest who originally gave them their names. It's true that his habit may have allowed him to ignore some matters of sex, but the end result is unforgivable. He should have known better. He should have named one of them María María and the other José José, thus eliminating doubt. Not all investigations are morbid; some are scientific.

REFRAIN

"This man is a woman. He puts on a disguise. He's got something under his hat even when he's hatless."

"This woman is a man. Her eyes glow when Rosa passes by. She'll overpower us if we trust her."

Never an explanation for them, poor things, not a single smile, from the tenacious dust that crackles between the teeth to the other crackle of human mistrust. It's too much to take. At the end of six days, on a Friday night to be precise. José María cannot muster enough strength to move his body and drag himself across the open fields for a friendly drink.

At the beginning, he leaves most of the bed to María José. But before long, things become confused: within the reach of his hand and other anatomical parts lies the warmth so badly wanted, the affection, the hope, the return to the source and so much more. It's best to stop here, in case there are youngsters about—and there are.

At the end of due time, a sweet creature was born, utterly unsexed. With the years the flat body developed in a contrary

The Legend of the Self-sufficient Creature

way, with peaks and cracks and a curious bulge and a slit of proven depth.

Far from the covered wagon, the villagers never knew which of the two was the mother.

Perhaps those who lived in the wagon never found out either.

The Sin of the Apple

They scrutinize me with the eyes of hunger, those abominable gluttons. I'm beyond your reach, gentlemen, and I don't intend to budge. I'm securely attached to the branch where my tree has placed me. I'm green, gentlemen, don't you see? Like the grapes above that famous fox. Besides, you'd need wings to reach me. No reason to look at me with such voracity. I'm green, and I haven't the slightest intention of falling.

After all, I'm the historical fruit, the most renowned, the most common.

Remember: I'm a descendant, as you well know, of Paris's apple, of William Tell's, of those of the Hesperides. I'm even related, in a direct line, to the scientific apple of Newton, the apple that has done so much for the human race. I'm a descendant . . .

Horrors! Why is that damned serpent approaching? Why does she stick out her tongue at me, why does she coil herself around the branches of my tree?

She's doing it on purpose, to remind me of the frailty of my species, the great shame of the apple. No one remembers Adam and Eve any more, no one thinks about the original sin. Yet this demonic serpent doesn't let me forget—me, particularly. I feel the shame mounting through the stem, it makes me hot, I feel myself blush. Oh, how red I am! . . .

"It's only natural," one of the men at the foot of the tree said as he took the first bite of the apple. "It's only natural, it was ripe and it fell."

The Alphabet

The first day of January he was anxiously awakened by an alarm clock, and that accident made him resolve to act methodically all his life. From then on he would act in accordance with all unwritten laws of art. He would respect the good old alphabet, which is, after all, the basis of human understanding.

In order to fulfill this resolution he started, naturally, with the letter A. So the first month he adored Anna, he traveled airborne from Argentina to Alaska, he ate asparagus, anchovies, avocado aspic, abalone Alfredo, and apples. He armed himself, attacked abortionists, and assassinated his aunt. He became an anarchist, an ascetic Aristotelian, amazingly good at anagrams, and he appended "Aha" and "Aho" and "Amen" to all his assertions. He acted aggressively by abusing an accountant, and he added an avocet to his aviary. He also developed an antipathy for alligators.

Things were quite neat, alphabetically speaking. The next month he burned some brassières, he borrowed a bicycle, betrayed Beatrice, blew up balloons, bombed a bank, burglarized a bookstore, and besotted himself with brandy. The third month he created a carnival, crossed a creek, and consumed caviar, cakes, chicken, carrots, and cauliflower. He courted Clara and curtailed all credit.

He was carrying on an experience that would have been essential for the advancement of humanity if it hadn't been for the unexpected occurrence that stopped him before he arrived at the letter Z. In the fourth month, without prior notice, he died of dysentery.

A Family for Clotilde

Rolo spent that morning, like so many others, watching Rolando. For his father, taking a rest meant exhausting himself physically: long jogs down the deserted beach, racing, leaping, one exercise after another. He was forty-six and still physically fit. Rolo was about to turn seventeen; it was a serious age, and unlike his father, he felt sick and tired of the world.

Standing at the top of a dune, or drinking an orangeade, Rolo watched the sun glistening on his father's golden back as he conscientiously did his calisthenics. Rolando was a good athlete and he knew it. Rolo looked at his own pale body, narrow at the shoulders, and understood why he was ashamed to walk next to his father when they were both in bathing suits. Even so, as the season progressed, and they rented a cabana, Rolo preferred going to the beach with his father to sitting in a beach chair next to his mother all day long. She was unusually emphatic in her attitudes, and if in November and December she was busy in the house and didn't take a moment's rest, for the remainder of the vacation she would forget the house and family and dedicate herself entirely to sun-bathing. She wanted to return to Buenos Aires looking as if she had had a good time.

That afternoon there was nothing to do, as usual, and Rolo sat on the fence and dreamed about dancing, about girls in bikinis, about friends he missed. At four o'clock Don Luis clambered up from the beach along the path between the dunes that led to Rolando's house. Don Luis's cart was massive, and corroded by the sea.

"Good afternoon," said the driver.

"Hi," said Rolo.

"You could make that sound more cheerful. I have the valises of the lady who's going to stay in the cottage in back of your house. Your family's lucky, I told your father, because at this time of year nobody rents or sells."

The horses pulling the cart rested after the hard trek. Only the pony was impatient and breathing hard.

"Uh huh," Rolo mumbled without enthusiasm, but he looked intently at the white leather bags and the enormous old-fashioned trunk.

"Looks like the lady's going to stay a long time, eh?"

"Uh huh."

"All summer?"

"All summer, part of autumn, the rest of her life. That goes for us, too; we'll never move away from here. Buried."

He dug his penknife into the trunk of a pine tree. He wanted to go away, anyplace. If only Pinamar were a port, then he could at least imagine trips. . . .

It was Sunday morning. With his jacket over his shoulder, Rolo walked through the trees surrounding the house, along the border of thickly clustered acacias, to the garden of the rear cottage. He had forgotten about the new tenant, but there she was to remind him, reclining on a deck chair in the shade, showing a great deal of white flesh and gleaming red hair. Rolo stopped short.

"Hi, darling. Where're you off to?" She had a warm, soft voice.

"To Mass," he answered grudgingly.

"To Mass?" Coming from her, the word sounded new and mysterious.

The sun was burning bright. Rolo wanted to stretch out in the cool air under the pines and simply listen to her. Instead he said, "Yes, to Mass. You may think our chapel small and ugly and unfinished, but that's not what counts if you want to go to Mass."

"Hmm. And if you were to stay here at my side and sip a gin and tonic, wouldn't that be nicer than going to church?"

"No."

"Well, your good father would prefer to sit here with me. He isn't like you. He doesn't go to Mass. Yesterday afternoon he passed by here on horseback five times. Just a little while ago I saw him in a bathing suit; he must be off for a swim. . . . Stay a bit."

She had deep-set dark-gray eyes. Rolo ran off without answering her.

I'll show that wild woman I'm not like my father, he thought. Who does the old man think he is, coming through here all hot and excited? I'll teach them. . . .

As the days passed, Rolando grew pensive. Rolo followed him all over the house, taunting him whenever he could. But Rolando didn't complain; in fact, it was practically impossible to drag a word out of him on any subject.

"Dear, don't put your feet on the sofa, you'll dirty the cretonne."

"Dear, move a little so I can open the windows and air the place a bit."

And the dear did as he was asked, without protest. Astonishing.

Rolo first became suspicious when he noticed that his father no longer got up at seven o'clock to take his early-morning swim. Then, one afternoon during siesta, he saw Rolando sneaking out through the kitchen door. Rolo raced upstairs to the attic and peered out of the small window just as Rolando entered Clotilde's house—without knocking, as if she were one of the family.

They're going to find out what I can do, and they'll have to learn the hard way, Rolo thought. They'll see. No one plays dirty with me. I was invited first.

Rolo had never thought of himself as patient, but sometimes virtues surface in time of need. Squatting on the dry, brittle leaves behind the bank of acacias, he waited two long hours for Rolando to abandon her body, the body that must be so white between the sheets, so soft to sink one's hands into. He thought of the other poor bodies he had known, withered and worn, smelling of his friends who had been there before him.

Clotilde must be different, he thought, and he had her in the palm of his hand. Now that he knew their secret and could denounce them. Soon he would show those two he also was a man. Rolo, little Rolo, would follow his father's footsteps to Clotilde's flesh. He would put his mouth where his father's had been, he would carefully imitate each of his gestures. The wait was long and torturous, but the compensation of Clotilde's hot, slippery body would come.

A blossoming azalea exuded a subtle smell that Rolo was not prepared to appreciate. Beyond the flowers, beyond the walls of the house, he imagined his naked father on the white Clotilde, and he knew his turn would come.

Rolando wouldn't take long. The door with the slightly flaky green paint would open just wide enough for him to slip out, and Rolo would only wait long enough to see Rolando recede in the distance. Then he would enter quickly and take Clotilde by force. She'd have no way to defend herself.

That wasn't how it happened at all, of course. Clotilde saw him, called to him, and he surrendered as meekly as a puppy. It was Clotilde who guided his hands along the trail of his father's hands.

"He asked me to swear not to say anything to you, and I swore and asked him to go on kissing me. . . . As if I cared . . ."

Rolando laughed a cold, empty laugh, but Clotilde went on

chattering. When she tried to cuddle up against his body, however, the muscles of his back arched one by one, and he leaped up, smashing his fist on the night table. A little while later, though, he sauntered into the bathroom as if nothing had happened. He came back looking calm and lay down beside her, but then doubt assailed him again and he shook Clotilde violently, shouting, "I'm better than the kid, right? Tell me I'm better than the kid!"

"Yes, yes," she said, and she thought of the boy who had never dared to sigh, and she felt tender toward him.

The following afternoon, Rolando told his wife that he was going out to get some cigarettes, and she seemed to believe him.

Rolo, however, couldn't say, "I'm going out to get some cigarettes," because he wasn't allowed to smoke. But he was allowed to come and go as he pleased, so he didn't have to make up excuses in order to visit Clotilde and engage in something far more serious than smoking.

As soon as his father left, Rolo, as usual, ran upstairs to spy on him from the attic window. The scene was always the same: Rolando, hurrying, furtive, ran into her open arms, and he, Rolo, felt happy because he would soon be on the path his father had paved for him, thus proving that he was no less a man.

But any man is a man, given certain attributes. In a sense, Clotilde was as much a man as either of them: she manipulated them as she pleased, frustrating them, pitting one against the other, favoring one over the other. She was the real man there, and she knew it. She reaffirmed it every night in the bed that often bore the weight and heat of one of them before the weight and heat of the other had faded. Clotilde. She would look at herself in the mirror, caressing her full breasts, smiling and showing her teeth, white, even, indifferent. Thinking was a tremendous effort for her: she simply felt happy and at times nostalgic. She also enjoyed tantalizing those who had the good fortune to touch her. And she felt no remorse about it.

In the big house on the other side of the dense acacias and the soft rosy mattress of pine needles, Estela, Rolo's mother and Rolando's wife, was also in the habit of looking at herself in the bathroom mirror. Her image emerged from the cloud of foam she used to clean the mirror. She ran the rag back and forth furiously, sometimes allowing only her eyes to appear, sometimes an ear or a corner of her mouth that revealed a hurt expression. She would have loved to rub that image out altogether, but there it was, facing her, inexorable, and all she could do was wash the mirror and hope a little of the cleanliness would rub off on her soul.

She knew it: her two men were gone forever, gone to the other woman because Estela was soft and easy, not hard and strong like the other one.

Rolo crouched behind the thick maze of acacias. He knew that the door would open at any moment, and he curled up even more in his hiding place. But it was a false alarm, or, more accurately, a false hope. His father was lingering longer than usual on Clotilde's body; it wasn't fair; Rolo was restless. What if she was detaining him? Could she have asked his father not to leave her? Still, the one time he had asked her how Rolando caressed her, she had answered, "Not exactly out of this world . . ."

"Please tell me what he does with you. I don't want to be less of a man."

"No, I like the differences. He's a brute. He beats me. Sometimes he slaps me across the face and shouts while he's making love to me."

She had turned toward him and put his uncombed head on her belly. "But you are soft, almost like a girl. I like to stroke your face, your shoulders, your back."

"Have you ever done it with a woman?"

"Hmm," she had answered vaguely. Sometimes he interpreted the *hmm* as yes, sometimes as no, depending on his mood.

He had been hiding behind the acacias for over two hours. Soon his mother would wake up from her siesta; he was furious. Clotilde knew very well that he was there, but there wasn't even a sign from her. That whore. She was worse, devouring anything that came her way—men, women, old people, children; a sexual ostrich.

To calm himself, Rolo walked behind the cottage. Hidden behind the shutters, the father watched his son's every move.

He doesn't know yet Clotilde isn't here. What the hell, let him suffer. I'm suffering too, Rolando kept repeating to himself.

Rolo stopped abruptly. Behind the climbing jasmines, in front of the bedroom window, there was a mound of cigar butts, some crushed, some smoked down to a nub, some only half smoked, all with a cork tip. His father had been there many times, probably hoping his son would leave Clotilde's bed once and for all so he, Rolando, could go back to her and have the last laugh.

Rolando knew his secret, he knew his son had also been there, just as he had been before him, just as he would be again. Always Rolando had to have the last word, the last loud laugh, the last act of love. His father always bested him, always flattened him out. It was Clotilde's fault this time for telling him everything, for not keeping her mouth shut. Whore.

Behind the shutters, Rolando felt jealous of his son and happy to see him standing there confused. Clotilde had left him a note saying she would be gone until evening. She must be avoiding him; she knew he would be coming that afternoon. And that poor boy, standing there disconsolate, believing his father was performing Heaven knows what feats, not realizing that those feats are usually a young man's prerogative.

A Family for Clotilde

On either side of the closed shutters, father and son stood overcome, defeated. He'll stay in there all afternoon, Rolo thought, all night, forcing her to forget about me. Finally Rolo decided to leave. He walked slowly down the path, kicking pebbles and telling himself that, after all, Clotilde must prefer women anyway, the struggle wasn't worth it.

Rolando watched Rolo move in the distance. He may be too thin, thought Rolando, and his back may curve, but still and all, Rolo is young and strong and intense in the way women like.

Neither of them could guess that Clotilde was fed up with the whole affair, with Rolo hiding in the garden while Rolando was with her, and then Rolando pacing back and forth in the garden like a caged lion, although he would never admit it. As if she didn't know that they were searching for each other through her.

That night, Rolo helped his mother wash the dishes, a thing he seldom did.

"Mama," he said after a long silence, "do you know the woman who rents the cottage in the back?"

"No."

There was an uncomfortable pause.

"You should get to know her. Make friends with her. She's very nice."

"I don't need friends. Not the likes of her, anyway."

"Why not make friends with her, Mama? After all, she's our tenant." It was a bold statement to make to a mother who must have known quite well what was going on. "You could go see her tomorrow and bring her a piece of that delicious cake you make. . . ."

His mother wiped the burners of the stove furiously, then took off her apron and went into the bedroom.

Rolando was in bed. He had not gone for a walk in the

woods, he was not reading in the living room. He was simply there, installed in bed as if he'd been waiting for her.

She spent a long time in the bathroom and came back into the bedroom in her nightgown.

"Estela," Rolando said, "Estela, you've been alone so much, too much lately. If we're going to stay here another two months, why not get to know people?"

"My friends are coming after Epiphany. . . ."

"That's a month away, Estela. Meanwhile what? Stay shut up in this house? The weather's nice now for the beach. You ought to have a friend to go with you."

"You have someone in mind?"

"In mind, no . . . the tenant, maybe. She seems pleasant enough."

It must be a conspiracy, she thought. They must be making fun of me. She was sick and tired of being treated like an idiot for trying to keep peace in the family. They wanted to see her act, well, she would act. The fight's on, she thought; let's see who wins. An inspection of the enemy camp can't hurt; that will give me an equal chance.

"Fine," she said, gently as usual. "If tomorrow's all right with you, I'll go visit her and bring some cake for tea."

Rolando was astonished at the ease with which he had convinced her.

The men in the family are sadder than ever. While they were enjoying themselves they could afford to overlook her pain. It had been a clean fight between men, altogether understandable. They had eaten with gusto, shown their happiness in an effort to make each other suffer. They had paid no attention to the woman who sat in front of them, doing her best not to burst into tears.

Now the situation is very different. Estela is exultant, she has turned into an eloquent conversationalist. She has acquired a new grandeur. She, Estela, now occupies an ample and warm place where the two men had once fit. Now Estela is alone and triumphant in Clotilde's bosom.

Listless, they never look at her or at each other. They only walk back and forth in the house that is no longer a home because Estela has neglected the floor, the meals. And she no longer bothers to put flowers on the table. She has other interests. From the last bite of lunch until sunset, she spends the day in Clotilde's cottage. A lightning friendship, one might say, blissful love at first sight, the reunion of queen bees, with the drones buzzing around like lost souls. Sometimes they circle around Estela, trying to get her back; at other times they attempt to get back to Clotilde. They haven't succeeded with either— no bread and no cake.

Finally, they were ready for a confrontation. But what could those two dispossessed beings say to each other, those two males who had learned that the only way they could reach each other was through silent competition?

The days went on until Rolo couldn't stand it any longer. He walked over to his old hiding place to spy on the cottage. He had hoped to set his mother against his father, but the wind had blown another way: good-by, Clotilde; good-by, love; good-by. Estela now took up all her time, all her gestures, all her words. She had shown herself to be the most astute: she had conquered Clotilde effortlessly. "You have a formidable mother," Clotilde had said to him the one time he saw her alone. And she hadn't said another word—no apologies, no gratitude for what had gone on before. About-face, march, and once again she was inside her cottage with the door firmly closed.

Huddled behind the acacias, Rolo is remembering the past with Clotilde. He knows that a few feet away, Rolando is taking his customary walk behind the climbing jasmines. Both are caught in the same trap, spying on the women who are devoted to one another and have no intention of parting.

Neither knows what he is waiting for, and each ignores the other's presence. They ignore everything except the world from which they have been excluded forever. They listen, and each in his hiding place receives on his face the lash of a kind of laugh, a submissive laugh, somewhat ashamed, that rises suddenly to cover up something and then lowers in tone, changing into a whisper that filters into the bones. Rolo leaps up and runs toward the bedroom window and, unexpectedly, collides with his father, who has also left his hiding place on hearing that laugh that threatens not to end. They look at each other accusingly, but neither says a word. They are both outside forever, and it is only because they had had the idea of putting Estela inside the cottage. Now Estela was never going to leave, for she had awakened Clotilde's laugh.

It is a well-tuned murmuring, like the pines, caressing, loving. Suddenly it begins to rain, softly at first, then with some fury. They remain in the garden, drenched, waiting until night falls.

Inside the cottage, Estela doesn't feel the cold, the rain, the night. She smiles with beatific happiness because her plan has succeeded. She makes Clotilde repeat once again the Act of Contrition and the Prayer to the Virgin. "Hail Mary, full of grace . . ." The prayer returns and undulates like a laugh that leaves Clotilde's contrite lips. And Estela, who doesn't really care about Clotilde's contrition, smiles because she knows that she has won back her men.

A Family for Clotilde

CLARA

to Michel Chodkiewicz

The Body

1 How boring to wait. Her left foot scratched her right
leg in a gesture of resignation. Her name was Clara, and she
had had it. Who else would have thought of wearing new shoes,
knowing all along she'd have to stand around and wait, and why
had she agreed to meet him on a corner where there was no
place to sit down?

And Victor telling me to be here before eight to avoid the
crowd. Now it's almost eight-thirty and there's still no sign of
him. I should know him better by now: he talks about tranquillity all the time, but there's no tranquillity. If I reproached
him he'd swear he didn't even remember we had a date.

As usual, Clara had been on time. She had been waiting since
before eight, while he, she was sure, sat at some bar talking
to some stranger, endowing words like "silence" with great sig-
nificance so he could savor the silence he himself had imposed.

In Victor's life, monotony and boredom had nothing to do
with one another. He repeated his repertoire so often that even
from miles away, Clara could follow his conversation with anyone who happened to be sitting next to him.

"Well, you have to take life with a grain of salt," the man
next to Victor would conclude, tired of the harangue.

Victor would never allow himself to be put off by an irrefuta-
ble platitude, nor miss the chance to have the last word.

"Not with salt, my friend. Salt makes fissures, it deceives
and distorts. Life, you see, has to be taken with its own pure
flavor, a flavor that satisfies hunger."

Unfortunately, Clara knew Victor's priceless clinchers very
well; what she didn't know was when he would use them. In
the beginning, she had listened to him attentively, expecting to
be initiated into what he called the secrets of harmony and
balance. However, she soon discovered that he said the same
things to everyone and that he had no special mystery to reveal

to her. So now she preferred to wait patiently and let him upset others with his need to be thought profound.

One by one, the streetlights went on around the square, the clock hands of the Torre de los Ingleses pointed pitilessly to eight-thirty, and, above Clara's head, the Parque Retiro's big neon star flickered as if it were real. The sky had turned a deep blue; it made her think about the sea, and for an instant she felt happy. It was that flash of happiness which at times redeems a day, a month, a year of indifference and insularity; for Clara, the sea was one of her fondest memories.

Through a scrim of wet haze, the people running toward the railroad station had the ponderous appearance of subterranean beings. Although the Southern Cross had not yet appeared in the sky, Clara's eyes were fixed at the exact point where it was hidden, and she tried not to move or be distracted for fear of missing it.

In that confused weariness, the weariness that comes of waiting, she expected everything. She even expected Victor—not with a great deal of hope, it's true, because everything came to her too late. Once, to console her, a friend had said, "Happiness never comes too late." The only words that had stayed with her were "late" and "never," permanently fused into a single, irremediable reality. It was that way with Victor. He remembered things at the wrong time, when they no longer mattered.

She raised her left hand to look at her watch, but suspended the gesture in midair; she remembered that three days earlier she had pawned the watch. Parting with it had been a great sacrifice, but they needed money, and Victor was a gentleman and would not let her walk the streets as she had done before. Victor was always there to tell her that he was a gentleman, and a gentleman would never allow his wife to be a prostitute.

As if we were married, Clara said to herself, but she chose to remain quiet, because with Victor no one was ever right. To

The Body

avoid hopeless arguments, she pawned her watch and the silver maté gourd her grandfather had given her. She did take the precaution of carefully hiding the pawn tickets for the day when she could redeem her treasures. She had learned her lessons well from Lady Experience, and did not trust Lady Luck.

The enormous Torre de los Ingleses, with its brick body and circle of light, didn't allow her to forget that time was passing. The grass squares of the park were no longer visible, and the water had stopped spurting from the slow-turning sprinklers. Victor, naturally, was nowhere in sight. He was fated to be late, just as he had been the night they met: she was, by then, imprisoned behind a wall of anguish that had built up slowly over the years and that no one could tear down now. She asked herself if it would not be too simple to blame everything on fate and in that way free herself of responsibility, but she realized her anguish was not of his making.

No, nor was it because her old work disgusted her or because she liked it: she did it without thinking, like when she came from Tres Lomas and got off the train at Once station. Back home, they had told her that in the capital the most beautiful place was the Palermo woods, with its lakes, its swans, and its neatly trimmed rose gardens. But when she descended the short flight of stairs from the station, she found herself facing a square and an inhospitable plaza with an inhospitable monument. She saw more people than she had ever seen before; they rushed along the wide avenues, breathing the fumes of millions of big and small buses, and for the first time she saw streetcars and heard them screech as they rounded a curb.

Carrying her suitcase, she took a walk around the plaza. Thinking of the woods she yearned to see, she asked an elderly man with a kind face how to get to Palermo. The man, thinking she meant the Palermo railroad station, told her to take the red minibus. When Clara arrived at Palermo, there were no trees, no lakes with swans, and the only roses were the ones wilting in the window of a flower shop that smelled like a cemetery. Next to the flower shop, though, there was a window filled with silk and lace blouses and flouncy skirts. She stood there looking at the window.

Her father had told her she was old enough to go to the city and find a good job. She hadn't the time to object, because her father had immediately locked himself in the bedroom, where Clara had once discovered him with the butcher's wife. There was nothing else for her to do but take off her apron, put on her coat, and meekly leave the house without waiting for her mother, who might return any day from her long trip to Quemú-Quemú. She walked the mile and a half to the station and boarded the eleven forty-five train. Now that she was in the city, however, the blouses were tempting her, keeping her in front of a shopwindow.

From a distance, a sailor with sparkling eyes had been watching her. He waited a little while before approaching her.

"Alone?" he asked; and then, "The blouses are pretty, aren't they, honey?"

"Uh huh."

"But you're even prettier."

She laughed. The boy seemed nice. He was in the navy, his uniform was blue, not a murky green like some she had seen. So Clara agreed to have a drink with him in the café across the street. Besides, she was hungry, although she didn't know how to go about asking for the dinner special. She drank the Martini in one gulp so she could get quickly to the olive. She kept sucking on the pit. Hunger, however, couldn't be fooled by a morsel, and she was afraid the bubbles she felt in her stomach would start to rumble. She asked a question to forestall that possibility.

"Is the sea pretty?"

"Believe it or not, I don't know. I've been in the navy for a year and we haven't left port once. The fellows say the ship's too tired to go to sea and it only stays afloat because the river's thick with muck."

He laughed. He was missing two teeth, which somewhat diminished his charm; also, it was rather depressing to meet a sailor who had never seen the sea. Without feeling guilty, she accepted a second Martini and a third. Then she took courage and asked for the dinner special, but he had a better plan.

"What do you say we take a little stroll upstairs? There're some nice, cozy rooms. . . ."

Clara's elbow was on the table, her chin resting in her hand. Outside, the cold fell with the night, and inside, the café was warm and inviting, with its many mirrors and curtains—dirty perhaps, but inviting all the same. She looked indifferently at the sailor. Everything seemed at once so beautiful and unimportant, and she had the sensation of floating. She shrugged, smiled wryly out of the corner of her mouth, and answered, "If you feel like it . . ."

On the second floor, the room with an iron bed wasn't pretty at all. It was cold. The man who had gone up with them ran to close the window. "Have to air out the place between one and the next, right?" And he left them alone.

Clara didn't even realize she was being undressed. Once they got into bed, she asked the sailor his name, but the question was lost in moans. In the morning, he rose at five to return to his ship. Pleased that he had taken her virginity, he left a hundred pesos on the night table and ran off to tell his buddies about the great catch he'd made on Plaza Italia.

Clara, on the other hand, woke up late, with a terrible headache and a strange dry taste in her mouth. Slowly she recalled what had happened, but the money under the lamp saved her from shame. She got dressed and, looking in the mirror, settled on a vague expression which she thought would serve to get her out of the elevator and through the café with dignity. But just as she passed the cash register, the owner approached her and she lost her composure.

"Nice of you to honor our modest establishment, miss. You'll find all the necessary comforts and discretion here, if you want to come again."

He cleared his throat, straightened his tie, and unobtrusively slipped thirty pesos in her coat pocket. Frightened, Clara looked around her, but there were only a few customers at that hour of the morning, and no one seemed to notice what had just occurred. She left the café thinking that life in the city wasn't too pleasant, but it wasn't as bad as she had been told either. She went into another café to have a hot chocolate and a sweet roll while she counted her money. Then she walked to the shopwindow where the blouses were, and this time she looked at the prices.

She lingered there to make sure the hundred and thirty pesos she had earned—she hesitated at the word "earned"; she preferred "gotten"—plus the twenty-six she had brought from home could not pay for something that cost the fabulous sum of one hundred ninety-nine pesos and ninety cents. She remained looking at the window and peering down the street, secretly hoping to spot the sailor again. Finally, she grew bored and walked toward the center of town, studying the uniforms that passed.

She forgot about shopwindows until she came to a German restaurant with a large sign that said "Indoor Garden." It was noon, and a cup of chocolate and a sweet roll weren't enough to fill the stomach of a person with a physically demanding occupation. Besides, the garden might very well turn out to be the park with the lake and swans she had heard about. She decided to go in.

The garden was small, but there were several tables in the sun with red tablecloths, and the steak and French fries were almost as delicious as the caramel-and-whipped-cream dessert. She did not miss Tres Lomas at all. When she left the restaurant, she realized her capital had been considerably reduced, but she wasn't too worried. She had enough money to last her through the night.

2   At last the Southern Cross appeared, dotting the clear sky, and there was no longer any reason for Clara to continue gazing upward, dwelling on her past. Victor was still not there. Her legs were hurting, and she was afraid impatience would win out. She always brushed aside negative feelings and refused to be carried away by anger or despair.

To shake off her unhappy thoughts, she decided to walk. She was rewarded when she came upon a low wall in front of a souvenir stand where she could sit down. There, at least she could be comfortable.

I hope Victor takes a little longer, so I can rest, so I can take off these tight shoes. I've walked too much since I came to the capital, or rather since the fourth customer I had on my own, the one who wore that battered hat he wouldn't take off even when he jumped into bed. I remember asking him, before we went upstairs, if we could have a drink, something to make it a little easier.

"A drink? Like hell," he had answered. "I pay to have you in bed, not sitting at a bar. Do you think money grows on trees?"

The customer is always right. Besides, you have to finish what you start, so Clara forgot about the drink. She would go to the sacrifice with a clear mind, like cows she had seen going to the slaughterhouse, surely knowing they were about to die.

The man didn't waste a moment with her. He finished his business quickly, leaped up, zipped up his fly, and clapped on the hat, which had fallen off his head in an involuntary gesture of courtesy. He shook Clara's arm.

"Get up, lazy. It's time to leave."

"You leave. I'm going to sleep."

"You think I'm paying for you to snore?"

"Don't get excited. It's the same price anyway." Clara yawned and covered her face with the pillow.

"Same price, your mother's ass! At this hour, I'm paying for every extra minute. Get up by yourself or I'll get you up!"

It was useless to argue with this fellow, so Clara chose to dress slowly and to go downstairs, doing both with her best expression of disgust.

As she passed the front desk, the man behind the register—the one who had given her the thirty pesos and who smiled whenever she came to the café—felt pity for her, a pity that had ulterior motives: he called her into the coatroom, felt her breasts, then tapped her cheek consolingly with one hand while patting her behind with the other.

"Take this key, child. Go up to Room Five and wait. I'll cheer you up."

When Clara arrived at Room Five—a luxurious room she had never seen before—she realized that it must belong to the owner. There were curtains, a flowered coverlet, and a wardrobe of shiny wood. She sat down on the edge of a chair facing the sink; she clasped her hands in her lap and lowered her eyes. One had to savor these moments of hope: the owner had asked her to his own room; someday, perhaps, he would marry her.

A few minutes later the man arrived. He immediately switched off the overhead light and switched on the bedside lamp—"to make it more intimate," he said.

He reclined the beautiful Clara on the bed and disappeared

behind the half-open wardrobe door. When he finally reappeared, stark naked, all Clara's hopes vanished. He was as white and blubbery as those strange creatures she had seen mornings in the fish market—God knows who had told her they were called squid. She secretly christened him "The Squid," and when he forced her to place her open hand on his belly, she was surprised that it was neither slimy nor cold.

She woke up the following morning and opened the Venetian blinds like a good housekeeper. The light that suddenly brightened the room brought her back to reality and, as always happened, to disenchantment.

Like hell he's the owner!

The man who had gone to bed with her couldn't be important in the hotel, because he didn't live in that elegant room: the wardrobe door was open and she could see that it was empty. The few hangers there seemed sad not to have clothing to support.

Dreaming's a waste of time. No one's going to want to marry me, ever: for that you have to say no, show restraint. I can't play those games any more.

A short while later she heard a gentle knock at the door and, without waiting for an answer, the man entered carrying a tray.

"Don Mario has breakfast for his precious. . . ."

So your name is Don Mario. So I'm your precious. You're bringing me breakfast. It's not all bad.

Modestly, she covered her breasts with the sheet and smiled back softly. Don Mario placed the tray on her knees, and she began to sip the hot café au lait, which pleased her senses more than all the love-making. But The Squid, of course, kept annoying her, and that destroyed all the charm.

"I don't understand how a fine girl like you can go around doing these things. . . ."

She soaked a croissant in the coffee. "Out of necessity."

"Where do you live?"

"Here, for the time being."

A few drops of coffee fell on the sheet, which smelled of bleach.

"Mother of God! I can't have you here. Don't you know the boss doesn't want to have anything to do with regulars? He says he has enough headaches already with the ones who come and go; he needs customers, he says, but not that bad. . . ." He touched her naked back with a caressing hand.

"Don't worry about anything, señor. I just sleep with men. . . ."

During the day she didn't like to talk about those things. She preferred to walk around the zoo or go to the movies. Near the hotel there was a theater with a continuous show, which was exactly what she needed, for at the end of three viewings there wasn't a detail left undiscovered. The first time, she simply looked at the images; the second time, she read the subtitles; and the third time, she tried to do both at once and figure out what the story was about. The last time was always the most moving, but she couldn't explain that to The Squid. Instead, she decided to repeat, "I just sleep with men."

"You're a dreamer, woman. If I wanted to exploit you, I'd get rich. But I don't take advantage of people," he sighed. "And besides, nowadays, this business has gotten very risky. But I won't hurt you, you'll see. I'm going to protect you like a father."

What good are fathers? If you only knew my story. . . .

"Yes, like a father . . ." Don Mario repeated to keep the conversation alive. "How old are you?"

"Twenty-one."

"Thank God, at least you're of age. You don't look it, though. I would have said eighteen, at the most. Tell me, how long have you been around here? You said you're twenty-one, right? You're already a woman. . . . Gee, I thought you were just a kid. I even told myself you couldn't be more than seventeen. It's a pity, isn't it?"

Who can understand men? First they say one thing and then they say another; first they say it's better to be almost of age, and then they pretend you're seventeen.

To please him, she wanted to tell him that until five days ago she had been what is called a virgin, but she didn't know how to phrase such a delicate matter.

'Well, don't you worry. I'll help you all the same. Do you have a little savings?"

"No."

"See, see? Just what I said! You don't even know the basics of life, my girl! Do you think you can spend the rest of your life like this? Without thinking about tomorrow, without a roof over your head or a penny in your pocket? If you count on those poor fish you catch at Plaza Italia . . . The one last night left you in the lurch. Besides, you can't live on what you get from one man a night; you have to find two, three, four, I don't know how many. Some find as many as ten. Don't look at me that way; you'll get used to it soon. But you'll need a corner where you can rest. . . . Look"—he went on as if he'd had a sudden inspiration—"look, I'll work it out with the boss to rent you a little room for a special price, and in exchange you can bring me customers. On the days when you hook more than three who have a few drinks, I won't charge you. Don't tell them you live here. Make them take another room. Then they have to pay, right? Don't be a fool."

Clara nodded in agreement, although she realized she was going too far along a path she hadn't chosen.

Maybe that's how things happen in life, whether you like it or not; probably because it's already written, as they say.

"The little room will cost you almost nothing . . . if you do me a little favor once in a while, of course."

To save time and to seal the pact, Don Mario wanted a little favor immediately; he lay on the bed almost fully dressed. Clara did what she could, but the pact was only half sealed, and that same morning she discovered that while any time is good for going to bed, there are men who are not so good at any time. It was a relief.

It's sad to think of Don Mario; he turned out to be all right, really; a squid with a heart of gold. . . . And I am all woman now, just as he said. And without having come too far along in life. It's a change, having someone to wait for, but it's not the same as getting ahead. Most of all I'd like to have someone waiting for me, like ladies do. One day my time may come. Who knows? Right now, though, the ledge of the wall is hard and narrow, and my feet hurt.

She walked to the corner, just for something to do, and she heard arrogant steps.

"Excuse me, miss. Your papers, please."

It was the voice of a hoodlum speaking out of the corner of his mouth. Clara turned around sharply, frightened, and found herself looking straight at a well-trimmed mustache.

"Oh, Officer. I don't have my papers. I left them at home."

"Sergeant," he corrected her, throwing his head back. Clara laughed in a high-pitched voice to show that she wasn't afraid and that she liked strong men.

"So you forgot them, eh? And what are you doing, walking around here all alone?"

"Waiting for my boyfriend, Sergeant."

"Has he kept you waiting long?"

"Well, long enough . . ."

"Come off it, kid. That boyfriend story is older than Methuselah. You've been sitting here forever. If you're looking for a real man, come with me. I'm the best in town." He laughed, showing a row of large white teeth.

The Body

"You're mistaken, Sergeant. I'm not what you think, believe me. I'm waiting for my boyfriend."

How maddening! Don't forget Don Mario's advice just because of a small blond mustache. Stay away from cops.

She had learned about cops soon after she had been given her own little room. Deciding to make the most of her new position, she had taken a handsome young rookie to the hotel café. To show him she wasn't a beginner, she sat at the table sideways and summoned the waiter with a nod. She was as well known there as anyone walking around, and the waiter would certainly give her a big hello. But he gave her no sign of recognition. Nothing. He came toward them, scrupulously wiping his metal tray with the towel he always carried under his arm, and asked, "What would you like?"

The rookie ordered a beer, and Clara was about to say, "The usual for me," when she noticed Don Mario gesturing desperately from behind the cash register. The cop saw Clara frown, but she could only look beyond him at Don Mario's frenetic hands alternately motioning her to the door and pointing at her as if they held a gun. At last she understood. She managed to smile at her companion and ordered a rum and Coke.

A few minutes after the drinks arrived, she looked at the clock on the wall and, like a perfect actress, exclaimed, "God! it's seven-thirty. My mother must be worried." She picked up her purse, jumped up, and, with her sweetest smile, said, "Officer, it was a pleasure to meet you. See you again, I hope."

If she had been on the stage her exit would have received a long ovation, but this was life and she was not at all pleased to disappear while the poor boy, with his mouth open, watched her infinitely repeated image finally vanish from the café mirrors.

She was on the street again. It was Don Mario's fault; after all, that young cop was the most promising customer she had found.

Young, handsome, just the right sort to help her find out if the business of going to bed could be more pleasant. She thought of Eulosia, the crazy one, as she was called in Tres Lomas. Eulosia had raved about going to bed.

She felt sorry for herself.

It's terrible, a young girl like me having to work all the time. And not a moment of pleasure. Horrible Squid, you forced me to get rid of the cop. Tonight I won't bring you a single customer. Drop dead, for all I care; you won't get anything from me.

An hour later she returned to the café, sat at a table, and angrily ordered a double brandy. From his watching post behind the cash register, Don Mario noticed she was upset and came over to comfort her.

"You know, it's better not to get mixed up with the police. When you least expect it, they'll ask for a permit we don't have and then lock us all up. Especially you. Us, we can pay a bribe and everything will be fixed, but you'd be lost. I did it for your own good."

My own good. Jealous pig.

"You don't have to jump at the first guy who comes along. Someday you'll meet a prince of a fellow, you'll see. Come on, cheer up." He made her drink another brandy and then followed her upstairs to her room on the third floor.

"Are you going to invite me in?" he asked as they reached her door. Clara nodded.

"Don't play with the bulls," he went on. "Uniforms are beautiful but dangerous. First they take advantage of a woman and then, bang! They finish it off by putting her in jail. Whatever path you follow, modesty is the best virtue," he concluded.

Pompous ass.

Nevertheless, Clara had absorbed that lesson and promised herself never again to be impressed by a double row of silver buttons or the little stars given after five years of active service.

The Body

When Clara made a decision, she was as firm as a rock.

"But my boyfriend will be here any minute."

"Don't try to kid me, baby. Don't give me that innocent act. I like my women simple and straight."

If only Victor would show up. Waiting isn't too bad when you can stir up memories you've set aside for years; but waiting when you're face to face with a blue uniform doesn't leave you a moment to think of anything else.

She leaned against the wall, and the sound of the Cuban orchestra playing on the other side reached her in slow waves. The sergeant said a few more things to her, but she didn't hear him because she was concentrating so intently on the hands of the tower clock. Victor obviously wasn't coming, and here was this other man, entrenched in his arrogance.

She looked at her nails, pretending to be distracted. Another woman passed by, almost touching her. The sergeant whirled around.

"Miss, may I see your papers, please. . . ."

Clara felt lighter when he left, as if the sergeant's solid body had been weighing on hers.

3   At times, waiting is as tiresome as working; muscles become tense, contracted. Clara found it difficult to understand why she was tense about Victor. They had been living together for more than three months, enough time for her to have become accustomed to seeing him arrive at the most unlikely hours.

Let your whole body relax, like in bed, beginning with your face to prevent wrinkles. Don't make fists. Don't dig your nails into the palms of your hands. Think about something else, anything else. Victor will never surprise me by arriving on time, not even once.

She had met him on the night when all her optimistic notions and good faith had forsaken her. The only consolation she had had was the pleasure of hateful thoughts, which made her feel stronger but which were also tearing her apart. She wanted to strike at something with her bare hands, to twist something, to rip it into shreds, to strangle it. Once she had believed in goodness, but she no longer had the strength to believe; all the desperation of her life was focused now on destructive desires, and she looked at the passing subway cars in search of some way to restore indifference.

He got off one of those cars, just in front of her, and stared at her. For a long while, he stood there staring at that woman, so pale, with such big eyes, so lost. She had a vague beauty, like an old engraving he had seen in a bookstore window. Her hair was straight and long, like that engraving. Finally, when the platform was almost empty, he approached her.

"I don't like tunnels, either," he said. "Let's go look at the stars."

Clara smiled bitterly, but someone was offering her a hand and it was difficult to refuse that hand. They went up the escalator and found themselves facing a dull, starless sky.

"The Three Marys must be behind the Coca-Cola sign, and the Southern Cross over there, near the church steeple," Clara said. But he wasn't listening.

"My name is Victor. And yours?"

"Clara."

"A pretty name. Transparent, like peace must be. You couldn't be called anything else. That's why I liked you. I had to take you out of there. I hate closed-in places and crowds and noise. You hate them too, I'm sure. What were you doing in the subway?" He didn't give her time to answer. "Life should be an open space, where everything is clear, Clara. Clear without chlorine, clear as clear water."

The phrase seemed perfect to her, and she relished it in silence. But then she thought he was waiting for her reaction, so she said, "I don't understand anything about life, but it seems to me that . . ."

He took her hand. "Shhh . . . Don't talk. The moment is too delicate, too rare to shatter with sounds," and he remained sniffing the air to inhale the moment.

They had just met, but Clara knew that with him it would be useless to open her mouth. The idea of not being able to talk didn't worry her too much, for no one could prevent her from continuing an inner monologue, silent but intense. That same night, sitting on the steps of the new church, they decided that since Clara didn't have a place of her own, she would move to Victor's house for a while.

The apartment was old and small, with a tree that grew so close it almost came through the window. Victor felt proud showing her the matrimonial bedroom suite he had just bought, as if he had had a premonition. The enormous wardrobe and double bed, the two night tables, and the chair cluttered the one room. The narrow passageway had nothing in it yet—a blessing, Clara thought, because there was no room for anything else, except possibly a mirror and a clothes tree. The kitchen was long and narrow and also served as a dining room. Victor told her he would have it painted green to keep flies away. She looked at him admiringly.

"Then you're rich, with new furniture and everything. . . ."

"Well, I have a little nest egg. I'm also thinking of selling that old radio and buying a new one; you know, one of those small ones with a golden dial."

Clara settled into her new home, happy to have a man who gave her socks to mend and shirts to wash. That way, at least, she could say she was a true homemaker. She also had dishes to wash and new saucepans, which Victor had brought home one afternoon because he was tired of eating ham and cheese sandwiches.

Clara did a lot of scrubbing because there was nothing else to do. Victor never allowed her to talk. By now she had lost the use of her voice, but she could still dream. Her favorite fantasy was the one about marriage. She had perfected it all the way, to its very ending—no winners and no losers. The truth was that she didn't want to marry Victor any more than he wanted to marry her. On days she had nothing to do, she would stretch the daydream to the infinite; when she was tired, though, she would sum it up in a few words: it wasn't worth marrying and having children, because, as Victor said, "it's too complicated."

Victor did have crushing arguments, and it was better to agree with him, even in thought. Besides, Victor was making an effort to be good to Clara, a fact she couldn't ignore. She was already too weary from wrestling with his defects to attack the few virtues he had left.

When their life together was going smoothly, he would call her Clarita and take her out for an evening. But when some problem arose, it was invariably her fault, and he would refer to her as "my wife." At those times Clara would tell herself how much better off she was not being married to Victor, even if it meant not having children.

Usually, though, their life together went well. Clara learned how to haggle with the butcher to get the most meat for the least money, and Victor appreciated her boiled dinners. Sometimes, it's true, she did dream of the blouses and necklaces she used to buy, and, feeling despondent, she would go for a walk around

The Body

Plaza Italia. But it was her vocation as homemaker that would win out, and instead of buying the pretty lace-trimmed slip she wanted so badly, she would come home with a chicken and a bottle of good wine. Since men's minds are conquered through their stomachs, Victor never took the trouble to ask how these delicacies reached their table.

The inevitable day arrived when Victor confessed to her that his savings were spent and that lately he hadn't been able to sell even one refrigerator. Clara told him not to worry, she would find some customers, but that infuriated him.

"Are you crazy? I wouldn't think of using you that way. Do you believe I've sunk so low? Do you expect me to send you back to the gutter I took you out of?"

He fell silent, and then his fury changed to humility.

"Look here, Clarita, the best thing we can do is pool our strength to weather the storm. Everything will be all right soon, you'll see. I'll pawn my cuff links and my pearl tie pin. The new radio, too, if you think I should, although I don't think that'll be necessary. You . . . well . . . would you have something to add?"

"Yes," she sighed, and went to get her grandfather's silver maté gourd. Then she took off her wrist watch and handed it to Victor.

She didn't care much about her grandfather's maté gourd: it only brought back memories of her fifteenth birthday, a day as boring as any other. The watch, though, was as much hers as her feet or her mouth. It was her medal, won in a moment of courage she might never repeat. One of her greatest pleasures was to watch the tiny wheels spin around while she told herself that she had managed to escape without too many scars from machinations as fiendish as those she was watching.

Of course, luck had been on her side.

Over and over, Don Mario had told her in that special tone he used when, as he said, he was trying to protect her from the evil of the outside world, "Never go after men with cars. Cars are very nice, and men wearing gold chains are attractive, but they're bad. Who knows where they'll take you and what they'll do with you. Your profession isn't one of the easiest, right? And if you give in to someone who won't stop until he has sucked your soul dry, don't come crying to me. I'm telling you now: no cars or men flashing a fat roll of bills."

Clara decided to follow Don Mario's sound advice to the letter. It's good to have someone guide your early steps. But she couldn't get the car out of her mind. She wanted to get ahead, and she knew there was a vast difference between a man with his foot on a gas pedal and one with his foot on the curb. There was a social difference, too. Besides, she dreamed of seeing the sea, and a car was necessary for that, one with soft reclining seats to set the mood for foamy blue waters. The sea couldn't have a train filled with fat women and snoring men as its prologue.

She had never brought up the subject of the sea with Don Mario. She enjoyed having secrets to ponder as she sat in the solitude of her room on the top floor, facing the window that looked out on a black roof spotted with the pigeon droppings. Sometimes she hoped the pigeons would change into sea gulls that would eat from her hand. And every morning she threw out bread crumbs, just in case.

Don Mario had also advised her not to get mixed up with the hotel employees. "They're a bunch of alley cats. You're going with the manager. That gives you a certain position in life. One has to have dignity, my girl."

He smiled with pleasure then, and remained still. She would take advantage of such moments to close her eyes and imagine that the man next to her was not Don Mario at all, but Carlos, one of the waiters on the afternoon shift.

Clara's dreams were divided between Carlos and the sea.

Carlos was tall and dark, and when one looked at him closely she could see golden spots in his eyes. Every once in a while, Clara would ask him to bring up tea and pastries at five in the afternoon, the fashionable hour, but he would stay only long enough to greet her and place the tray on the night table. She always promised herself that next time she would receive him with her robe slightly open, but she never did, because Carlos was shy and she didn't want to make a bad impression. For the same reason, she went out to work after nine, after Carlos had left the café.

But one afternoon her confinement became more than she could bear, and she left her room before eight, dressed in her new lilac dress even though it was too low cut for the cool October night. But if she had felt confined in her room, on the street she felt worse. She stood in front of the café windows watching the neon lights changing colors. Suddenly a voice tickled the flesh on the back of her neck.

"Are you waiting for somebody, Señorita Clara?"

She turned her head, startled, and whispered, "Oh no, no."

"Are you busy?"

"No."

Now that she faced him, she didn't know what to do, but she ventured to say softly, "The night is so beautiful. . . ."

"A beautiful night to be enjoyed. 'Ambition rests . . .' " he said, quoting the words of a tango. "Since neither of us has anything to do, why not have a drink together?"

Clara looked at him as if she were dreaming. "Yes," she answered in a voice thin as thread, and she moved toward the café door.

"No, not here, Clara. May I call you Clara? Let's go someplace else. Change the setting. I know a nice bar in Rosedal, facing the lake. We could even take a twirl around the dance floor."

"I don't dance very well. . . ."

"That doesn't matter; they keep the lights dim there, so no one will be able to see us."

They looked at each other and laughed. It was the first time Clara had laughed with a man. Usually, she would laugh at a man before he could laugh at her, or she would laugh to please him if he said something intended to be funny. But she and Carlos laughed together, and when she spoke, it was without watching her words.

"All right, the bar by the lake, and if no one can see us, we'll have fun."

He took her by the arm firmly, and they turned into a dark street. They walked in silence. Carlos was holding her arm and she was afraid to break the enchantment. "We can call each other Clara and Carlos," he ventured. "We've known each other for months."

"That's true."

But they continued to walk in silence, with the lights of the avenue dwindling into small white spots.

They strolled at an easy pace, their steps marking the rhythm of the night. Carlos let go of her elbow and put his arm around her shoulders; Clara felt stiff and clumsy, her arms hanging at her sides. As they were crossing a street, Carlos stopped her in the yellow circle of light that fell from a street lamp.

"You are too pretty," he said.

Clara shivered as he pressed her against his chest.

"Are you cold?" he asked, and she shook her head, which she rested on his shoulder as they went on walking.

First he caressed her forehead and then he took her hand.

"Is the bar much further?" Clara asked, although she never wanted to get there, despite the lake and the swans.

"You're tired, let's rest a bit," he said, as he sat down on a low wall that bordered a garden. Carlos drew her to him gently

The Body

and sat her on his knees. She lowered her head, afraid that the feelings hammering inside her temples would escape, and he took advantage of the moment to kiss the hair at the nape of her neck. Then Clara raised her eyes and found the little golden spots in his eyes.

With a tremendous effort, Carlos pulled himself away from her and put his arm around her shoulders again as they moved on. He whispered into her ear words that were full of magic.

The lights of a new street stunned her eyes. There were no streetcars or buses, only cars that sped by. Clara let Carlos decide the right moment to cross the road, and she let herself be led, eyes closed, enjoying the sensation of being cared for.

On the other side, the woods were barely lit by the street lamps. Beyond, there was the thick darkness of blooming trees.

Carlos led her to the darkest part of the map drawn by the shadows of tree trunks. He took his jacket off and spread it flat on the ground, under a big eucalyptus tree. He stretched Clara out on the jacket and lay upon the soft mattress of her body.

Disarmed with passion, Clara was afraid of what she was and of what she was no longer, the part of herself that she had given up without regrets when she came to the city. A moment of fear as he separated from her, that long emptiness so full of man and earth, a step closer to the gods and, at last, after so many rehearsals, closer to happiness.

Back at the hotel, Clara wanted to feel forever as she felt now, with the sensation of Carlos's body floating on hers. She sat at the bar and ordered a cognac, smiling blissfully and looking at Don Mario without seeing him.

"Clarita, my girl," Don Mario called from behind the cash register. "You look strange. You must have been out drinking. Go up to your room and get some sleep. In the morning I'll bring you a nice hot cup of coffee and an aspirin and you'll see how much better you'll feel."

Don Mario kept his promise and brought her an aspirin along with the coffee, though Clara had never felt better. She was radiant. Then Don Mario shattered the enchantment into a thousand pieces.

"How many times have I told you not to go out with anyone who works at the hotel? A pretty mess you got me into! Last night Carlos's wife came in like a madwoman, looking for her husband. Pichi told her he had seen him with you. Imagine what an uproar there was! And I got all the screaming. To make matters worse, now we're without a waiter. That bitch won't let him come back here."

Those few words had the taste of death. Clara leaned against the pillow, drank the coffee, and swallowed the aspirin, trying to understand why she had to pay so dearly for every minute of happiness.

Now, with Victor, she at least lived quietly: she was not excessively happy, but then again she was not afraid that the relentless judges who rule life would make her pay for these monotonous days. At the most, they would give her the penance of waiting without a show of impatience, of facing the enormous clock that intensified the awareness of time. It wasn't like the time she had waited for Carlos: three days and nights without eating, without sleeping, without leaving the hotel. She hadn't wanted anything to distract her from her waiting.

She consoled herself by telling herself that he had deceived her—after all, he had never told her he was married. But she also blamed herself.

I deceived him, too. I never told him how I earned my living. I'm to blame for everything. Yes, he'll come back; he hasn't come yet because his wife is an ogre and has him locked up. But he'll escape. It doesn't change the fact that he deceived me, though. At least I wasn't betraying anyone, but he had his own woman. Maybe even children.

Even so, she waited. But Carlos never appeared again.

On the last night, as they were putting the chairs on top of the tables in order to wash the floor, Don Mario took her by the arm and said, "I'm going to put you to bed. You need it."

Clara let him lead her out of the café and into the elevator. He didn't even try to fondle her between floors.

When they got to the room, he forced her to sit next to him on the bed and said reproachfully, "I told you not to go out with waiters, but you didn't listen. Those kind of men play with women and then disappear. I hope you've learned your lesson. Now you won't disobey old Mario again, eh?"

He helped her to undress and tucked her into bed; he turned off the light and sat down on the chair at her side. He wanted to make love to her, but he knew that Clara needed sleep; then she would forget everything and things between them would be the same.

Obedience. Lots of obedience, but if it weren't for you, old Squid, Carlos would still be here and I could see him as much as I wanted.

She slept until the next evening, when Don Mario had one of the maids bring her a cup of hot chocolate and a ham sandwich.

An hour later she went down to the café and, as she passed the bar, she realized that she could no longer live there. The despair sat hard in her gut, and she left the café resolved to give up the life at Don Mario's and find a man who would take her to the sea in his own car.

She began to study the long cars that went by, the fancy two-toned ones with tail fins, but most of them were driven by uniformed chauffeurs and she knew that an important man couldn't reveal to a subordinate that he needs a hooker.

He has to pretend he can have all the women he wants by simply lifting his little finger. Of course, there are some ladies who are too difficult and some who are too easy, but unfailingly they are also too expensive and full of airs. That's why every so often these proper gentlemen have to look for a woman whose price is fixed, but they can't do that in front of everyone, and least of all in front of their own chauffeurs.

Nevertheless, Clara continued waiting for the right car. She even refused a blond sailor, and sailors were usually the best customers around Plaza Italia. Each time she saw a car with a man alone in it, she bent down to smile, but they were all in too much of a hurry to notice her. Finally, a car pulled up at the curb in front of her. She hadn't smiled at that one because it was an old-fashioned model, but the driver said "Get in!" with such authority that Clara obeyed.

As she settled into the car, she noticed that the seats were fairly comfortable, and they might even be able to get as far as the ocean if the motor didn't break down. It occurred to her that perhaps the front seat could be pushed back to make a bed, like that drawing on the cover of a magazine that the Catholic Action in her town had condemned as immoral.

Ridiculous! How can a drawing of a car ever be moral or immoral?

She had not dared to defend it before the Committee, but when she went to confession the following Sunday, she told the priest about her bad thought. She still remembered how he had admonished her:

"My daughter, bad thoughts are like flies on candy: one alone seems inconsequential, but soon others are attracted, and they accumulate and cling to one another until they form a putrid body. Say six Hail Marys and three Our Fathers. . . ."

Clara tried to think of other bad thoughts she had had since; she could find none. Until now, as she again wished for a car that would change into a bed and take her to the sea. Therefore, she concluded, if she hadn't had bad thoughts, she couldn't have a putrid body. That idea was soothing, and she smiled.

The Body

She casually ran her fingers through her hair and said to the stranger, "Let's to go the Almafuerte bar. It's very pleasant there."

Awful habit. If I go back there, I'll think about Carlos again and I'll never be able to make this one take me away.

The man seemed to read her thoughts. "You think I'm a taxi that'll take you wherever you want to go?"

Clara looked at him, wide-eyed. The stranger lit a cigarette and brought the lighter perilously close to her face.

"Do you have an obligation to go there?"

"No, no obligation."

"Who's in charge of you, honey? This isn't the first time I've seen little innocent you cruising around here."

"Nobody's in charge of me."

Clara thought that was the right moment to sigh, to be elegant and sad at the same time, but she never had the chance because the car shot ahead. "Then let's go where I want to go."

A few blocks farther on, they had to brake to let a truck go by.

"What's your name?" the man asked.

"Clara."

"I am Toño Cruz. My buddies call me Devil Cruz."

That was only a half-truth, of course. His classmates in the second grade had called him Devil Cruz, but no one since then had used the nickname. Certainly not at the bank where he had been working for fifteen years at the same job, and where he was considered quite respectable. Nevertheless, he repeated, "Devil Cruz, ha ha!" and slapped her on the back.

He stepped on the gas again and kept his foot pressed hard on the accelerator until they stopped abruptly in front of an austere building with a brown marble façade. The car moved slowly toward a garage door, which opened automatically to admit them. When Clara turned around to see how the door worked, it had already closed behind them and they were surrounded by darkness. The shadow of a man approached, making such obsequious gestures that Clara didn't have to be coaxed to get out of the car and to follow Toño Cruz and the porter into the somber, carpeted corridor.

When they were alone inside the apartment and the bright light was turned on, Clara saw that Toño Cruz was shorter than she had thought, and that there were white streaks in his hair. His chin came to a sharp point, and the top of his head was flat, but Clara knew that the perfect prostitute doesn't worry about her customer's physical appearance. He was studying her, too, but that was fine, because a customer can waste his time in foolish games; after all, he's paying for it.

When he finished inspecting her from a distance, he approached to touch her, rolling his tongue over his lips.

"All right, undress. Now we'll try you out."

Clara undressed meekly and made a move to turn off the light, but he told her to leave it on. She came toward him slowly, like a cat, and rubbed against his body.

When they finished, Clara figured that playing the cat had pleased Toño, because he had tried to please her. She decided she would play the cat with all men from now on. Don't think of Carlos, don't think of Carlos, she told herself. The phrase was lulling her to sleep when a roar cracked the air.

"What's that?" she asked, startled.

"Nothing, woman . . . a boat whistle . . ."

"Are we near the sea?"

She knew very well that you had to travel at least five hours to reach the sea, but they had driven so fast . . . A city-educated boy from her town had explained to her once that if one goes very fast, time no longer exists. She hadn't understood him, she had been afraid of him, and she never wanted to see him after that, even though he had asked her to marry him. That had only made her more afraid, sure that he would fill her head with peculiar ideas simply to make it easy to abuse her and forsake her. Now everything was different: no one could abuse her and she could clearly understand that they had moved so fast toward the sea that they had escaped time.

But Toño, Devil Cruz, brought her back from her comforting illusions.

"What sea are you talking about, dummy? We're near the harbor. Don't you know the harbor?"

"No."

"And the Rio de la Plata?"

"No."

"And this neighborhood?"

"No."

"Then what *do* you know?"

"Well . . . very little."

Toño Cruz decided to play his trump card. "The best thing you can do for yourself is come with me. I'll teach you everything you need to know."

"Seriously? But I have a room in a hotel. . . ."

"You're alone, aren't you? Then what the devil do you care? Come to my house and make yourself at home. A classy apartment on Junin Street, lined with shops."

"And leave my work?"

"Your work? You're not a maid, are you?"

"Oh, no. This is my work."

"Ah, this isn't work. It's a pastime. Don't give it a thought. You'll be much better off with me. When you have time to relax, I'll keep you company. I'll get you organized and you'll even be able to save. What do you say?"

Clara thought of Don Mario, and of his advice. She thought of the hotel, and the bar where Carlos no longer was. She felt an urgent need for change, and she asked Toño, "Will you take me to look at the sea?"

"During your vacation, maybe, if you behave . . ."

"What do I tell the people at my hotel?"

"Don't tell them anything. You'll get your things early in the morning. I'll wait for you in the car. Do you have much?"

"A few things, but I don't have a suitcase to put them in."

She had thrown away the one she brought from Tres Lomas because it was old and shabby. Later, she had bought some blouses and skirts and two dresses, but not a new suitcase. I don't really think ahead, she said to herself, and she laughed at the thought that when she left the hotel she also would leave behind all her sad memories, and, in addition, she would finally be taking a step forward.

Undoubtedly she took a step, but it was more sideways than forward. Things were neither better nor worse than before. It had pained her to see the hurt expression on Don Mario's face as she was leaving, carrying a clumsy bundle.

"So you're going," he had said, simply. "I guess I couldn't keep you forever. I'm an idiot."

But his humility irritated him, and he screamed:

"Go, just go! If you prefer living with a pimp, what do I care! But don't ever put a foot in this door; I never want to see you again!"

Toño's apartment was on the ground floor, in the back. It was a good size and had a small private patio, although that turned out to be useless since the sun never reached it and the neighbors threw garbage out of their windows. Soot fell like black rain and stuck to the freshly washed clothes Clara hung there to dry.

Nevertheless, the hope she felt in those first days there compensated for the disappointments of the past. With the exception of some details, Clara worked as before; she was acquiring a great ability to handle her customers more efficiently. The hotel she went to most often was ugly and small, not like Don Mario's.

She missed her old neighborhood of Plaza Italia, and all those young boys and servicemen. There were even times when she would allow herself to think nostalgically of Carlos.

She remembered, back at Don Mario's, the time a group of tourists had arrived, such happy people, singing and playing guitars, and she had heard their music and laughter from the rooms below. What she missed most, though, was Don Mario's encouraging smile when she would arrive with an old or ugly man. Hoping to find another smile that would give her the courage to go on, she once asked Toño:

"Wouldn't it be better if I brought my customers here? It would be much more elegant, and we could charge them the price of a hotel room. . . ."

Toño looked at her, astonished.

"Are you crazy, woman? What will the neighbors think? What will the janitor and his wife and daughters think? And that woman in 1C is a real lady! She'd be horrified to learn she lives one floor above a prostitute. She's a friend of the landlord and could have us thrown out. You can't offend the modesty of ladies."

So as not to offend anyone's modesty, Clara had to keep going to a dirty hotel and give Toño all the money she earned. First he had asked for it to pay the rent; later it was for the gas; after that, food, until one day Clara screamed.

"Toño, what I give you is enough for you to pay the food bills, the rent, the gas, the electricity, the hot water, and to keep a car running for all our neighbors!"

But he wasn't intimidated. "I knew you'd be ungrateful. Didn't I give you some class? Didn't I give you a home? Of course, you have to complain! You know, I'm not stealing from you; I'm investing your capital in stocks and someday you'll be rich. If I let you do whatever you want with your money, you'll spend it all on junk. Well, I think for you: with the stock, you'll have a magnificent pension. A whore can't keep on working forever, you know. The time comes when the body is worn out and nobody wants it."

To hell with the stocks!

While that was a comfort, she was much more impressed with the threat of her worn-out body. When she finished that night, she rented the hotel's most luxurious room and looked at herself for a long time in its only mirror, which was on the ceiling. It wasn't too easy to look at herself lying down, but she could tell that it would be many years before her body was worn out. That made her happy, and thanks to Toño's stocks, she could retire from her profession while her body was still good.

She worked more eagerly and with more hope until Toño told her that he had quit his job at the bank—although he continued to leave the apartment every morning, freshly shaved and wearing a tie. She was too tired to get dressed and follow him. She didn't even have the strength to ask him where he was going until he returned home one day wearing a pair of gold cuff links with big topaz stones.

"I'm sick and tired of working for you!" she cried. "I can't buy myself a pair of earrings and you go around like a big shot, and at my expense! But this is it! Give me my stock now. I'm getting out. Do you hear me? I'm getting out!"

Toño stuck out his chest and raised himself to tiptoe. "Go ahead, beat it. I'll just go to the police and turn you in! Are your papers in order? Do you think you have the right to do the work you do? You're not going to get rid of me that easily!"

Clara closed her eyes, and as his words spun around her head, she realized that this was not the right moment to force the issue. But she wanted to force a promise out of him.

"All right, I'll go on working for you. But you have to take me to the beach for a few days."

"You've got to be kidding! Gas is expensive, and I'm not here to play around."

Tears rolled down her cheeks, and Toño felt pleased. He told himself that the way to handle women was to mistreat them; from now on he could do what he wanted with her because he had command of the situation. He began to abuse Clara and to scream at her from that day on.

"Two hundred pesos! Two hundred pesos! You've been out for twelve hours and you bring me two hundred pesos! You're nothing! What do you expect me to do with your lousy two hundred pesos? I need money, money!"

Or: "Why're you back so early? You think you've done what you're supposed to do? Well, in case you're interested, you haven't done anything. Rain is no excuse to come back after two customers. Or is the baby tired?"

He screamed so much and his voice was so resonant that Clara thought he must be hollow inside, like a drum. To get some relief from him, she went out one day earlier than usual and returned later. As she undressed in the dark, Toño saw a sparkle on her wrist.

"What's that you have there?" he shouted as he switched on the light.

"A wrist watch."

"Oh? So now you go around buying gold jewelry without my permission, eh?"

The watch was solid gold, with fifteen rubies inside. It had a one-year guarantee. Thinking of the guarantee made Clara smile with satisfaction, and that smile so angered Toño that he jumped out of bed and slapped her.

Clara stared at him, wide-eyed, but she didn't even raise her hand to rub her smarting cheek.

Pleased with her reaction, Toño returned to his bed. "Man, do I know females!" he said to himself. "This'll quiet her down for a while." Aloud, he added, "Tell me where you bought that ridiculous watch and I'll go tomorrow and exchange it for something I can use."

Clara didn't have the slightest intention of exchanging it, and the following day, when Toño returned from his daily visit to the lady in 1C, the landlord's friend, he found that Clara had left for good, taking with her all her clothes and even a handsome imitation crocodile-skin suitcase that belonged to him. Toño was alarmed and ran to the wardrobe to search among his winter underwear. Also missing were the thirteen hundred pesos he had hidden there to pay the smuggler who was going to bring him French perfume for the lady in 1C.

"A place for everything, and everything in its place," the man who had snatched her from Toño's hands had said when he wanted to put her in a brothel. Waiting by the side entrance of the Parque Retiro railway station, Clara felt as out of place as a mouse in a rainstorm. Staring at a brick clock tower wouldn't let her ignore the waste of time.

Years ago, during a long summer siesta, she would say to the daughter of her mother's employer, "Let's listen to time go by." But that had been a small town, where lost hours are not important. She and the other girl would shut themselves in the dark living room and lie under the table to look up at the sheet-swathed furniture and listen to the ticking of the pendulum clock. Back then, time was a man with a cane and a wooden leg who walked in circles while he slowly grew old. But in front of the gray station, there was no man with a wooden leg; it was simply adult time, an elusive and irksome time slipping away as Clara waited for a man with legs of flesh and bone, who should be arriving at any moment.

Twenty to nine, and the clock hands keep moving, without

The Body

worrying about me. Of course, time itself is strange. There were no problems about that with Toño; he used to let me come and go as I pleased—as long as I handed over the cash, of course, fresh bills, one by one. It was a way of buying time and of being able to use it any way I liked.

But that was so only until she decided to buy herself time seriously, in palpable form, in the shape of a wrist watch.

After leaving Toño, her big experience with time cost her dearly. Her birthday was approaching, and she didn't want to face it. Though she tried, she couldn't delay it for more than forty-eight hours. She wandered about the streets, went into tearooms, window-shopped, and when her conscience told her it was time to do something, she would look at her watch, which she hadn't wound since she left Toño. It always showed the same time—ten past four. Eventually she grew bored and wound the watch. An hour later, she was angry that the time had moved so quickly, so she turned the hands back a half hour. She continued to do this whenever the hands advanced toward her birthday faster than she wanted them to.

Lavalle Street had become her passion: people hurrying by, and scores of movie houses. She wanted to hurry along, too, but the movie posters were irresistible, and she would cross from one side of the street to the other just to look at them. Occasionally a man would approach her and ask, "Alone?" in a confidential tone.

At one-fourteen it was really nine-thirty. Clara was hungry, so she went into a cafeteria. Then she decided that she wanted to sleep, so she did something she had always wanted to do: she rented a room in a hotel with revolving doors.

As she was going to bed, she thought that being twenty-one was all right, but twenty-two was an adult, a painful age. Although she had seen "May 22" printed on the register at the hotel desk, she assured herself that she wouldn't become twenty-two on the twenty-fifth of May, because, thanks to her little watch, that day would never come.

The thirteen hundred pesos once set aside for French perfume evaporated in other ways. Clara ate as much as she wanted and slept as long as she liked. She even saw the same film three times in a movie house where she had to leave and then pay to get in again. But she only gained two days in her fight against growing older. On the third morning, it was obvious that Clara's efforts had failed. All the houses were decorated with flags, and the music of military bands was driving the pigeons away from the square. No doubt about it, it was Liberation Day, the twenty-fifth of May. Schoolchildren were self-conscious in their immaculately starched white smocks, each with a badge pinned on at the left side.

The fatherland on your heart, the teacher used to say. I really liked the big pleated badges with the tiny metal circle in the middle, and Mother insisted that I wear that horrible one she had made, with the narrow pleated ribbon. Year after year I wore that same badge so we wouldn't have a useless expense. If you think about it, though, useless expenses are the only ones worth having—everything else is a necessity.

She thought the moment had come at last when she could buy the badge of her dreams, and right at the corner was a man who sold flags and other patriotic items. But she changed her mind; first she should straighten out her situation. After all, she had until Independence Day, the ninth of July, to buy a thousand badges, and also to make herself a necklace, white and sky blue, and an eagle in the sky with wings as blue as the sea.

She opened her purse, unfastened the pin in the lining, and took out a scrap of paper she had hidden there, with the name and address of a very distinguished lady who would find Clara a job.

The Body

Her suitcase in hand, she boarded a streetcar. There was nothing more pleasant than a trip by streetcar, Clara thought. On hot days, with the cool air racing through the windows, it gave her the feeling of being out in the open. When the weather was cold, it seemed like a glass cage carrying her along, enclosing her in its ringing bells and groans.

Clara was pleased. A job was waiting for her, in a fine house facing a park. "Just the right place for you," the man had said, and she thought perhaps he meant a job taking care of children. She would take them to the park across the way; ever since that night with Carlos, she longed to be surrounded by trees.

When she arrived, she was told that the woman had gone away.

4   Clara's thoughts returned to the subway and her appointment with Victor. The happiness of being free from Toño had lasted only briefly.

How good can freedom be if you're alone and broke, with just a few coins in the bottom of your purse, hidden in the lining, the forgotten coins nobody cares about.

She was floundering in the middle of a blank space, unable to look back because she felt she would retch and unable to look ahead because there was nothing there. Begging was the only thing left for her to do.

"Ah, Clara, Clara, forgive me for being late. Some character detained me with a line of double talk and wouldn't let me go. I'll tell you: he insisted modern life is all violence and movement and all that matters is realization. A leftist, a crypto-communist, who knows what. But I didn't let myself be impressed. He went on and on and I didn't open my mouth, because if I had, he would have been left cold. He had the hardest of hard heads I've seen in my life. A rock; worse, pure granite. I cut it short by taking the catalogues out of my briefcase. Enough philosophizing. Right there and then, I played the salesman, and I didn't hear another word of his nonsense. He let me make my points about the refrigerator, and when I finished, bang! The guy tells me I'm going against my own theories, that instead of selling Bibles, which is what I should be doing, I sell refrigerators, which are pure noise, which means movement, which is a symbol of the future, and that there's nothing better than drinking a glass of good ice-cold red wine or a little cold beer when you come home exhausted from following the course of modern people dedicated to action. He said man dominates everything, including electricity, which is just floating around—push a button and the light comes on and that's it.

"I was sick and tired. Sick and tired of his ranting and raving, and I was ready to leave him there, planted in his own doorway, when suddenly a little light went on in his head—from so much talk about electricity, I guess—and he decided to buy the refrigerator after all. He talked himself in circles; there's nothing like letting your customers talk. No salesman knows that secret better than I. Let them talk and they'll sell themselves. Naturally, he'll pay in installments. Two years. Imagine, all that talk and he doesn't even have enough money to pay cash for a miserable refrigerator."

Clara was about to interject, but Victor had paused only long enough to catch his breath.

"Talking about refrigerators, you iceberg, you haven't even given me a kiss."

Talking about refrigerators, creep, you can go to hell. I don't have to wait an hour and then have to put up with your story.

But Victor, the enthusiast, grabbed her by the arm and led

her to the admission booth at the entrance to the amusement park. "Let's go buy a bit of happiness," he said.

Clara turned around to glance again at the people running to the station, at the Torre de los Ingleses, and at the sky, which no longer seemed like the sea because it was dotted with stars.

It was Monday night, a day of bad moods, the beginning of a week that was endless. Inside their booths, the ticket sellers looked sleepy and dejected. The gigantic wheels turned, empty and listless, parting the heavy air; even the colored lights had lost their brilliance.

A few couples were seated at the small tables outside the bars, and a handful of soldiers were looking up at the planes on long chains that circled above their heads. The planes were empty, and the silence hanging there was made of a sad and distant music; a place meant for people, and people had deserted it.

Clara decided not to let the depressed atmosphere affect her. She longed to recapture the happiness she had felt the first time she had been in one of those planes. She tugged at Victor's sleeve.

"Let's go, let's go on the planes. They're so thrilling. Let's get in one of the big ones that fly very high. Not everyone goes up on those, not everyone flies. And if the chain breaks, we'll really be flying. And if we crash, it'll be without a care!"

"Don't tell me that nonsense gives you pleasure? What do you feel when you're up there, turning around like a mule on a treadmill?"

"I feel like laughing and screaming, and I feel a beautiful dizziness that tickles me inside."

"If that's what you want to feel, let's go home and screw."

"It's not the same."

"Show me a woman who's happy with what she has, and I'll faint on the spot. Always new ideas, always wanting more. I ask myself why they were put in this world. . . ."

129

"And what's the answer?"

"That you were put here to make our lives impossible. You're like flies, always buzzing around, bothersome, and even stinging sometimes."

"The ones that sting are the horseflies, the males."

"You're the one who stings me. Trying to make me lose control, right? Jangling my nerves. Why do you have to utter idiocies every time you open your mouth? All right, all right, don't look like that. Come on. Let's try our strength over there."

He led her to an area where there was a steep vertical track with a heavy iron disc that had to be thrown hard enough to send it up the track, then down, then up again. Victor paid, blew on his hands, and dried them against his trousers. He grabbed the disc, shifted his body into position, and shot it upward with an unconvincing pretense of effortlessness. The disc, which should have peaked two or three times, didn't reach the top of the track once. Victor paid for another round, explaining that skill was more important than strength. He prepared to throw again. He was about to hurl the disc when his glance fell on a man in a dark suit and black hat who was leaning against a wall in the shadows and who seemed to be watching him. The grin stretched Victor's mouth wider, and to make a better show of himself, he took off his jacket. Then he threw the disc with all his might.

"Almost two hits!" he exclaimed with satisfaction, but the look vanished from his face when he realized that the stranger was not watching him, but Clara, and that she, in turn, was staring back.

He took her by the arm and spoke in a loud voice. "Let's get away from here, honey. Let's go to the shooting gallery. I'm a first-class shot."

From the corner of his eye he saw the man following them, so he continued talking loudly.

The Body

"Remember when I came back from the country? Forty ducks, not counting the partridges. I prefer duck, though; with an orange sauce there's nothing more delicious, of course."

With Toño, Clara had learned how to handle conceited men, and so she said nothing.

"Come on, beautiful, leave that jerk!" the man whispered to her, but he turned and walked away without waiting for a reaction from Clara. Victor was indignant—his steps quickened, and they left the shooting gallery. He bought two tickets for the Phantom Train.

As the car lurched forward amid whistles and grunts to enter the tunnel, Victor embraced Clara and held her close. She was preparing herself for the corpse that springs out of the coffin after the first turn, but Victor kissed her and she didn't see the corpse, she only felt the make-believe spiderwebs grazing her face. She wanted to push Victor away so she could get a good look at the dancing skeletons, but he was getting quite enthusiastic, stroking her under the skirt with one hand and caressing her breasts with the other.

Between chilling howls and shrieks, the car kept moving, until suddenly, without warning, it left the darkness of the tunnel and jerked to a halt in the bright light where the ride had begun. Clara felt all the heat of the lights concentrate in patches on her cheeks, and Victor searched his pockets for the tickets.

The man at the controls had seen them before they saw him.

"Did you see the way that man leered at us?" asked Clara.

"Envy, sheer envy. Those people get mad because everyone is having a good time while they have to work."

A woman dressed in bright green, her hair dyed red, approached Victor and rubbed against him with her hips. Indignant, he took Clara by the arm, and said, "Women like that would be better off in jail."

Of course he said it to set Clara apart from those women, and himself as well, but it offended Clara nevertheless. Since they had started living together, Victor was determined to hate pitilessly all women of the street.

"Let's go have a drink, get away from this mob."

"Why not go dancing?"

"You go from bad to worse, my dear. Can't you think of anything better to do? Exercising on these great machines is the best way to give the body a vacation and let it rest."

He really has good arguments; no wonder he sells so many refrigerators. Still, he makes me furious.

"Don't you see there's no fun here? Everything's dead, deadly dead, and buried. A funeral would be more fun. If you don't take me dancing, I'll go home and leave you to have fun alone."

The word "alone" acted like a magnet: three women, who had been cruising around looking for someone to pick up, suddenly materialized. Victor walked ahead quickly and blindly; Clara followed, hanging from his arm, happy to leave behind that world of mechanical monsters.

In the center of Parque Retiro there was a square yellow building with a canopy and a doorman who kept repeating: "Come right in, ladies and gentlemen, the Dance Palace welcomes you. Wonderful Cuban and tango orchestras, exquisite drinks, abundant pleasures." Glancing over his shoulder, Victor saw that two of those hateful women had followed them and were close behind. He took Clara's arm and pulled her inside.

They sat at a table near the orchestra. Victor dried his forehead with his handkerchief.

"What nerve! They even follow a man who's accompanied! These women don't have the slightest respect for anything. Sticky as flypaper—flypaper that pursues its victims instead of remaining quietly in place waiting for them to fall upon it."

Nice idea, the one about flypaper.

"My mother knew what good manners were because she washed and ironed for the Brunettis, people of the best kind, and she never handled those disgusting strips."

But then she went with the two youngest to spend her vacation at my aunt's house in Quemú-Quemú, one of those vacations that never ended, and my father let the women neighbors talk him into it—I know now it was the butcher's wife—and he hung very long strips from one end of the kitchen to the other. He never took them off. The butcher's wife must have had some scientific information about flies. Luckily, I left all that, the hut and the smell of fresh blood that was everywhere because the butcher's wife didn't even wash her hands when she came to visit my father.

At least she still had pleasant and sweet-smelling memories of Tres Lomas, like when the grocery boy—the one with blond curly hair, not the obnoxious one who came later—gave her a bunch of white roses in full bloom, a bit wilted, perhaps, but like the roses the druggist's mother used to wear in her hat, and she was a real lady from Santa Rosa de Toay who only came to Tres Lomas the first Friday of each month to visit her son and make a confession to the parish priest, who was a friend of the family.

Make friends with the judge, the proverb says. I never thought it worth while to make friends with the priest, too. It's a good idea, though; I'm going to look for one and become good friends with him before I make my confession so I don't have to spend the rest of my life saying Hail Marys and Our Fathers to cleanse my sins. Good thinking.

She smiled at Victor to show that from time to time she too was satisfied with herself. Victor liked that smile and asked her to dance, for once putting aside his firm resolve simply to sit there and watch the dancers.

The Cuban orchestra was playing a mambo. Victor held Clara in his arms and led her around the dance floor in small bouncing steps. When they passed in front of the orchestra, Victor made two or three quick turns, and once he dared to release Clara so that she twirled away from him and then came back under his arm while he moved his hips from side to side like the couples he had seen in the center of the dance floor. Clara laughed, carefree; she delighted in showing off before those men in their white shirts with full sleeves. They were all wonderful, singing and shouting incomprehensible words to the rhythm of the music. The mambo ended and a merengue began, but Victor didn't pay attention to that. He continued to dance in the mambo rhythm, spinning around the floor at great speed in order to be in front of the orchestra again as fast as possible.

The music stopped abruptly, and the players rested: some of them shook the saliva from their horns. Clara and Victor walked to their table holding hands. They sighed together, happy, as they sat down. Victor smiled and Clara looked at him affectionately. The waiter took advantage of the moment to approach with a tray under his arm to ask them what they would like.

"A stein of beer for me. What will you have?"

"The same."

"No, no, Clarita. Have a strawberry soda, the kind you like so much."

Clara nodded and settled back in her chair. All around them, couples were laughing and moving from table to table. At the other end of the ballroom, several men were sitting, alone, smoking and drinking with studied dignity, their legs crossed to show the well-pressed trousers and the black patent-leather shoes trimmed with white suede.

A little past them, several girls were sitting alone or in pairs, also with their legs crossed, showing high-heeled sandals.

The Body

They all have wonderful drinks, the color of the sun, in tall, slender glasses. I'd like to drink one in a gulp and get the bright cherry at the bottom. Those girls are smart, though; they sip slowly and make their drinks last all night.

The musicians were disappearing from the platform one by one. A man took the microphone.

"Ladies and gentlemen, we are honored to present to you the great tango orchestra of Maestro Julio Ortega [piano arpeggios], who will be joined by a face new to the tango—Ruben Chiesa, the San Telmo Kid! and, as always, our great international singer— Carlos del Arrabal! A big hand, please, for these giants of the tango."

Victor didn't applaud. He looked at the announcer with disgust.

"Tangos! Just when we'd gotten to know each other's style and were dancing so well . . ."

Clara, too, was a bit disappointed. However, the San Telmo Kid sang with enthusiasm, and his tangos were surprisingly cheerful. On the dance floor, the couples were taking short steps and then long gliding ones, making lively patterns with their feet while their faces showed only serious and concentrated expressions. A few of the men in the back had approached the girls, and they led them around the dance floor, holding them close. They moved slowly, dragging themselves. Clara wanted to be part of that enormous inching worm of human bodies, and she asked Victor to dance.

"Hell, no. This kind of song is meant for listening, not dancing."

She had to console herself by watching a girl who was slowly rotating her hips in a skirt so tight it seemed ready to burst. She sat quietly while the San Telmo Kid sang his three songs. Then Victor took advantage of the break to call for the check.

"Let's go."

"Oh, no, let's stay. It's so much fun. Maybe the next singer will be good."

He looked her up and down, as if to shame her, and said sarcastically, "You didn't work all day like I did, that's for sure. There's nothing relaxing about going from door to door. There's nothing relaxing about having to wait around and argue. I'm dead tired from making the rounds. Getting home fast is all I can think about now. We've had enough fun."

He started to walk away to give more weight to his words and to avoid any further cajoling from Clara. She slowly put on her knitted jacket and picked up her purse. As she pushed her chair against the table, the bandleader announced the name of Carlos del Arrabal, and she felt an overpowering urge to turn around.

An instant was enough to restore every memory as she recognized the sure step of Carlos, the same Carlos she had known with his quick movements between the tables of Don Mario's bar. And she realized that if she had scarcely thought of him recently, it was because the memories of him were embedded in her, together with the certainty that one day they would meet again. That day had arrived, without warning, without premonitions; it had caught her off guard. She had to lean against the back of the chair and breathe deeply to bring herself back to reality. But his image didn't fade, he was still there on the platform, adjusting the microphone and preparing to sing.

She closed her eyes and saw the Palermo woods, the moon, and Carlos in front of her. It was inevitable that she would meet him again, for they had never reached the lake and the swans. She opened her eyes again and was able to smile at him. He also smiled, showing his white teeth, but Clara didn't accept a smile that was meant for everyone.

Victor was calling her now, with desperate signals. Slowly

she walked toward the exit, but she couldn't resist the temptation to turn around once more to look at the enormous bare room where only Carlos's body was shining under the dim light that fell from the ceiling. She hurried to get out of the ballroom.

The uniformed doorman handed her a small pink card; she put it in her jacket pocket. Once they were past the doorman, Victor grabbed her arm and spoke gruffly.

"What took you so long?"

Transition

1   The printed card said:

The Board of Directors of the Dance Palace is honored to have had your gracious presence and hopes to see you again in our grand ballroom. Present this card to the waiter and he will serve you, free, a delicious cocktail, our bartender's specialty.

Clara was still treasuring the warm flush that had run through her spine, still treasuring, too, the exquisite torture of imagining the text on the card she had so casually put in the pocket of her linen jacket. While Victor slept at her side, she had spent the long hours of the night in uncertainty, unwilling to get up and run the risk of waking Victor and of then having to reveal her secret. After all, the card might very well carry a message from Carlos. She could envision the most thrilling sentiments written there, phrases like "Clara, I love you," or simply "Tomorrow at 6:30," or "Don't return; it's too painful for me."

She saw Carlos going in and out of the cheap bars of the Bajo, looking for her. At last he would find her in the Dance Palace, and together they would sing an endless love song, like the one in that Technicolor movie she had seen a few days before. She would be wearing the lilac dress, the same one she had worn that night in the woods. Little by little, they would put together a great orchestra, and on the drum they would paint their initials, C and C, interlocked and identical.

She neatly avoided thinking of Carlos's wife. Instead, for the first time in her life, she tried to imagine happiness. First she saw herself with Carlos on a beach, then in a small house in the woods, and finally at the tearoom by the lake. She was always wearing the lilac dress, and he was always singing sweet love songs in her ear.

He crooned so soothingly that finally Clara fell asleep. When she woke up, it was ten-thirty and Victor had gone to work. The thought that he might have taken her pink card alarmed her, and she jumped out of bed. Luck was with her—the card was where she had left it. Just finding the card helped to soften the disappointment of discovering that there was no message from Carlos on it, but she couldn't push away the thought that Carlos was like the rest who didn't believe in love. Victor didn't believe in those sentiments either, but he, at least, was generous.

He gives me a home and food and he asks for very little. He must have some love for me, otherwise why would he put up with me?

She decided it was wrong to be unfaithful, even if it were only in her imagination. She went to the bathroom to wash his shirts.

As she hung the shirts over the bathtub, she remembered another shirt, which needed the collar turned. When Victor returned at twelve-thirty, she was still sewing. Lunch was not ready.

"Don't you realize I come home hungry?" he screamed. "You don't do anything all day. The table isn't set. It's bad enough to have to rush through lunch without finding there's nothing ready!"

Clara set the kitchen table and took the cold meat out of the refrigerator.

"Roast, roast!" he shouted. "We've been eating the same roast for days. I ask myself how you would manage if the place where I work hadn't lent me a refrigerator. It's a good thing you have it, so you can keep the same meal for months. Give me the salami I saw in there."

Clara shrugged. She was secretly surprised at the extent of her indifference to Victor's outbursts. When she still had illusions about him, she was confused, she wanted to hit him or bite him or mangle him. Now, she felt nothing, and she was somewhat lost in the face of her lack of feelings.

"I'll make you a salad, the kind you like, with mayonnaise sprinkled with garlic."

"Garlic! Are you crazy, woman, with all the customers I have to see today? And at Rivadavia, no less, a fashionable neighborhood."

There was a pause while he cut himself a generous slice of salami. He peeled it, put it on a buttered slice of bread, and said, "Make me the mayonnaise and salad anyway."

He polished off the cold meat, the salad, and two bananas. He was in the doorway, drinking the last drops of his coffee, when he realized that Clara had not eaten at all.

"You didn't have a bite. What's bothering you? Are you mad?"

"No. Why should I be mad?"

"No reason. Let's drop it. Look, I'll be back late tonight, I have a meeting. Eat something and go to the movies. There's a fifty-peso bill in the night-table drawer. Have a good time. Your face looks like it's ready for a funeral."

It isn't worth it to work until they think you're a slave, Clara thought as she ate the end of the salami and sucked on the string. She cleaned the mayonnaise from the plate with a piece of bread and ate the last banana. Then she went to the bathroom to look at herself in the mirror and take inventory: young, without bulges or wrinkles, perfectly pleasing; a bit anemic, perhaps, if she turned down the lower eyelid, but who was going to turn down her eyelid?

Sometimes, though, they look you straight in the eye, as if they want to reach your soul. But that's where it ends—no hint of going deeper, no desire to learn your intimate secrets. That's dangerous, bad; you run the risk of falling in love. But no, it's not even that. You don't fall in love with someone's defects and weaknesses, but with the fact that you know he has them and you can empathize. Well, back to myself: firm body, slender waist, pretty legs. In the lilac dress and new bra, I'll look fantastic.

She ran to the bedroom, where the narrow mirror of the wardrobe reflected her body's length but cut off her generous hips. She looked at herself front and back: ample buttocks and breasts. Not bad. She could be a painter's model.

She stretched her hand toward the drawer where her dress was, but common sense forced her to halt her gesture midway and ordered her back to the kitchen and the shirt with the unstitched collar. She took a razor blade and attacked the cuffs, which were also worn out.

"Everything is worn out," she sang in a low voice. "Even Victor who comes home, shouts, and goes away. Wo-orn o-out."

She stopped in time, however, before she started feeling too sorry for herself.

I shouldn't complain. I was worse off before. Now everything is stable, respectable, smooth. Respectable. And I still complain. I'm coldhearted, ungrateful, mean. Poor Victor with his damn customers. Damn blade, it won't cut! He doesn't have to take his bad moods out on me. I don't play around all day. I keep the house neat as a pin for him. Like that time he came home hours late and found me still awake. "What's up? Did you go to the movies?" he asked. And I said, "No, I washed the kitchen walls. Don't you see how they shine?" "Not bad, not bad," he said, "but you could have finished. Still some stains on the wall over here . . ." Men don't realize you can't get to heaven, even on a clear night.

She raised her eyes; the blade had deeply pierced the skin of her left thumb. She lifted the finger to her mouth and sucked it carefully. The repulsive, hot taste of blood made her ill. The shirt was stained with a few bright-red drops that would soon harden and turn brown. As she ran to the bathroom to put the shirt under the faucet, she remembered the stains on the sheet after the first time with that sailor. What a job it had been to wash them away the following morning. She still had the blade in her hand, and she wanted to squeeze it. Instead she broke it into tiny pieces and threw them into the toilet.

So thin, treacherous as a thin woman. Fortunately, my father shaved with a straight razor, much safer, a blade that always held its edge. He was furious when I took it to sharpen pencils. Victor shaves with an electric shaver, naturally. Faster, but much less picturesque. It eliminates soap, foam, and even grimaces. But it doesn't cut his whiskers evenly and they're hard and prickly.

She put her bloody finger under the faucet. The spurt of cold water felt good, no more heat and throbbing. She wrapped it tightly with a handkerchief and went to the window.

The warm breeze made her want to go out. Only a little distance, perhaps a step, was between her and the night table with the fifty pesos. She sat down on the bed and opened the drawer. Tidy confusion: the gas and electric bills, neatly held together with a paper clip, rested in a nest of refrigerator catalogues. Clara looked for the fifty-peso bill and found it inside a paperback copy of *How to Win Friends and Influence People*. The only book in the house.

The bill was new, green, and crisp as a dry leaf. Clara held it in both hands and felt that the piece of paper was transmitting an unfamiliar pleasure to her. She placed it against the light. She felt sorry she had to spend such a new bill; those she would get in its place would surely be dirty and rumpled.

Victor had told her to go to the movies to change her ideas, but she didn't want to change her ideas, bad as they were, for at least they were hers. She wanted to keep it all, the new bill and the old ideas.

Suddenly she realized that all her disparate thoughts were circling around the pink card in her jacket pocket. By stretching her arm, she could touch it. It wasn't new like the fifty-peso bill, its edges were gray and worn. She wouldn't feel sorry to part with it, and the free drink would be a big saving. In her purse she had a few extra pesos she could use. She wondered if perhaps she would have to dance with strangers, but dancing was the least of it.

She would see Carlos again. She stopped for an instant in the middle of the room and tried to imagine how she would feel when she saw him. She was afraid that a knot would form in her throat and choke her. The best thing to do, she thought, was to stay home and sew. Immediately, she accused herself of being a coward, of being afraid that Carlos would reject her or perhaps force her to leave the comfort in which she was living.

At four-thirty she finally decided to go to Parque Retiro. She wouldn't speak to him or search for him. She would sit at a table in the back of the dance hall, listening to him sing.

At seven o'clock she still was not ready. First she had had to stand on the table to reach the box on top of the wardrobe to look for the only brassière that went with the lilac dress. Then she had had to iron the ruffles on the skirt and starch the special petticoat. She had decided to rest awhile, but she could only endure five minutes in bed. It had taken her almost an hour to pluck her eyebrows and put on make-up. When at last she boarded the bus, it was with the firm resolve that she would not go near Carlos.

2   When she handed the waiter the pink card, she felt some of her old shyness. She sat at the table farthest from the orchestra and listened with forced attention to the Brazilian rhythms played by musicians dressed as Cubans. Before long a man with

a kerchief tied around his neck asked her to dance. She stood up unenthusiastically, unwilling to offend him, and went to dance.

Just shake the skeleton. Twirl around a few times. Shine the floor.

She tried, but her mind was elsewhere, and a couple of times before the dance ended she stepped on the man's feet. He sighed with relief when he took her back to the table.

I never do anything right. I rushed too much, arrived too early, and now I have to do exactly what I didn't want to do: wait. Always waiting. Maybe today is Carlos's day off and he won't even be here. I'd better go home; I have too much to do to be wasting my time here. Crazy. Maybe he'll come with his wife.

She felt frightened when she remembered Carlos's wife. Her chest ached; the mistake was wearing that low-cut dress. She shouldn't go around showing herself that way. The waiter had already served her the bartender's special, but she couldn't drink it. It was better to escape now, quickly, before they announced the tango orchestra and probably Carlos's name. She grabbed her purse and stood up.

"You new here?" a young woman asked.

"Yes," Clara said hesitantly.

"That's why you're bored to death. I'm bored too. I'll sit with you and we can chat awhile." And she hurried back to get her drink.

"I bet you think I always sit around," she said when she returned. "A regular wallflower. No, sir, I dance all the time! I'm worn to a frazzle. That crazy music makes my feet ache. Thank God the tangos are next! They're restful, right?"

The girl took a sip of her drink and shook her curly brown hair. "My name's Mary Magdalene—Monona to intimates and women. What's yours?"

"Clara."

"Nice name, but a little inappropriate. I can see you're new to this business, green. Now me, I know this place like the back of my hand; I can tell you whatever you want to know. You floor me, you know? Must be that innocent face. But you aren't innocent, are you?"

"No."

"That's good. This is no place for a fairy-tale princess. You have to know what's going on in this life. And in the next one, too. I struggled hard to get where I am today. I'll tell you all about it sometime."

She downed the rest of her cocktail in one gulp and summoned the waiter with a nod. "The same," she said, pointing to the two long, thin glasses. Clara's glass was almost full, but Monona insisted that she finish her drink and have another. Clara obeyed and sadly watched the waiter take away the untouched cherry, which she had been saving at the bottom of the glass.

"But the card only gives us one. . . ."

"So what? I'll pay for the next round. I'm dying of thirst. You'll see, another drink will make us feel real good."

The waiter brought the drinks and Monona quickly emptied half her glass.

"I feel good. Cacho didn't come tonight, notice? He's the soul of the dance. And he's mine, you know, even if once in a while he does go off with someone who happens to be floating around. Doesn't bother me. I've got my own tricks. Life has to be worth while in some way. But he was going to spend tonight with me. Do you think he's jealous of the guy I took home yesterday? A big guy, with muscles like meat pies. Cacho knows I like him, but I'd never tell him that because he was born conceited. Besides, you have to be mysterious with men or they don't bother with you."

Clara made every effort to listen, although the San Telmo Kid had already started to sing and she knew that it would be Carlos's turn soon. She finished her cocktail and stretched her tongue to get the cherry at the bottom of the glass.

Monona was quiet for a while and then looked at Clara mistrustfully. "If you're not one of us, what the hell are you doing here?"

"I'm a friend of Carlos Arrabal," Clara answered, with the cherry in her mouth and triumph in her voice.

"Carlos's little friend? You don't say!" She laughed so hard that her breasts shook. Her laughter came in short yelps, and she began to choke. Clara patted her back while Monona screamed, "You, you!" between hiccups. Clara was nervously wondering what Carlos could have said about her.

Terrible things, I'm sure; enough to give anyone the shakes and make them laugh like the ghouls on the Phantom Train. Tel me right now; calm down and tell me!

By now she was shaking Monona violently. Finally Monona took a handkerchief from inside her low-cut dress, blew her nose, and dried her tears.

"So you're the mysterious mistress of Carlitos! That's the funniest thing I've ever heard. Covered with jewelry, he says, her hair in an enormous bun. A lady, not like you, kid. That's what he says. What nerve! Funny. Very funny, that you turn out to be one of us. A poor kid. No better or worse. Or maybe worse. And he said you went around in a car with a chauffeur. What a bullshitter!"

"Maybe he wasn't talking about me," ventured Clara, although the idea didn't please her. "Maybe he was talking about another woman."

"Oh, no. Don't give me that, little girl. Don't try to cover up for him. He was bragging that you were unique, that you didn't let him breathe, he said, so he couldn't give us, the gang, the time of day. A dirty lie! Cacho suspected it all along; he's got intuition about people. More than once he told me that the tango man runs away from bitches because he's impotent. Crippled by sex. He must be right, or Carlos wouldn't go around making up stories about a kid like you. Cacho's just the opposite. You'll find out someday if you meet him. He's like that with everyone. Today's my turn, though. God! I wonder why he's not here!"

"Maybe something happened . . . an accident."

Monona raised her head and shook her hair. "It must be that. An accident. Otherwise he'd be here. Nothing serious, of course, a car brushed against him or something. He must be fighting to get them to pay for his suit or whatever. He's shrewd. . . . Naturally, after that he won't be up to dancing. But I'm sure he'll come and pick me up."

Monona's thoughts returned to Clara. "Tell me, honey, Carlos isn't supposed to know you're here, right? I'll bet he forbade you to come so he wouldn't get caught. Well, it's too late now; he won't be able to strut around giving himself airs. *Did* he tell you to come?"

"Of course not. The last time I saw him was centuries ago, before he even dreamed he'd be working here. Yesterday I came to the Dance Palace with another gentleman, and I saw him. It's an old story."

"Really? Then it's true about the rich lady?"

"How do I know? When I met him, he was a simple guy. He worked as a waiter in a bar. I knew him, more or less, until one night when he took me to the woods and I got to know him well. It was wonderful."

"Were you a virgin?"

"No, a whore."

There was a pause.

"Hmm," Monona finally answered. "So he was the one who really got to you. Tell me, did you see him again afterwards? Did he take all the money you had and leave you?"

"He didn't take a penny from me. He just went away and that was that. His wife locked him up."

"Ah, he's married! That's terrific! Cacho will laugh. But really, you in love with the tango man . . . And you never saw him again?"

"No."

"What makes him your friend, then? If you were a friend to every guy who passes over you . . ."

"You don't understand. He's different because I love him."

"Me, not understand? With the crush I have on Cacho! Look, I'm not a bitch. When he finishes moaning, I'll tell him to come see you. The Dance Palace, ladies and gentlemen, ennobled by a great love!"

The announcer had just finished pronouncing his name. "Carlos . . ." Clara repeated, and shouted, "No! I don't want to see him! I'm going with someone else who'll be jealous."

"What the hell do you care about someone else if this is the guy you like?"

"The other one wants to marry me."

"Marry!" Monona laughed again. "Marry . . . There's no marriage for the likes of us. Once a whore, always a whore."

"But I wasn't born a whore. Things just happened that way. When I was a girl, I went to Mass every Sunday. That's why I don't want to see Carlos."

"You're strange. But how could you be any other way with that name? Clara—a nun's name."

Clara turned pale and held her breath.

"Quiet, here he comes," she whispered, squeezing Monona's arm. Then she gripped the edge of the table to keep herself from screaming, from calling out to him.

Transition

"Clara . . . A name like that's confusing. No guy would dare touch a woman called Clara. In my case, Cacho named me Mary Magdalene, after the most important whore in the world. She was after Christ, but He wouldn't give her the time of day. He was so serious. Nowadays, nobody's serious, and any idiot with half a brain realizes I'm not called that for nothing."

Carlos was singing a ballad, and Clara felt her whole body vibrating with his voice.

The indefatigable Monona went on. "You shouldn't pretend in life, my friend. You are what you are, and it doesn't pay to look for the fifth leg of a cat."

Carlos's voice was deep and rich. Clara tried to enclose herself in a cocoon of silence that only his voice could penetrate, but it was no use.

"Cacho also invented the name Monona. I have lots of names, like artists and thieves. If he gets to know you, I'm sure Cacho will give you another name, you'll see. Imagine, my name was Daisy. What could be more ridiculous? Cacho says daisies are good for pigs. He's a man with lots of intelligence and knowledge. He'll also tell you your neckline isn't bad but a full skirt is for girls at convent school. You have to be aggressive, girl, if you don't want to be stepped on. Look, I swear I'll bring Carlos over when he's finished singing, but I have to talk to somebody now or I'll burst."

Clara would have liked to scratch her, to dig her nails deep into her and then twist her fingers until she tore out her flesh, but instead she said in a slow and restrained voice, "I don't want you to bring him to me; I told you, I don't want that. I only want to listen to him, if you'll let me."

"Jesus, what you need is a good drink."

Monona signaled the waiter.

"Two more."

"You still owe me for the other two."

"Don't be stupid. Bring me the drinks."

The waiter stood there, uncertain.

"Bring me those drinks, I tell you. If I can't pay you, Cacho will."

"Not Cacho. He doesn't pay anyone else's bills."

"Son of a bitch, drop dead," Monona growled at the waiter, as Carlos was desperately holding on to the last note. "That bastard doesn't want to bring me a drink because he says I'm broke. As if I ever owed anybody anything. He's a tight-ass; I'm going to tell Cacho, I swear. Nobody plays with Cacho's woman. . . ." The tone of her voice suddenly changed. "Clara, Clarita, would you have a few pesos tucked away somewhere to buy us a drink?"

"I don't want another drink."

"You never want anything. You've got tomato juice for blood. You don't want another drink. You don't want to see the tango man. You don't know *what* you want."

Clara grabbed her glass. "What I want is for you to shut up," she shouted. "Let me hear this last song, for God's sake."

Carlos had already taken the microphone back. Monona's eyes sparkled restlessly.

"I'll shut up if you'll pay for another drink. And the first ones, too, because I don't have any money today."

"I don't have any money either," Clara said in a low voice.

"Go on, a sensible girl like you doesn't go around broke. You've got the face of a penny pincher, girl, so don't give me that story. Pay him and I promise I'll shut up. Cross my heart."

Carlos deserved at least that. She opened her purse and took out the fifty-peso bill. As it passed from her hand to Monona's, it rustled like a sigh.

Monona kept her word. She finished her drink in one long swallow and laid her head on the table between her crossed arms. Clara settled into her chair; she shut her eyes and held her breath. But Carlos was singing a comic tune, not a love song, and she felt cheated. Then the lyrics of the tango—". . . and you rolled up those bills like you were stuffing a sausage . . ."— seemed to her prophetic, and she knew she had done the right thing to sacrifice that new bill for Carlos.

Life doesn't have to be sordid; money buys everything, even a little peace.

She looked at Monona with disgust, then quickly turned her eyes back to Carlos, under the spotlights. She felt a lump in her throat, and she thought she would cry.

When Carlos del Arrabal finished his last tango, Clara didn't even have the courage to applaud. Some young men who had been dancing started to shout, "More! More!" and she supported them with all the strength of her thoughts but she did not want to part her lips for fear that she would destroy the enchantment.

Suddenly the spotlights went off and the stage was empty. Monona jumped up from her chair.

"Now I'll bring him here."

"No, I don't want to see him!" But Monona was gone.

Clara remained seated, her eyes fixed, her hands in her lap. The three drinks she had drunk unwillingly helped to confuse and blur events.

"Clara. Hello."

Carlos's tall silhouette blocked the lights, and when Clara raised her eyes she couldn't see his face because it was hidden in shadow. His gestures were vague and indecisive. Clara was touched; intuitively, she sensed his vulnerability. Behind him, Monona's eyes were getting small with irony. Clara drew strength from all those things—the irony, the vulnerability, the inability to see Carlos's face, the three drinks—and she said casually,

"Well, Carlos, how are you?" and stretched her hand out to him in a perfect gesture of courtesy. He pressed it between his limp, damp hands.

"I didn't want to bother you, but Monona insisted."

"Thank you, Clara, thank you."

Monona didn't want to be left out. "Blah, blah, blah. Stop yapping and let's have a drink to celebrate the reunion. Order me a gin while I go to the john. I'll be right back." She got up unsteadily and walked away swinging her hips.

"She's drunk," Clara said.

"She's always drunk," Carlos confirmed. Then he spoke to Clara urgently, taking her hand.

"Clara, Clarita, what have you been doing all this time? What brought you here? Whenever I remembered that night, I felt awful. Nothing was ever as great as that little time we spent together."

"Shh, here she comes."

"We have to get out of here, fast. I can't take her any longer."

"Let's go."

"Too late. Tell her Cacho's looking for her. Tell her he sent for her. Tell her anything," and he let go of her hand.

"Now I feel better," Monona exclaimed as she fell into a chair. "Where's my gin?"

Under the table, Carlos moved his leg gingerly and pressed it against Clara's. She looked at Monona with her purest expression of innocence.

"We didn't order it because a man came by looking for you. He said Cacho is waiting for you."

"Cacho? Where?"

"Well, I think he said 'the usual place.' "

"What did he look like?"

"Dark, with a mustache, I think."

Transition

"You think, you idiot! Cacho's waiting for me, he sent for me. I have to run!"

She grabbed her purse and rushed out, pushing aside tables and chairs. After she had disappeared behind the swinging doors, Carlos broke into laughter. "Funny," Clara said. "She was laughing at you a minute ago."

Carlos sobered up immediately. "That bitch, laughing at me? What did she tell you? How can you be friends with her? And with that Cacho?"

"I don't know them. I never saw Cacho in my life."

"What about 'the usual place'?"

"Lovers always have a 'usual place,' don't they?"

"Why ask me? I don't know anything. You know everything."

"Don't be so bitter," Clara said. "She said . . ."

"I don't want to hear what she said! Everybody here hates me because I won't join the gang. All I ask of them is to leave me alone."

Clara bit her lip.

"Forgive me, Clara. I don't mean you. You're different. Different from all the women I've known. You can't imagine how much I've thought of you since my wife died."

A mixture of pity and happiness prevented Clara from grasping the meaning of his words. After a prolonged silence, she whispered, "Poor Carlos."

"Let's get out of here, Clarita. How about a walk to the harbor? Do you have time?"

"Of course," she answered softly.

The rides in the amusement park, still and silent now, formed a thousand shadows. Carlos and Clara kept up a steady pace as they passed through the turnstile at the exit and walked on silently toward the harbor. They could see the flickering lights on the masts, though they were still some distance from the harbor.

Carlos broke the silence. "Do you remember Don Mario's hotel? We weren't too badly off there, were we? We could have seen each other often and gone off to the woods now and then, like we did that one time. When I got home that night, my wife knew everything. She forced me to leave that job. She had a delicate heart, and any upset made her ill. She was my wife; I couldn't kill her, could I? When we were married she was beautiful, dressed in white. She never wore that dress again, though. Or any other. She spent her life in a bathrobe. Maybe because she was sick."

They passed a wooden barracks, and the night air carried the drifting voices of sailors singing in a foreign language.

Carlos went on with his confidences. "You know, before I married, I was a tango singer. Like now. My wife didn't want me to sing, and she found me the job as a waiter. With the tips, I made good money, but when she heard about you, she went wild. Almost choked to death. Luckily, the doctor came and calmed her down, but I had to swear that I'd never see you again. Then she found me a job as an usher in a movie theater on Corrientes Street. Always a job with tips! But I enjoyed it, until she became jealous again. If I wasn't home on time, she'd call the theater. The boys kidded me, so one night I did go out with a girl, to show them I wasn't afraid. When I got home she was in bed, hardly breathing. I called the doctor, but it was too late."

Clara took his hand and kissed it.

"I am so sorry," she said.

"But you ought to hate her. She kept us apart. Don't you care about that?"

Clara wanted to say yes, to tell him that she cared more about that than anything else. But she felt ashamed.

"One should never hate the dead. One should think kindly of them. After all, they can't do us any harm."

"Yes, they can. When she died, I felt terribly guilty. But when the doctor told me that it was to be expected, my conscience eased and I felt happy. Yes, happy. Finally, I was free. After a month of mourning, I looked up the bandleader here. He's an old friend, and he hired me right away. You don't know what it is to go back to an empty room. When I hear my neighbors fight through the thin walls, it feels strange to be without my wife. But instead of thinking about my wife, I think about you, I wonder what you're doing."

He stopped to light a cigarette, and Clara sat on one of the mooring posts. Carlos knelt at her side and hid his face in her lap.

"I looked for you everywhere, Clarita. I even went to Don Mario's hotel. He told me you had left and that it was all my fault. I was very sad. He was sad, too, and made me promise that if I found you I would take you to see him. Do you want to go tomorrow?"

But Clara didn't want to see Don Mario, she didn't want Carlos to take her back to the past now that she had decided to start a new life.

"Not tomorrow. Another day. I have to get used to seeing you before I can see Don Mario." She stood up. "Let's go back. I'm tired."

"You're not offended, are you? You know I love you."

Why hasn't he kissed me, then? Clearly, love is something I haven't discovered yet. What about the rich woman Monona spoke about? But Carlos is mine now that I've found him again.

He kissed her good-by at the bus stop, but he didn't offer to accompany her. Instead, he made her promise she would come back the next day. On her ride home Clara asked herself why Carlos had seemed so distant.

3   Fabulous luck for a change: last night, she had arrived at the apartment just before Victor and had had enough time to undress and to pretend that she was asleep. This morning, Victor had told her he was going to Rosario for three days. Clara had to restrain herself from singing as she cleaned his tie and pressed his pants. She took him to the station to make certain he didn't miss the two-thirty-seven. Victor rewarded her with a chocolate bar. Clara put it in her purse, waited until the train pulled out, and ran to the subway.

At six o'clock sharp, she arrived at the main entrance to Parque Retiro. Carlos was there, waiting for her, and that made her think that her life would be different from now on.

Carlos took her by the shoulders and said, "Parque Retiro is yours; we can go wherever you like."

Clara looked with lust at all the rides spinning and snaking and racing around her. "Let's go on that one! The Caterpillar! The Hammer! Marvelous, I'm dizzy already!"

Carlos had a book of tickets for twelve rides. Clara was wildly enthusiastic. They kissed every time they reached the top of the ferris wheel. On the next ride, they laughed as they were whirled around at great speed and then thrown against each other. They squealed with delight and hugged each other in mock terror on a train that went into a dark tunnel and then fell suddenly into water. They didn't ride the Hammer, because that would have meant sitting apart, and they wanted to be together always, even upside down.

From the roller coaster they could see ship masts in the harbor. Clara wanted to scream with joy, but she stopped herself just in time. Just one word could destroy it forever. She was determined to preserve happiness now that she had found it.

They still had four tickets left when Carlos had to rush off to the Dance Palace.

"Try to hide from Monona, or she'll scream at you about yesterday," he warned Clara.

Carlos rounded the corner and entered through the stage door. Clara sneaked to a dimly lit corner. Soon she spotted Monona on the dance floor.

A few minutes later Carlos was announced, and Clara moved to another table in order to get a better view of him. When he began to sing, Clara thought of Monona again: what if she came over and plopped herself down to talk and talk? But Monona was among the swaying bodies, dancing close to a tall, thin man. That must be Cacho, Clara thought, relieved.

A mustached man asked her to dance. "I can't, thank you. I'm waiting for my boyfriend." She was glad that she hadn't had the cocktail with the elusive cherry, that no one could force her to dance. When the waiter came, she ordered an orangeade.

Carlos, meanwhile, was attacking a love song with great vigor. His voice was crooning to her through a speaker just behind her head. But Clara was distracted briefly. Monona was only a few steps away, allowing a man to kiss her neck while she stood in a position that seemed undignified and uncomfortable. She wished she could make Monona notice that the strap of her dress had fallen off her shoulder, that her bra was showing, that her skirt was so tight it was rising above her knees. Perhaps she signaled to her inadvertently, because Monona raised her head, pulled away from the man's lips, and looked toward Clara. She winked in greeting, got rid of the man, and threw herself into the empty chair opposite Clara.

"They made fun of me! They made fun of me, the pigs! I'll show them. Listen, I want you to tell me all about that guy who came here yesterday. The one who told you Cacho was looking for me."

"Why?" Clara asked with innocence.

"Because Cacho wasn't looking for me, you idiot. He was shacking up with the redhead from the night club. And I raced to his place, out of breath. . . . Shit, I was so damned embarrassed. You don't know Cacho, so you can't understand. Around here everyone's jealous of him. They'd do anything to screw him. They knew damn well he was with the *gringa*. You've got to help me. We've got to make that miserable creep pay. Point him out to me when you see him. I'll tell Cacho. Cacho doesn't fool around. He's not holding a grudge against me. He promised that if I behave, he'll take me to the Mar del Plata this weekend." And Monona leaped up and disappeared.

It's worth it, to get to the sea. I'd do anything to get to the sea. What does Monona have to do to be taken to the sea? When I was a kid, behaving meant helping Mother scrub the floor and wash the dishes. Going to Mass every Sunday. Later, behaving meant not letting boys kiss me in the dark. What the devil does it mean now?

Monona was dancing with the same tall, thin partner. Clara signaled her, and she left him standing on the dance floor.

"You saw that guy?"

"No, but I wanted to talk to you."

"Fine, the bean pole will wait. What's up?"

"I just wanted to know what you have to do to get Cacho to take you to Mar del Plata."

"I have to get him at least three grand."

"Three thousand pesos! You need so much to go look at the sea?"

"What sea? Cacho and me, we play roulette. Gamble."

"And you never look at the sea?"

"From the window of the casino, sometimes. But we don't usually. When the casinos are open, we're there like horses at the starting gate. When they close, they have to throw us out.

If you could only see Cacho; even when he loses he looks like he's winning. If he loses, I catch hell back at the hotel. But I don't care, because when he wins we come back like royalty on the express train. Win or lose, it's always great. Do you think three grand is too much?"

Strange people, who go to the sea and never look at it. Maybe Cacho is great and when you're with him nothing else matters. But what could be more wonderful than the sea? If I'm wrong, I'd sure like to meet a man like him.

She needed someone to make her forget the life she had lived. Not someone like Cacho, but rather a quiet, wise man she could trust, as impressive and mysterious as the sea. She felt sorry for herself because she always met people as weak as she was. Even Carlos had let himself be dominated by his wife.

Monona went on talking about Cacho, but Clara was no longer listening. She sighed and repeated one of her mother's favorites:

"What will become of women now that there are no real men!"

Carlos was approaching, and she regretted having such unpleasant thoughts. She was a fool to want to search for new dreams, she thought, now that her old dreams had come true.

Carlos looked at Clara with great tenderness, but his tenderness faded away when he turned to Monona.

"You're still here?"

"Yes. I'm still here. So what? I was telling your little friend that nobody makes fun of Cacho."

"Ah, Cacho . . ."

"Yes, Cacho. What did you do about the rich broad, may I ask?"

"I told her to take a walk."

"The great sacrifice, right?"

"What sacrifice? I'd do that and much more for Clara. The lady, of course, was very sad."

"Sure, sure, losing you. Well, I'm leaving; the bean pole's waiting for me."

And as Monona walked toward the dance floor, Carlos and Clara walked out of the dance hall.

"Look, Clarita, I don't want you to see Monona any more. She's crude, bad company. Tomorrow, wait for me outside so you don't have to be with that bunch."

Clara didn't answer him. As they climbed up the hill at Plaza San Martin, she thought how marvelous Carlos was to have left a rich woman to be with her. An ordinary girl. Just thinking about it thrilled her and made her laugh. A lady covered with jewelry, with diamonds, and he had had the strength to tell her no. A real man. He knows what he wants. She pressed close to his side, and he kissed her.

"Don't you want to come with me tonight?"

Now that she had conquered a man, she was determined to make herself important.

"I can't. I live with a strict aunt. She'll worry."

"Tomorrow, then?"

"We'll see. . . .'

"What time do we meet?"

"At six, like today."

"That's so late."

"You must be patient."

"Do you love me, Clara?"

"Yes," she answered, and shyly buried her face in his shoulder.

A question was burning in her mouth, and she decided to ask it just before getting on the bus.

"Are you sorry you gave up the rich lady?"

Transition

"Look, Clara, that's all nonsense. I made up the story about the rich lady."

4 Goddamn dreams. They sure get in the way when you're happy. What you thought was perfect turns out to be a factory reject. Or something like that. Carlos is good and loves me, but Victor also loves me, or why would he have sent me that pretty card of a bride and groom covered with silvery speckles? Each loves me from his own corner, but neither loves me completely, as I'd like them to.

The following morning Clara got up earlier than usual and, without even eating breakfast, got to work on a dress she had cut the week before. She didn't want to disappoint Carlos: with a couple, if one is disappointed, both suffer. All his illusions would remain intact when he saw her in her fashionable flower-printed dress. To get there on time, she had to forget about the sleeves, but she would put them in later, in the fall. She looked at herself in the mirror and felt satisfied with her work. But she couldn't forget Carlos's rich lady.

"It doesn't matter," she told her reflection. "As soon as I forget the Carlos I imagined, the real one will seem divine."

She left the apartment late and ran the five blocks to the bus stop. She arrived at Parque Retiro forty minutes late.

Carlos was upset. "I've been waiting an hour for you."

Clara spun around. "I have a new dress."

"Now we have to rush or I'll be late." He grabbed her arm and dragged her toward the corner.

"Where are we going?" Clara shouted, surprised.

"You'll see."

"Aren't we going on the rides?"

"Not today."

"But you still have some tickets left."

Carlos wasn't listening to her. He hailed a taxi and pushed her inside. As she sat down, Clara didn't bother to arrange her skirt. It didn't matter if it got wrinkled. It no longer mattered, because, obviously, now it was not going to fly in the air and puff up like a balloon.

At the motel, Carlos ripped open a seam that was not securely finished. The dress lay limp on a chair, along with Clara's old enthusiasm for Carlos.

On their way back to Parque Retiro, he made an urgent request.

"I don't want you in the Palace when I'm singing. Wait outside. Take a few rides. I'll give you the tickets."

"Don't you want me to listen to you?"

"No. You make me nervous. And I don't like you hanging around with that bitch Monona; not to mention Cacho and his gang. Promise me you won't come."

A promise has to be fulfilled, even if it weighs you down. The quick stop at the motel had left her with an empty feeling in her stomach, the way she felt when she drank a lot. With drinking, there was a reason to feel that way, unaccustomed as she was to alcohol, but the other shouldn't disturb her. With Carlos she had wanted it to be different, but it had been so very much the same.

Clara felt as lonely as ever.

When there's someone in your life, loneliness is hard to take, she thought, but when you're alone, loneliness keeps you company.

She wouldn't have felt so lonely if it had been the deep of

night, but sunset is guilty of desertion. She strolled over to a food stand and bought a bologna sandwich wrapped in cellophane. Anguish was making her hungry, and the sandwich was a distraction. As she walked toward a tent of multicolored stripes, she heard a group of boys shouting:

"Is it good, beautiful?"

"Give us a bite?"

"Come here, doll; I want to smell the flowers on your dress. . . ."

Finally she reached the multicolored tent.

"Gather around, ladies and gentlemen," a barker was shouting into a megaphone. "Step right up if you want to know what fortune the stars have in store for you. Don't waste a moment; your future is in the hands of the swami, recently arrived from India. Step right up, ladies and gentlemen! Don't push."

Two soldiers, with girls on their arms, moved closer. Clara moved closer, too. The swami was sitting on a pedestal, motionless, his arms and legs crossed. Rays of light darted like arrows from the enormous ruby set in his turban.

Clara was so close to him that she could touch his wide, shiny black satin pants. His long, fine hands fascinated her. She looked straight into his calm, olive-colored face and deep-set gray eyes. She guessed that the man up there, so out of her reach, was even lonelier than she. But unlike her, he was indifferent to loneliness. It didn't make him hungry or thirsty, or melancholy. She would have liked to touch him and become infected with that indifference, but she was even afraid to hand over a peso to have the seer predict her future. A fat woman carrying a child did pay. She giggled.

There was a glass cylinder in front of the swami. With hesitant movements, almost liturgically, he threw into it a powder that exploded. Blue and red smoke rose before him, changing him alternately into angel and demon. When the smoke cleared, he put his hand inside the glass container and took out a scrap of paper and handed it to the fat lady.

Clara stood there spellbound, staring at that still, indifferent figure. While the fat woman strained to read the slip of paper in the tent's dim light, Clara wanted the swami to deliver her destiny to her with his long dark hands. And she opened her purse to look for the peso that would buy her future.

The barker went on shouting as she timidly handed him her peso. From his pedestal, the swami was watching her.

The blue and red smoke was brighter for Clara than it had been for the fat lady, and the swami rocked the cylinder to make the smoke rise faster. The yellow paper sent a shiver along Clara's spine, and as the swami handed it to her, she tried to touch his fingers. His eyelids didn't flicker, and their fingers never touched.

What marvelous indifference. I must put the yellow paper away carefully in the bottom of my purse; it's good to carry your destiny in your purse. In life everything is preordained. To know your future is the same as moving ahead too fast and running the risk of reaching the end before its time. I'm not afraid of death. It's too far away.

Two soldiers were reading their fortunes aloud, guffawing. Clara wanted to shut them up; it upset her that they didn't take the swami seriously. But the swami was above it all, and he sat on his pedestal, legs and arms crossed, not moving a muscle.

People came and went, as Clara stood there mesmerized. She gave the barker another peso in exchange for another piece of paper.

This one is violet. I have two destinies, like supernatural beings. I'll keep them both in my purse so they won't feel lonely. Strange. One loneliness plus another loneliness doesn't result in a larger loneliness. Rather, they cancel each other out.

Clara noticed that the swami was watching her from the corner of his eye. She opened her change purse, counted out some coins, and handed them to the barker. The swami repeated his routine with the cylinder. Clara stared at him, wide-eyed. It was better than seeing the same movie three times: here the protagonist was flesh and blood, and he was delivering the plot straight into her hands. The secret remained between them.

She had three destinies now. Perhaps she could choose one. She would have liked to ask the swami about that, but she thought it unlikely that he understood her language.

Three destinies, and I'll have to choose one without knowing what they all are.

She put her hand into her purse and picked one.

It's the red one, the brightest one. Red, a color that becomes my face.

5   Carlos begged her to stay with him all night because he needed her. But Clara yearned to feel a need rather than to feel needed, and she left him standing at the Parque Retiro exit.

The next morning, she decided to stay at home, to make no decisions. It was Friday; Victor would be back the next day. In the afternoon, she began to feel lonely and full of regret for having abandoned poor Carlos without an explanation. She began to wax the floor to distract herself. She tried to iron. She had a headache. She was dizzy. She undressed and took a long shower. But nothing calmed her. Finally, she decided to go back to Parque Retiro.

She bought her ticket and walked over to the swami's tent. Between the Caterpillar and the Phantom Train she caught a glimpse of the yellow lights of the Dance Palace, and they pierced her heart. She decided to ask for Carlos's forgiveness, to explain that she had chosen another destiny.

It was early, and there were only a few people in the ballroom. She zigzagged between the tables, and when she passed by the bandstand she stretched out her hand as if to say good-by. She remembered the emotion she had felt when she had seen Carlos again.

It's a shame, the sensations that make your legs tremble and clutch your throat don't last long. When they pass, they leave a void that's difficult to fill.

"Are you waiting for that jerk? It's the wrong time, friend; today he sings late."

It was Monona. She grabbed Clara's arm and dragged her toward a group sitting at a table in the back of the room. Afraid that Monona would steal her new red destiny, Clara freed herself and ran out of the dance hall.

Clara ran past the shooting gallery, past the games of skill, past the stand where she had bought a sandwich the previous day, to the swami's multicolored tent. All there was to see was a dark curtain covering the upper part of the pedestal.

She couldn't think, she almost couldn't move. She decided to unfold the scrap of red paper and let it decide what she should do next. She sat in the doorway of a stand opposite the tent. She placed her elbow on her knee, her chin on her hand, and she drew circles in the dust with her left foot. People passed by, but she didn't bother to raise her head. Suddenly, a few steps away, a pair of misshapen brown shoes came to a halt and a sarcastic voice asked, "Waiting for someone?"

Clara thought it was a scene she had been through before, like the one with Monona. But when she looked up and saw the dark face with the aquiline nose, she realized that this had never happened before. It was the person she was waiting for. She opened her purse and took out a peso.

"Tell me the future," she said in a weak voice, handing him the money.

"Keep that; be my guest today. How about some coffee?"

They went to the bar that had metal tables outside. Overhead, the planes were flying in monotonous circles.

"I thought you didn't speak Spanish," she said, just to say something. He understood her feelings sufficiently not to laugh.

"I know Hindu secrets, but I'm really from Buenos Aires."

"Really? That's strange. How do you tell the future?"

"There's magic in that. Give me your left hand. . . ."

Clara hid her hands behind her back. "No, no. I've chosen my future, but I don't want to know what it is."

"Have it your way. I'm sure you have the most beautiful heart line though."

"Ah, well," Clara sighed.

"I'm never wrong." And he moved his chair closer to Clara's. "So you've chosen your destiny?"

"Yes, the red."

"Then you must be careful with bulls."

"I'm not afraid of animals. I'm afraid of men."

"They're the same."

"You think so? What about women?"

"I dont want to offend you. Ask me a different question."

"It's harder to offend me than you think."

He stared at her awhile, and then said in a low voice, "Yesterday you were in front of my tent almost an hour. Why?"

"I don't know. I liked your little machine, the one that smokes."

"That's not the reason," and he squeezed her arm.

"Well, if you know the reason, why ask me?"

They looked at each other defiantly. Suddenly he kissed her on the mouth.

"That's why," he answered, sitting back with a sigh of relief. Then he lit a cigarette and added, "Now let's talk about you. Tell me who you are."

Clara again discovered the indifference she had observed in him the night before, and her admiration returned.

"There's nothing about my life worth telling. My name's Clara, but they say it doesn't suit me and I'm going to change it. What name do you like?"

"Clara."

"But that's the same . . ."

"No, it isn't. Before, you were anybody's Clara, but from the moment I said your name, you've been my Clara."

"And your name is swa . . . what?"

"That's my name for others. For you, it's Alejandro."

"Alejandro," Clara repeated.

"What are you doing tonight?"

"Nothing."

"And tomorrow, and the day after, and every day?"

"Nothing, nothing, nothing. I had a job, but I left it."

"You should never leave your job, or you're lost. I wanted to be an architect, but I couldn't make it."

Like Doña Ramona's son: he went to the capital to become a doctor, but a year later he came back to his village to plant carrots. Like his father.

"It's so expensive to study."

"It wasn't the expense. I had a scholarship. But in a student riot, I broke a professor's nose. They expelled me. I just couldn't go back to books. Now I pull rabbits from top hats. I read minds. I'm a magician. Come home with me and I'll show you all the tricks I know."

Clara's eyes sparkled, but her common sense won out. "You have to work now."

"This is no job for me. They can all go to hell! I'll manage somehow. Hey, kid, come here!"

He called a young boy who was hanging around and gave him five pesos.

"Take this. Go and tell the guys shouting at the swami's tent that the swami got sick and went home. But be sure you tell him, okay? Or the next time I see you, I'll kick your ass."

"Yes, sir," the kid answered, running off.

6   The bus pulled into the terminal, and the few remaining passengers descended the steps slowly. Alejandro led Clara to the edge of the Riachuelo River, and she laughed with pleasure when she saw the houses clustered there, each painted a different color.

"How pretty, Alejandro; how beautiful they are."

"They're not beautiful. They're a mess, a slum. Come on, let's not waste time around here."

"Do you live in a house that's brightly painted?"

"I certainly don't. I hate brightly painted houses."

Clara thought that having been an architectural student had forced him to develop a kind of austerity, and she didn't persist.

They arrived at a house of several stories with walls sheathed in sheets of zinc. They had to walk down thirteen steps to the entrance; Clara carefully counted each step.

Children were fighting in the courtyard. They went up a rickety staircase where kitchen smells and vapors collected; Clara felt nauseated and leaned on Alejandro's arm. On the first floor, a baby howled. On the second floor, an old man coughed, a woman sang, and a bunch of men were arguing. All these noises rose to the third floor, where Alejandro lived. The door to his room was unlocked.

"Aren't you afraid of being robbed?" Clara asked.

"Robbed? Of what?"

Inside, the unmade bed was surrounded by piles of books; it was deep and warm, like a nesting hen. To one side of the window, there was a big drafting table cluttered with papers and rulers; beyond that, a washbasin with a corroded mirror above it and a shelf with paints and brushes. A curtain covered a corner that served as a wardrobe. More books on the floor, an old shapeless armchair, and a stool completed the picture.

Alejandro looked at it with pride.

"Bohemia," he told her, and she believed it.

Since he didn't have a key, Alejandro pulled some heavy weights out from under the table and stacked them against the door.

"They weigh a hundred pounds. I don't think anyone can move them."

Then he came close to Clara as if he were about to kiss her, but he shifted away and went to the table, opened the drawer, and took out a package of crackers and a few slices of boiled ham wrapped in grease-stained paper.

"Here, eat. I don't have butter because it melts in the heat."

He pulled a bottle of wine out from under the bed and rinsed the only glass he had.

"Sit down," he told Clara, pointing to the bed. He handed her a glass of wine.

Clara sat and ate as if she were at home, although she had never seen a home as strange as this one. She stole quick glances at the titles of the books. On the cover of one, there was the palm of a hand crossed with many lines and a few stars; the others said things like *Dogma and Ritual of High Magic, The Golden Branch, Oriental Occultism*. She told herself that Alejandro must be the studious type.

He had seated himself on the table and was watching her. When the ham was finished, he took a package of cherries from among the papers on the table and popped them into her mouth as quickly as she could eat them.

"Hand me the towel," he said at last. "It's there, next to the pillow."

Clara stretched herself across the bed to reach the towel, but she pulled back sharply with a scream—something warm and furry had moved under the covers.

Alejandro remarked calmly, "That's Asmodeo," and he cradled in his arms an enormous black cat. The cat looked at him adoringly.

"The indispensable companion of the perfect magician," he added, caressing its back. "But now you have to go, Asmodeo. You frighten the lady."

He went to the window and opened it with a jerk.

"Go on, go eat some birdies on the roof," and, in spite of the heat, he closed the window again. But Asmodeo didn't move, and from the other side of the windowpane, his eyes followed his master's steps as he moved toward the bed, toward the woman who had displaced him and whom his master now began to kiss.

Asmodeo's green eyes were large and unblinking, as if to catch every detail of the feverish movements on the bed. When they were still again, he began to meow desperately. He would have liked to join them and to rub against those naked bodies and go to sleep, like his master, with his head between the woman's warm and generous breasts.

He stayed outside all night, meowing, forced to content himself with watching what was happening inside.

Clara didn't dare move. She didn't want to disturb Alejandro. Her head rested on his shoulder and her leg was flung across his belly. She savored a leisurely look at his perfect muscles and aquiline profile. She felt lethargic, but he had made her happy and she wanted to show her gratitude. Alejandro stretched his free hand to reach for a cigarette; he lit it and began to smoke.

Clara remembered his indifference when he was on the pedestal, and she tried to imitate him, to be like him, to complement him. Sleep was coming to her in waves. Every time she opened her eyes, she saw him in the same position—smoking, with his eyes fixed on the ceiling. She persisted in her efforts to keep from moving and, although her face was contracted and pained, sleep overcame her.

Finally, at dawn, she was able to feel more at ease with him. She no longer felt that unpleasant numbness in her leg and hip. Suddenly, someone banged furiously at the door, and she tensed with alarm.

"Señor, don't you hear your damned cat howling like someone's dying? He's keeping the whole building awake!"

Except for removing the cigarette from between his lips, Alejandro's expression was unchanged. "Leave Asmodeo alone, lady. He's looking for a she-cat."

"You're the one who goes after she-cats. If you don't shut that animal up, I'll get Don Anselmo to shoot him."

Alejandro got up slowly, went to the window, and opened it noisily.

"Come on, Asmodeo," he said.

The cat jumped inside and rubbed himself against his master's legs; Alejandro remained in front of the open window looking at the orange sky. Clara took advantage of the moment alone in bed to cover herself with the single blanket and to forget both the cold she had suffered all night and the cat's meowing. She was just about to fall asleep when Alejandro called her to his side. She had to get out of bed and go to the window naked, but then he was naked, too, and she wanted to do whatever he did.

Alejandro took her by the shoulders.

"I've thought about it a lot. You're going to stay with me forever. Too late to say no. When a woman spends all night with a man, hardly sleeping and not talking, then she has no right to walk out on him."

Asmodeo looked at her from the armchair, and his green eyes were shining with a mixture of admiration and hate.

7 The next day Victor arrived at one in the afternoon, dropped his suitcase in the hall, and asked Clara to bring him his slippers.

"What a lousy job," he complained as he kissed her indifferently on the cheek. "You have no idea how hot it was in Mercedes. And the train! A bunch of gossips who never stopped cackling. Bring me a bottle of cold beer. I'm dying of thirst. I sold two refrigerators. A nice little commission, right? Of course, I worked like a horse, galloping from here to there during the hottest part of the day. Now I'll be able to buy the blue cotton suit I saw the other day. I know, I know, don't interrupt me: you want the blender. Next time, baby, and don't argue

—a traveling salesman has to be well dressed, and that suit is just what I need this time of year. I'm too hot in the twill one. On the way to Mercedes, I met a man by the name of Menendez who was really pleased with his cotton suit. It's washable. Just think how much you can save in cleaning bills. A great guy, Menendez. I've got to meet him at two-thirty at the Café Paulista in Callao Street. He's got good connections. A traveling salesman in salami and sausages. Maybe we can work together. He put it so well—to keep salami fresh you need a good refrigerator. Talking about salami, I hope lunch is ready.

"Yes," Clara answered.

He left his jacket and tie on the bed and went into the kitchen.

"Cold chicken with mayonnaise!" he exclaimed, rubbing his hands. "My favorite dish."

He sat at the table and sliced almost half the chicken for himself. Clara cut herself a wing and put it on her plate with a teaspoon of mayonnaise. Victor helped himself to what was left and wiped the dish clean with a piece of bread. When he finished eating, he finally decided to look at Clara.

"You don't look right, baby. You're pale. You've got circles under your eyes. Don't tell me you're pregnant?"

"No."

"Thank God. That's all I need."

"Something worse is happening."

"Worse? Impossible; nothing could be worse. You're sure you're not pregnant?"

Clara shook her head.

"Then don't exaggerate, woman. It's just something temporary."

"No, it isn't temporary. I'm going away. I'm leaving you for good."

Victor choked, "You're going away? Where?"

Transition

"I don't think you should care about that," she said sadly.

"Are you out of your mind, woman? I always said you'd lose your head one of these days. Look, don't rush; think it over. Don't leave all this comfort for nothing. I've given you a home, food. I've got to run now because Menendez is waiting, but I hope when I come back you'll tell me it was all a joke."

When he returned, Clara and all her belongings were gone. She had left a note on the night table which said, "Sorry and thanks." She also left him the two pawn tickets, since she could never reclaim her watch and her maté gourd with the money Alejandro earned.

The first three days she spent with Alejandro made her intensely happy. He had sent word to his partner, the barker, that he was ill, unable to go to Parque Retiro. Partly to justify that lie, they spent hours every day in bed, only getting up at sunset to walk to the Riachuelo, or to go up Avellaneda Bridge to watch the ships, or to go to Vuelta Avellaneda to sit silently on a bench. When they felt hungry, they would go to some cheap restaurant and eat fried fish, or buy bread and sausages to take home. Sometimes they would stand in the doorway of a café listening to the music of an accordion.

A threatening letter from his partner and the lack of money to buy even basic necessities forced Alejandro to forsake his peace. He was dressing to leave when Clara stretched out her hand for the dress she had left on the chair.

"No, I don't want you to come. What will you do there? Stay here and keep Asmodeo company. There's a piece of spinach pie left. Eat and go to bed early; I'll be back about one."

He gave her a hurried kiss and disappeared before she could protest. Clara leaned out of the window to watch him cross the patio, but the food smells floating up made her feel nauseated.

Asmodeo, who had reclaimed his favorite spot at the head of the bed, looked at her fiercely. She rested at the foot of the bed with her legs hanging over the edge and her head leaning against the wall.

Alejandro doesn't want me to see him glowing in that mysterious smoke I like so much. When he's close to me, I narrow my eyes and I can imagine him on his pedestal. So distant, so secure. And now he won't let me go there. It doesn't matter, though. If I close my eyes really tight, I can picture him forever.

The back of her head hurt from being pressed against the wall for so long, but Asmodeo slept peacefully on the pillow and it was better not to wake him. All she could do was leave the light on against her fear of the dark and the creaking of unknown steps in the corridor. She thought that probably now ships were passing under the bridge, just as they did when she watched the river with Alejandro, and that the tenement houses had the same cheerful colors under the same lights, but now that he was gone, she couldn't gather enough strength to dress and to descend the three flights to the street.

When Alejandro returned at one-thirty, he found her asleep at the foot of the bed, her legs still hanging over the edge. The light was still on, and Asmodeo had found refuge under the armchair. Alejandro was tired and a bit disgusted, but he wanted to settle her more comfortably without waking her. But she opened her eyes and said, "Never look back. . . ."

Alejandro realized that she had been afraid to be alone, that she wasn't strong enough to lift the weights and put them in front of the door; he would have to buy a padlock or a bolt. A bolt was a modest and useful object, inexpensive, but he opened his wallet and knew he didn't have enough to buy it. He caressed her hair, softly, and told her in a low voice that she must fight her fear. If it were up to him, he would work during the day or change jobs, but the idea of working simply to earn money disgusted him, and he cursed her for reminding him of his poverty.

As soon as she opened her eyes the next morning, he told her, "Don't let me catch you sleeping with the light on again. After all, I'm the one who pays the bills."

Clara was up early, looking around the room, wondering what to do. She wanted to tidy his worktable, but he had forbidden her to touch his papers. She wanted to sweep, but she couldn't find a broom. She wanted to wash herself, but he always got angry when she splashed water on his books.

"Sit down, once and for all! Stop hopping around like a bird in a cage."

Asmodeo was sleeping in the armchair. Clara had nothing to do but go back to bed. She stretched out on the bed and waited. At noon, Alejandro put his last few pesos in her hand and sent her out to buy wine, cold cuts, and bread.

There was a long line at the bakery. The man in front of her turned around and smiled pleasantly.

"I think we've seen each other before. Am I right, señorita?"

Clara looked at him indifferently: she had met so many men like him that she could no longer tell one from the other.

"Of course! We live in the same house," he continued, "on Pedro de Mendoza Street."

"That's right," she answered, biting at a piece of cuticle around her fingernail.

"You must be new in this neighborhood, or you wouldn't shop in Bianchi's grocery store. Don't think I've been spying on you; I just happened to see you go in. Listen, Don Pepe's store is much cheaper. Not as well stocked, though."

Clara raised her eyebrows.

"Surprised? Well, a bachelor gets to know the little secrets of his neighborhood. . . ."

Clara decided to smile. After all, he was being very friendly. When it was his turn, he let her go first. She asked the clerk for a loaf of Italian bread. Then he quickly bought three rolls. As he followed her out of the store he said, "It's better to come fifteen minutes earlier for the Italian bread; a new batch comes out of the oven then, and it's nice and hot."

"You know everything about this neighborhood!"

"Well, in my profession you have to keep your eyes open. . . ."

"Oh?"

"All this chatter and we haven't introduced ourselves. I'm Anselmo Romero."

"Clara Hernández," she said, extending her hand. She realized then how few times in the last years she had mentioned her surname. At least that gave her a certain dignity.

"We don't want the neighbors to talk. You go in alone, I go in alone. Some of our neighbors have such wagging tongues. . . . Good day."

While he rushed ahead in order to get to the tenement ahead of her, Clara tried to remember where she had heard his name before.

By late afternoon she had forgotten her new acquaintance, and she asked Alejandro to perform one of his funny tricks. He became indignant; he was reading about the sacrifice of eleventh-century heretics and thinking, like them, that hell is in this world. He felt capable of plummeting to the very depths of mysticism, of finding some form of truth. But this woman was forcing him back to reality, asking him to do magic tricks designed for fools. It was this mood that made him lose patience.

"Do I look like I'm ready to play games? Don't be ridiculous. Pass me the wine; I'm thirsty."

That night Clara slept in the dark. She fell asleep telling herself that under her roof she had a friend named Don Anselmo.

When Alejandro returned at dawn, he stood and stared at her

for a long time. He thought of his own frustrations, rejoiced in his failures. He felt he had touched rock bottom in that tenement, living with a prostitute, and, in his way, he was happy. One by one, things had gone wrong for him. If failure was his fate, he was determined to fail mightily, not halfway. He thought of the Marquis de Sade, of Giles de Rais, and of the possibility of torturing people physically in order to find himself. Sitting at Clara's feet, he decided that that was too toilsome, and finally he woke her up to make love; after all, he was giving her food and a home.

8   Alejandro had forbidden her to talk to the neighbors, but after spending five mornings lying in bed and watching the dust accumulate, she couldn't stand it any longer. She asked the woman in Number Nineteen to lend her a broom. The woman looked at her suspiciously, but then realized that Clara was the woman who lived with the eccentric young man in the attic. On impulse, she gave her the broom and even offered her the dustpan and feather duster.

Clara thanked her and promised to return everything in a half hour. That day she felt as lonely as ever and in need of distraction. Earlier that morning, Don Anselmo had told her that the following week they could not meet to shop together.

"I have to work the morning shift," he explained to her. "Of course, I can't complain. It's a good job. Quiet. I don't have to direct traffic, and those six hours go by fast, just like that."

The remark about directing traffic struck Clara, and suddenly the alarm bell went off in her mind. She recalled the first night she had spent with Alejandro, when the woman screaming about Asmodeo had said, "Don Anselmo, the policeman . . ." So that's who he is. Because of her old profession, she couldn't be a policeman's friend, and yet she needed a friend so badly. Alejandro was sullen and sparing with words, a characteristic that accounted for a large part of his charm, but she had lived with Victor for too long to tolerate such a sudden and radical change. In addition, everything surrounding Alejandro—Asmodeo, for example—was hostile toward her. Even his possessions broke in her hands when she handled them.

The faucet dripped with a maddening regularity, splashing water over everything. The lamp switch was impossible to turn on at night. And the one-burner stove put out only a small, totally useless yellow flame. Everything broke when Alejandro was not at home, and when he returned, the simple touch of his fingers was enough to restore the objects to their usual efficiency.

She began to suspect that perhaps he was a real magician, although she knew perfectly well that real magicians don't exist. In spite of that, Alejandro had the same power over her that he had over objects. When he caressed her, he did it so well that she couldn't deny him anything. Unfortunately, he didn't caress her often enough, and sometimes an entire day would pass during which he only talked to her about household essentials.

"Go to the grocery store." "Hand me the bottle." "Open the window for Asmodeo and give him some liver." Clara would stay at his side, admiring him for his perfect profile and his ability to spend hours without moving or sleeping, concentrating on his own dark thoughts.

But Clara needed someone to talk to once in a while, to unburden herself, she so chatted with Don Anselmo, who was, as he himself had said, a real gentleman. Her need for human warmth, more than her mania for cleanliness, made her borrow the broom from the neighbor. She busied herself by sweeping in corners and under the bed, not moving the books piled on the floor. She cleaned thoroughly, tidied everything, and added a touch of charm by spreading her green shawl over the dilapidated armchair. Then she went downstairs, two steps at a time, to return the broom.

She knocked at the door and waited. She was greatly disappointed when children appeared, but she handed the broom and feather duster to the tallest child, who looked about ten. The boy was offended and handed the items to his little sister.

"These are women's things," he said, and then, in a quieter voice, standing on tiptoe, he added, "Hey, lady, do you have a pack of cigarettes you could give me?"

Clara was indignant. "Children shouldn't smoke!"

"Smoke? If we want to smoke, we grab butts from the old man. He smokes dark tobacco, the good kind. I just want the backs of the boxes, the kind that have silver paper inside. It's to decorate the Christmas tree."

Clara was enthusiastic. "The Christmas tree, how nice! Where are you planning to put it?"

The boy looked down at his feet. "Look," he said firmly, "I don't believe in that stuff. But I go along with it. I'm sure we're going to have firecrackers, too."

Clara's expression brightened. "If I get you a lot of silver paper, will you let me see your tree?"

"It's not mine. It'll be in the courtyard. Pocho's old man—he's a gardener, you know—he brings us a big branch of real pine every year, and he pots it in a bucket. We decorate it with what we find around. I do it for the kids," he said, pointing to his little brothers and sisters. "They still believe, and my mother says there's time for them to learn for themselves."

"Can I help you decorate the tree?" Clara asked boldly.

"Can you bring firecrackers?"

"Well, no, not firecrackers . . . but I could make little dolls."

"Little dolls?" the boy mumbled. "If you think that's fun . . ."

"It is fun. Won't you let me?"

"The tree's for everybody. Even grownups come down with fruitcakes and cider on Christmas Eve. What I like is the cider. I bet I could drink a whole bottle without getting smashed. I could walk a straight line and everything. But if you bring firecrackers, it'll be much better."

"I'll see if I can get you some rockets."

"Great. Make the little dolls, too, because this year the tree's going to be real big. The guy next door is giving us candles. I think he works in a funeral home. Look, if you bring the rockets we'll even let you trim the tree. In my gang, we like to do everything ourselves. I'm the boss, though. If I tell them to let you help, they will. But you have to bring a lot of little dolls and stars and all that crap. And don't forget the rockets."

"It's a deal."

Clara gave him her hand and the boy squeezed it with all his strength to seal the pact. Then he looked at her triumphantly and said: "They call me Bumps, because I'm always knocking into things. Who're you?"

"Clara."

"Don't you have a nickname?"

"No."

"Well, don't worry. We'll find you one."

There were only four days left before Christmas Eve, and Clara knew it was impossible for her to save any money. Alejandro spent it as fast as he earned it. On good days he would take her to a restaurant, and on bad days they would eat a can of mackerel. She was sick and tired of mackerel, and she hadn't been able to save one penny for the rockets. Alejandro had become more taciturn than ever and talked to her as little as possible.

He spent his time reading books and trying to penetrate the secrets of the cabala. He would become agitated, restless. Sometimes he would draw strange symbols on the wall with charcoal. The room began to take on a sinister aspect for Clara, especially when he laughed suddenly and without reason or warning. At times Alejandro would remain quiet for hours, and then she was as afraid to disturb him as she was during those times when he was upset.

One morning, while she was stealing glances at his profile, admiring his features and his indifference, she realized that what she wanted most was for him to leave for work. Usually she hated the time when he put on his coat and kissed her goodby; the night seemed endless when she was alone, and Asmodeo's company gave her the chills. But that morning she knew she would not waste the night trying to catch the sleep that always slipped past her eyelids: Don Anselmo had lent her a pair of scissors, and she had collected enough round pieces from the necks of Alejandro's wine bottles to make a sky full of stars.

At last he left, and Clara cut out many stars, each one different and all perforated, as if they were made of lace. She was happy; even Asmodeo purred briefly. She wanted to paste all those stars on the ceiling before Alejandro returned, but she wanted to surprise him on Christmas Eve.

Only Don Anselmo knew of her project. She had to confide in someone. Furthermore, Don Anselmo could help her. In addition to lending her the pair of scissors, he had promised to pick up cigarette packs he found on the street. Clara pasted the silver cigarette paper on cardboard and then cut out little dolls. It was, however, much more fascinating to make the stars. The paper circles had to be folded in six parts and cut at random and the results were always different and surprising.

It was only two more days to Christmas Eve when Clara decided she had enough stars to decorate a whole tree. There were twenty-three stars. To Clara, that represented a corresponding number of quarts of wine collected in ten days. Suddenly, she realized where the money Alejandro earned had gone, and she felt like crying. Tears began to flow as she thought of all the rockets she could have bought for Bumps, if it weren't for those damned bottles of wine.

She cried for a long time, until she noticed a bright and cruel glint of happiness in Asmodeo's green eyes. Asmodeo's eyes were identical to those of his master: brightness showed in their eyes when their lips should have smiled. Alejandro and Asmodeo laughed only with their eyes, mocking the world.

Clara remembered an afternoon when Alejandro had had a day off and she had decided to clean in spite of his grumbling. On the table there was a small clay statue. As she brushed it with the feather duster, it wobbled slightly. Alejandro shouted, "Careful!" and leaped from the bed to grab it. He held it lovingly in the hollow of his hands.

"You're very fond of that little statue."

"It isn't a statue, it's an idol. And I'm not very fond of it at all. I'm not attached to material things."

"But you like it a lot. Look at you caressing it."

"Caressing it?" he said, astonished. And he tightened his fist deliberately until the delicate legs of the statue broke.

"See?" he said, opening his hand so that Clara could view the destruction. "I'm not attached to material things."

Clara stared at him, holding back tears. Finally, she asked him, "And Asmodeo? Don't you love Asmodeo either?"

"Why? Are you jealous of Asmodeo? Do you want me to break his legs, too? But Asmodeo isn't so easy to destroy: that's why I like him. He was only a few weeks old when I found him in an alley. He followed me home, so I put him in a box with a saucer of milk. Weak as he was, he didn't die, so one day

I took him out of the box to give him some sun. And there he is. In perfect health."

Clara looked at the two of them and realized that they were laughing, together, with their eyes.

He had brought her there out of pity, too. Like Asmodeo, she was determined to survive. That cat had no reason to laugh at her, not even now, when she was crying over the loss of the rockets.

"I'm going to do something neither of you expects. You'll see," she said to the cat threateningly. "No more showing off from you or from your master. Or from anyone else. If I need money, I know how to get it."

9   She put on her lucky lilac dress and went to that neighborhood where sailors, her specialty, were plentiful. But despite the favorable circumstances, she couldn't approach one man. Opposing forces were struggling inside her, and she didn't know which side to take. On the one hand there was the temptation to get the rockets, with their implicit promise of trimming the Christmas tree and the pleasure of laughing at Asmodeo. On the other was the absolute conviction that she would never be able to laugh at Alejandro.

"I'm not attached to material things. You go to hell," he would tell her, without getting out of bed, without even changing his position. He would throw her out without a thought. She would have to start all over again, and she was so tired of doing that, repeatedly, when the new beginning always ended the same as the old one had, the familiar, the despised. She sighed with dismay. A man passing by, mistaking the meaning of that sigh, took her by the arm. Clara freed herself with an abrupt shrug and began to run desperately.

She ran through streets and turned corners without stopping until she arrived at the tenement. By the light of the street lamps she saw a familiar silhouette approaching.

"Don Anselmo!" Clara shouted when she recognized him. He was her salvation.

"Clara, dear. What are you doing on the streets at this hour?"

"I don't know. I went for a walk. I was restless."

"I understand. But this neighborhood is dangerous for a girl like you; something terrible could happen. Do you want me to accompany you?"

"Accompany me? But we're at the door already."

"We could go for a short walk."

"Well, okay. But you know, Don Anselmo, I can't stay out late."

"Of course, of course. We'll just go a little way, that's all."

He put his arm around her waist; Clara had decided to let him comfort her, but she thought of Alejandro again and suddenly she stiffened. He noticed it.

"You seem agitated. It's very hot. Let's go for a beer. There's a bar just four blocks away."

"Yes, it is hot. Let's go."

They only stayed in the bar a half hour, but Don Anselmo had enough time to display his cordiality and good will. He did it so well that Clara dared to ask him if she could borrow some money to buy rockets.

"Of course, anything," he answered, taking out his wallet. "Naturally, you'll have to invite me to see the tree, eh?"

"Of course. The tree is for everyone. You'll be able to see the rockets, too. They're so pretty. The children want firecrackers, but I don't like them because they explode. But once the rockets are lit, they fly like falling stars. You're allowed to ask for three wishes."

"Are you going to ask for three wishes? I would be satisfied with one."

He looked into her eyes, and under the table he moved his leg next to hers. Since she didn't seem aware of his touch, he put his hand on her knee.

"Look, we're going to have a lovely party," he said to distract her. "I'll see about the firecrackers the little ones want. They're illegal, and a policeman shouldn't do these things, but I'll make an exception. After all, it's not Christmas every day. We're going to enjoy ourselves as we've never enjoyed ourselves before. The other years didn't count for me; only this one is brightened because you're here. I promise you I'll get the firecrackers."

He's so nice, but I shouldn't get his hopes up. I'm going to be with Alejandro during the party.

"It's getting late, Don Anselmo. I have to get home." She stood up.

"Ah, I forgot about your duties. It's a pity that those things exist. It was a pleasure to talk to you. I'll walk home with you—if it won't cause you any trouble, of course."

Clara thought of Alejandro. "I prefer to go back by myself," she said. "But please, watch me from a distance. I don't like to be alone on these badly lit streets."

"Certainly. Thank you for your company."

Clara gave him her hand with an almost childish seriousness. She walked along happy because she believed that at last she had found a man who respected her. She had asked him to watch her while she returned home not because she was afraid of the men she might meet, but because she didn't want him to know what she really was.

Alejandro arrived minutes after she did. He found her fast asleep.

The next morning she asked Alejandro to take her to Parque Retiro to see the preparations for Christmas.

"What preparations? Do you think anyone there is bothering with that foolish holiday? I figure maybe I'll catch a few more customers, but I'm not even sure of that."

"But I want to see you."

"See me? I have no intention of playing the clown in front of you. I'll never give you the chance to laugh at me, so don't insist. I don't want you to come to Parque Retiro, and that's that."

"Bring your machine home tonight, Alejandro, and play the smoke game for me. Tell me my fortune. I love it when you do that."

She wanted to caress his forehead, but he turned over, and lay with his face toward the wall, his favorite position.

Clara felt like crying, but she knew that he hated scenes and that the slightest irritation could put him in a bad mood. He had been so affectionate with her ten minutes before. She didn't understand him, nor did she make an effort to understand him: she knew that men are much more complicated than women. All she could do was make the good moments last as long as possible so that she had memories to sustain her during those lonely hours with or without him.

As she was looking out of the window that afternoon, she saw the children bringing the tree into the courtyard, and she decided that fighting with Alejandro to go to Parque Retiro was not worth while now that she had another diversion. She went back to lie at his side, and she spoke to him in a very soft voice.

"Forgive me. I didn't want to make you angry. I only wanted to keep you company, but if you don't want that, it doesn't matter. I won't talk about it any more. Be nice. Forgive me. Give me a little kiss."

He didn't seem to hear her. But from the corner of her eye, Clara could see the tips of the rockets sticking out of the old pitcher where she had hidden them, and they gave her the courage to go on insisting. She insisted so unhesitatingly and so well, caressing him gently as if she were afraid to offend him, that Alejandro finally succumbed.

"All right, I forgive you, but don't plague me any more about coming to see me. I'm sick and tired of that job anyway; I should be doing something else, something I really like."

While he was slowly undressing her, Clara knew that her experience with men was of some use to her, after all.

Sadness had left her, but it returned when he said, just before going out the door: "I'll be back later than usual tonight. I've something important to talk over with my partner. Oh, and I forgot to tell you: I'm not working tomorrow."

Clara screamed for joy and ran back to the room. Crouching on the floor, she pulled a box out from under the bed. She opened it lovingly and studied once again the stars and little dolls she had made. The moment to put them on the tree had arrived at last. She would leave the rockets where they were, certain if she gave them to Bumps in advance, he wouldn't be able to resist the temptation to light them.

She ran down to the courtyard in great excitement. The children didn't greet her with much enthusiasm, but she didn't let that bother her. The tree was there, and she felt that it was hers.

Piece by piece, she took the treasures out of the box. The children looked at them with unconcealed surprise as they handed her pins and hooks. Finally, all the tree needed was the big star for the very top, and since Clara had made that star, it was her privilege to place it there. A boy brought her a chair, and she stepped up without hesitation.

The children made a great circle around Clara. Clara looked at them and saw the sparkling Christmas tree reflected in their dazzled expressions. She was proud of her work, of having enchanted the children, and she would have enjoyed staying there forever to savor their happiness. It was getting late, though, and mothers were beginning to call them to supper; the mood was slowly fading. Clara and Bumps were left alone in the middle of the courtyard.

"The tree looks great, doesn't it?" the boy said enthusiastically.

"It was a good idea for me to help you, wasn't it?"

"Yes, but you didn't keep your promise. Where are the rockets?"

"I've kept my promise. I have them, but I won't give them to you until tomorrow night."

"Tomorrow? Why not today? Give me one, just to try. Just one, to make sure the powder isn't wet."

"No," she said resolutely. "There are only a few, so we're going to keep them all for tomorrow, for the right moment."

"Just one. Come on, don't be mean."

But Clara knew how to be decisive. Bumps had to leave in a hurry because his father was calling him, threatening to let him have it with a leather strap if he didn't obey. Clara remained alone in the courtyard, admiring the tree, until finally, she resigned herself to going upstairs.

The night was turning dark and heavy, and Clara couldn't see the tree from the garret window. She waited patiently for the moon to rise, but shortly after midnight, she couldn't bear another moment away from the tree. She took Asmodeo in her arms and tiptoed downstairs.

When they arrived at the courtyard, Asmodeo jumped out of her arms and ran to look at the parakeets that hung just out of his reach. Clara was disappointed: Asmodeo hadn't even glanced at the tree.

She remained studying each star until she heard steps behind her.

"The tree is beautiful," a voice said. "I'm sure you did it all alone. Those kids are no good for that. Or for anything else."

A man's arm grabbed her around the waist.

"Oh, Don Anselmo!" Clara complained, moving aside. "You frightened me. Do you really think it's pretty?"

"It's wonderful. Let's see if tomorrow we can give you a few candles so it will be even brighter. Too bad I'm on the night shift, but as soon as I finish, I'll be here. You'll wait for me, won't you? I'm going to bring you a little surprise for Christmas. What do you think of that?" He paused, then added, "Why don't you come to my room for a little snack? I have iced tea, and we could chat a while."

He put his arm around her waist again and tried to kiss the back of her neck but only succeeded in grazing it with his mustache. Angrily, Clara realized that he was far from thinking her decent, as she had hoped. Certain attitudes and background must reveal themselves on people's faces. She didn't want to show her anger, however, and mustering all her calm, she said amicably.

"I have to go up now. I wanted our cat to see the tree, but he's not interested."

"Dogs are interested in trees, not cats," Don Anselmo answered gruffly.

Clara looked for Asmodeo and then rushed upstairs.

"Did you see the tree last night?" she asked Alejandro the following morning.

"What tree?"

"The Christmas tree, in the middle of the courtyard."

"I didn't notice. I don't walk around looking at trees. I've got other things on my mind."

Clara moved the chair next to the window and looked out across a tile roof.

"Come here. You can see it from here. It gleams in the sun. Come, look."

"I'm not getting up for that. If you feel like falling from the third floor, go ahead, but I think you'd better get down from that chair. Did you buy some wine?"

"Yes, one bottle. Come see the tree. I trimmed it for you."

"I knew you were stupid, but not that stupid."

Clara closed her eyes.

"Why don't you look at it? I did it for you."

"For me? I don't give a shit about your tree."

Clara bit her lips and carefully stepped down from the chair. "I'm going to the bathroom," she said, and ran out of the room.

She stayed in the bathroom long enough to calm down. Then she slipped the bolt open and rushed upstairs to the indifferent and warm refuge of nestling against Alejandro's back.

In the late afternoon she went to the store to buy wine because Alejandro was thirsty. As she walked down the street, she hoped to avoid meeting Don Anselmo. When she got back, Alejandro wasn't there. She decided to take advantage of his absence to get dressed. The prospect of the party had put her in a good mood, and she hummed while she looked for the box that held her flowered dress, the one she had been wearing when she met Alejandro. She combed her hair carefully and used a muslin scarf for a ribbon.

Deep down, Don Anselmo is like all men, insensitive. What women have, above all, is sensitivity.

She smiled at herself in the mirror. Dressed up, she looked delicious. There was no reason to worry, least of all on Christmas Eve.

Ah, Christmas Eve. The rockets. She had to act quickly to get them to Bumps before Alejandro returned. When he came into the room, he found her sitting on the bed.

Transition

"You look pretty," he said, and sat down next to her, not to hug her as she had hoped, but to drink from the bottle of wine on the night table. Then he stretched himself out across the bed and toyed with the ends of the scarf on Clara's head.

"Why are you all dressed up?" he asked.

"To go to the party."

"The party? What party?"

"Downstairs. We're all going to get together in the courtyard and have a good time. They've put out tables and chairs. Didn't you notice? Everyone is chipping in to pay for the fruitcakes and cider."

"Fruitcakes and cider? Fruitcakes and cider," he sang in a low voice. "How nice. Pure and simple. Good-neighbor policy. What do you think I am? An idiot? Do you think I'll waste my time and money with those fools? You might as well take off your party dress right now. You're not going to need it." The tone of his voice was aggressive.

"You mean we're not going?" Clara asked, hoping it was all a joke.

"No, beautiful, we're not going. We'll have a much better time here. Alone."

"But it's Christmas Eve, Alejandro. That's an important night. It's a time to celebrate and enjoy. You don't understand."

"I understand everything, girl. Your Christmas makes me sick. Hand me the wine to settle my stomach a bit."

His eyes looked gloomy; he had drunk too much. He was becoming dangerous. She didn't dare deny him the bottle.

"If you want some diversion, beautiful, we can have a very good time right here, without anybody's help. I'm just beginning to feel like it."

"But I promised to go downstairs."

"And who did you promise, if I may ask? That mustached cop

who struts around with his chest stuck out? Aren't you ashamed to make promises to a cop? You disgust me, but to show you I'm not one to hold a grudge, I'll do you the favor of allowing you to break your promise. Give me that bottle again; those sons of bitches are making them smaller all the time! Christmas! Hand me the cup, too. I don't like to drink alone. And don't look at me with those cow eyes. Drink, drink. Let me see, turn the cup upside down. Not one drop left. That's the way."

Three times he filled her cup, and three times he forced her to down it all. The empty bottle rolled under the bed.

"Now we'll really have some fun," he said. Taking her by the shoulders, he forced her onto the bed.

Pleasure comes slowly, and Alejandro was allowing himself to sway with a pleasurable dizziness, as if he were sailing in a boat on a sunny morning.

Suddenly there was a soft whistle at the door. Alejandro leaped off the bed.

"It's that filthy cop. You're a bitch. A bitch. Whore!"

The wine gave Clara courage. "I know I'm a whore. Everybody knows it. You don't have to shout it. Even the cop knows it. That's why he's after me. But not because I did anything bad with him. I never did anything with him, never. I wanted him to think of me as a decent woman. . . ."

"Swear you didn't fuck him."

"I swear it! You can choke me as much as you want; I swear I didn't go to bed with him."

"You're a shitfaced liar."

All at once he quieted down. Clara was looking at him expectantly. Finally he said, "Nobody takes me for a fool, you know. You're not going to laugh at me so easily. If you feel like cheating on me, don't hang around any more, understand? Now come here; I don't like to leave things half done."

10　　All Clara saw of the party was three of her five rockets shooting past the attic window; she didn't even hear the laughter and the songs. Her disappointment rocked her softly, and she fell asleep little by little, like someone walking into a warm, dark river.

After a deep sleep, she woke with a pleasant sensation. When she opened her eyes, Alejandro told her he wanted to marry her.

He proposed to her casually, without preamble, but he had thought about it the entire night. After all, he needed someone to torture, subtly, and Clara was ready material. Besides, he enjoyed her in bed; she did anything he asked, and she wasn't like so many women he had known who never stopped talking. Once they were married, she would have to follow him, and with her he could easily leave Parque Retiro to go around the world looking for that something that would give him the measure of his own worth.

"We're going to get married, you hear," he repeated.

"But I don't know if I want to get married," she objected.

"Of course you do. What else would you want?"

"Want? I don't want anything. It's true that in the past I did want to get married, but now I don't know. At least give me time to think it over. You aren't in a hurry, are you?"

She's playing hard to get, Alejandro thought; as soon as I turn the other way, she'll run off with that cop. Aloud he said, "I'll give you until noon. Don't take too long, or I might change my mind."

Clara got up and dressed to go to the store, but instead of putting her wallet in the shopping bag as usual, she carefully took out her white purse. She wanted to consult the little red paper with her fortune, the one Alejandro had handed her at Parque Retiro. On the second-floor landing, she took the red paper out of her purse and unfolded it.

I'm a coward, always dreaming of marrying, and now that someone is proposing I'm pulling back.

On the second-floor landing there was enough light to read the note, but she crushed the paper, afraid to find out what it said.

She preferred to carry the weight of her own decision, knowing full well that whatever is written will come true in any case. She had repeated that to herself at Catholic Action meetings every Sunday for ten years back home, so it must have been an undisputable and irreversible truth. However, she couldn't trust Alejandro completely, for he had given her three different destinies, and he probably didn't even remember that she had chosen the red one. Perhaps he wanted to change the established order of things and keep the prerogatives for himself.

The street door was closed, and Clara walked through the hallway in the darkness. Suddenly a man's silhouette blocked her.

"Bad girl! Why didn't you come to the party last night? I saved some butter cookies for you and a bottle of something very special."

The full rush of anger Clara had felt when he had come whistling at her door revived now, and she clenched her teeth and puffed up her cheeks.

"Why didn't you answer when I whistled?" he persisted, closing in on her and trying to put his arm around her.

Wretch, degenerate. Taking me for a hussy.

Clara felt disgust for this man, who had the gall to touch her when she was about to make a serious decision.

"Let me go," she said.

"Why should I let you go, sweetheart? You're all right here."

"I'm not all right here! And you won't be all right either if my fiancé comes down."

"Your fiancé," he said scornfully.

"That's right, my fiancé. We're getting married next week!"

She pushed him away and opened the front door.

Transition

Things are so easy and simple: we're getting married next week.

It wasn't her fault that the man had pushed her into marriage. Now she couldn't turn back. The serious decision was made. Relieved, she breathed easily again, and as she waited her turn at Don Pepe's store, she wondered if she had the right to wear a white dress and a veil over her face when she entered the church. She thought probably she would have to forgo some of those traditions. Too bad.

She ran up the stairs with the bottles she was carrying, and arrived at the third floor panting.

"Let's get married," she said to Alejandro as soon as she stepped into the room.

"Are you happy?" he asked after a pause.

"I don't know. It hasn't dawned on me yet. I suppose the life we live won't change much, will it?"

"Who knows? We're going to go far away. I'm sick and tired of this tenement."

"Do you love me?"

"No. I don't love anyone. But I'm comfortable with you."

The next day he made an appointment at City Hall in the same way he might have made a doctor's appointment. He didn't return from Parque Retiro until one-thirty in the morning, but Clara was still awake, biting the end of a pencil as she figured out expenses.

"I can make the dress myself with three or four yards of taffeta," she told him. "The church here is small. We won't need many flowers."

"I'm not taking you to the altar, girl. If that's what you have in mind, look for another husband. A civil ceremony is more than enough; you suggest priests and altars to me again and I won't marry you at all!'

The third of August was as oppressive as any other summer day. After lunch Clara put on her flowered dress, fought with

Alejandro to get him to wear a tie, and went with him to City Hall. They had some difficulty finding witnesses, but at the last moment they persuaded Bumps's mother and Marcovecchio, the barker. They arrived a little late, a few couples were ahead of them. Clara looked at the brides with envy: they wore fancy hats, and in a few days they would surely marry in church. One smiled shyly at the groom, as if she were a virgin. None of them, however, had as good-looking a future husband as she did, and that was reassuring.

When their turn came, Clara and Alejandro went into an enormous room. Ten minutes later, they were married, with signatures and a seal on a certificate, and even a white booklet. They went to a bar to celebrate, although Bumps's mother declined to join them.

Clara studied the booklet Alejandro had tossed onto the café table. There was enough room in it to register as many as twelve children. As she carefully looked through its pages, she heard Marcovecchio say that although Alejandro was insistent on trying his luck elsewhere, he didn't care for the idea of moving around like gypsies instead of staying peacefully in Parque Retiro where the work was reliable if not very exciting. Clara didn't care about such things at the moment. The words the man at City Hall had intoned kept spinning in her head: the wife must obey her husband, be faithful to him, and follow him wherever he goes.

The Head

1   Clara filled the washbowl with the water from the pitcher and, for the third time that day, washed her eyes, her hands, and her arms up to the elbows. "Keep the shutters closed," the owner of the hotel had advised her, "or flies will come into the room." Her eyes hurt from working in the dim light, and the palms of her hands were sticky with sweat. From the kitchen came the sickening smell of the stew she had eaten at lunch; they were probably reheating it for dinner. It was late, and she had to find Alejandro at the fairgrounds. She picked up her sequin embroidery; the dragon on the left side glittered in the dim light. Clara thought the one she had just started on the right side was giving her the evil eye; if she made a mistake, she would have to undo it and begin all over again.

Spangles are like that; when you want to remove one, all the others on the same thread come tumbling off. It's the same with some men: when all you want is to get a little honesty out of them, you just tug a bit, and so many things come tumbling out that suddenly you have quite a different person on your hands.

Every afternoon, in every town they passed through, she had to seek out Alejandro when he finished work or else he would walk into the first bar he could find, embrace a gin bottle, and try to remember things he had forgotten for years. Nevertheless, at siesta time, before leaving the hotel, he would prepare his act with great care, meticulously hiding the playing cards and colored handkerchiefs in mysterious pockets, in a top hat, or in a double-bottomed box. By the end of the day he was dispirited, and Clara had to give him some reason to return to the hotel. He was a success with the children, but the more he made them laugh, the more gin he needed after his exit.

Clara walked the dusty streets yearning to share Alejandro's dreams, the dreams she couldn't discover when his eyes were fixed on something she couldn't see. It was two months since she had begun wandering behind him, and there had not been one word of his intentions, his plans, no reference to his feelings for her; Clara always came up against his silence.

She had left the main street behind and was walking past the low and gloomy houses. The women had put their wicker chairs out on the dusty sidewalk and they knitted while they waited for a breath of air that never came. Farther away, an old man was sprinkling water on his section of the packed dirt walk, and children took advantage of this to play in the mud. Clara was not interested in this life shipwrecked in dust; she had known it well enough back in Tres Lomas, although the dust of Tres Lomas was more like sand and brought with it some memory of the sea. Now Alejandro wanted to lock her in a circle where there was only room for him; little by little he was managing to attain perfect isolation. "I forbid you to come see me perform. You make me nervous." And Clara, obedient, would stay in the hotel trying to busy herself with embroidery, not daring to want anything more. She rolled from town to town like a ball, bouncing from the hotel to the general store or bar where her husband would be soaking himself in gin. There was one hope that repeated itself with each new train ride. I'm going to have a child, she would say to herself. But looking at Alejandro made her realize that could never come true, because whatever happened to her would be ruled by the will that did not believe in affection.

A car passed by, and instinctively she covered her face with a gauze scarf; she remained waiting with her eyes closed until the cloud of dust disappeared.

When Marcovecchio was with them, at least things went smoothly because he organized the trips and the acts for different fairgrounds. At least he was cheerful; with him Clara met other people, people who were a true part of the fair and who got together at night to drink wine and sing songs while someone strummed a guitar.

But a fight between Marcovecchio and Alejandro was inevitable. Alejandro created something impalpable between the two of them, meting out vague complaints and generating tension until the partner of many years couldn't stand it any more.

"I'm sick and tired of all this. I'm going back to Buenos Aires! You can go on rotting away in these shitty little towns. Burn yourselves out, but do it without me."

Clara looked at him with envy. At least there was someone capable of shouting at Alejandro, capable of leaving him. Marcovecchio didn't see that sparkle in her eyes, and when he slammed the door, he left forever. Alejandro, finally, smiled. She returned to her embroidery.

"Rotting away," those were his words. "Burn yourselves out." Little by little there would be nothing left of them in these towns; everything would fade, a bit at a time, under a white cloak of dust. They were locked in a coffin, locked in the middle of the inscrutable and alien countryside.

At least in my town every tree was my friend. Now I'm a stranger to everyone. The magician's wife. A nobody.

Alejandro's smile had lasted only an instant. Thick drops of sweat ran down his forehead. "Now that we're free, we could go to the sea," she had said to cheer him up, but her words embittered his triumph.

The heat felt heavy on the back of her head; the sun was following her through the streets. A group of girls, not much younger than she, had congregated in front of a bakery, eating ice cream and gossiping. Although she would have enjoyed having an ice cream, too, she didn't have the courage to walk past that female wall.

The fair had already closed down when she got there. She went directly to the general store nearby. Alejandro was leaning against the counter, staring at the black rope sandals piled on the shelves.

The owner of the hotel was kind. He had let her sit in the dining room during siesta because her room hadn't enough light by which to embroider. There was only a small window high on the wall, almost at the ceiling, and a door that led to a back yard where trash cans and empty bottles were piled.

Clara's eyes hurt and she decided to rest awhile and count the people as they passed on their way to the fair. But no one was passing by; siesta time in those towns was always desolate and deserted, and the deeper they moved inland, the later in the afternoon people appeared in the streets.

Alejandro had a knack for making changes almost imperceptibly. They had never been in a hotel as poor as this one, and, worse still, they occupied the cheapest room. The fair was no longer the same either. Alejandro couldn't go on for too long with the same people. Now he was doing his tricks among peddlers and fortunetellers. If only Marcovecchio hadn't left them.

However, Alejandro knew an extraordinary number of tricks which he said were from Malabar; Clara had spied on him one night while he was practicing a new one. Her eyes were half closed, and a vibrant, voluptuous current ran through her spine. Red, yellow, orange scarves appeared and disappeared, almost touching her face. If she could find out where he hid the scarves, she could get up some night, without making a sound, and wrap them around her naked body and dance and twirl and remember the time when she had had all the men in the world for herself. Alejandro's touch once must have been like those of all very young boys, shy and caressing, warm and fleeting, asking for much more than they could give. The scarves would fly and tie themselves to each other and untie themselves again. Alejandro always made the scarves and caresses disappear and then stood alone in the center of the room, in control of himself and of Clara's emotions.

In that town where everything was gray, she had been able to buy more golden spangles. Poor Asmodeo, he could have kept her company in spite of his mistrust, as he had when she had been alone in the tenement. But Asmodeo had gone down for the last time; she had been there when Alejandro put him in a weighted bag. The last thing he had done before leaving the city was to throw that bag into the Riachuelo, without remorse, because he couldn't take Asmodeo with him. "He's mine, I can do whatever I want with him," he had said, more to himself than to Clara, to whom he owed nothing, not even an explanation.

She had dragged herself down because one day in August she had sworn to be true to a husband. Alejandro was too proud. He should let her earn some money, share her a bit with others, and stop yelling as if she were to blame for everything that went wrong.

Of course, in such a miserable town she wouldn't be able to find a decent customer; she would have to go back to Buenos Aires where there was no dust and heat, where one can live at night. With a new pair of shoes and a good permanent wave, she would dare to walk down Florida Street in search of wealthy men. It would be even better, much better than Florida Street or Santa Fe Avenue, to go to Mar del Plata. There, by the sea, she would find rich customers, as well as waves, foam, and sand. She felt her body expand in anticipation of this happiness.

"If I worked, we could even go to the sea," she dared to urge Alejandro.

"So you want to work, eh? You think you're capable of doing something. All right, if you want to work, I'll find you a job. But don't come to me later saying it's too hard for you."

Hard, nothing would be too hard; nothing could be worse than these hotels and this loneliness.

What was truly hard to bear was her hatred of this life, a

hatred flat and round as a coin; she felt it growing inside her, agitating and stretching her as if it were a child.

She tried to smile at Alejandro, but it was too late; he had already begun to think that Clara was slipping through his fingers. She was volatile, subtle. She was slipping away and he couldn't stop her. To dominate her, to consume her completely, it wasn't enough to leave her alone in a hotel room. She would always find an escape. To possess her in any way he had had to marry her. He would now have to humiliate her, perhaps break her in two, to get her to surrender.

Clara smiled at him again. Hell, he thought, she is slipping away. She was like gelatin, slippery, but he always had her at his finger tips and one day he thought he could catch her. She had to be humiliated, why hadn't he thought of that before?

"I know of a job that's just right for you. You can't do anything, so I have in mind a job doing nothing. Exactly right for a person like you. This morning I met a guy who runs a traveling fair, and he told me he needed an Aztec Flower, a head without a body. It's perfect timing, but don't come to me later saying you don't like it. If we accept, we're committed. Tomorrow I'll buy what we need to get the act ready."

2   Clara felt happy. It was an inexplicable, unfamiliar, almost forgotten sensation. It overflowed her body, she was in the center of a halo of happiness that made her jump and dance. Alejandro would say, "Hand me the hammer," and she would hum, "Hammer, hammer," and twirl around it without seeing it. "Come help me hold this board," Alejandro would say, and she

would hold the board, frowning with concentration, eager to do her job well. Neither the heat, nor the flies, nor the poor light in the room bothered her any longer. At last, she was shoulder to shoulder with Alejandro, helping him, building something with him. Never, except in bed, had she felt so close to him, and bed didn't count because that was another matter, a different kind of closeness. This was the way marriage should be, complete, each of them working to create something that would go on after them.

He seemed content, too, and murmured under his breath, "The box is working out just right. We'll have to paint it before we put in the mirrors, and that should do it."

Such pretty mirrors, and all for me. Eight well-cut mirrors. Eight great mirrors just to cover me. We'll have a spot in a real amusement troupe. We'll travel around the world like circus people. We'll be with happy people, people who laugh. Now nobody can stop me from going to the fair, because I *am* the fair. And traveling from city to city, one day we'll get to the sea.

"The sea, the sea, the waves of the sea," she sang.

"What did you say?"

"Nothing. I was just singing."

"I heard you say something. See what?"

"Not to see; the ocean, the sea. Do you think we'll get there someday?"

"Oh, you and your sea! When you get an idea in your head, God Almighty can't get it out. I tell you, madam, I repeat; in the summer we can't go to the Atlantic coast because the beaches are filled with rich people who wouldn't dream of coming to see us. We're only good for the backwoods, where miserable provincials have never seen anything worth while in their lives."

"You say that, but my act will be sensational, the wonder of the century, something people will fall all over each other to see."

"Sensational? There are millions and millions of Aztec Flowers who have done, are doing, and will do the same thing as you, and nobody cares. Millions and millions of severed heads. Alive. And all the same."

"Maybe I'll be . . ."

"Maybe you will. Let's do it without tricks: I'll behead you and you'll manage to smile coquettishly, gracefully. And I'll hold your head in the palm of my hand and we'll become millionaires."

"You're disgusting. You want to cut off my head, and you expect me to pretend I'm alive!"

"Hell! You don't even want to try to be different."

She shrugged. Life was a bitch. It didn't give her a chance. However, it would be nice to try; she'd have to investigate some magic formula. She started to compose a song:

I'm the head without a body, hurrah for me, hurrah for me.
I open my eyes, I close my mouth, hurrah for me.
I'm pure head, I'm God's wonder, hurrah for me.

"Don't make such a racket. Stop jumping around. You're making me nervous. Stop acting like a crazy kid."

"I'm not a crazy kid, señor. You're mistaken. I'm sane. Don't you see I'm all head?"

Alejandro scratched his neck with indifference. "All right, we did enough for today. It's getting dark. We'll finish tomorrow."

"Tomorrow? Don't be so mean. Let's finish today so we can rehearse."

"Rehearse? The most stupid woman could play the Aztec Flower. We can finish it tomorrow, because I don't have to go to work. I have to make the box. The rest is nothing. Now let me measure your neck for the hole."

He put his hands around her neck as if to strangle her, pushed her softly to the bed, and threw himself on top of her.

The Head

After making love, Alejandro reached for his cigarettes on the night table. He lit one, but forgot about it until the hot tip burned his fingers. He was confused: he had been able to possess Clara through happiness and not, as he had believed, through shame or humiliation. The realization made him feel almost bad. Clara, so mysterious, hid dark thoughts behind her childish phrases. Clara, who never talked about herself, would let herself be disarmed without a struggle in exchange for a simple, slight, and almost useless moment of happiness. His mission would be to make her happy, always, so that he could reach and know every particle of her. But he felt weary in anticipation. It was hard work to make people happy, hard and without rewards. It wasn't the same as causing pain. Making someone suffer produces a pleasant warmth in the belly while the sufferer moans and twists.

He crushed the cigarette against the night table and lit another, thinking, Cigarettes and people are made to be crushed, you're better off without them. Some people don't crush cigarettes, they just throw the butts away, carelessly. They're the passionless. On the other hand, those who mercilessly squelch a butt in the ashtray, break it as if it were a flower, those are the ones to love or to hate and, above all, to fear.

Clara didn't smoke; she could avoid wasteful diversions and concentrate completely on her new-found happiness. She spent a sleepless night, but she realized that at last her destiny would come true—the red one, the passionate one, the one she herself had chosen. Everything she had done until then, the horrible and the inconsequential, had to be erased, discarded. She stirred in bed, unable to control her excitement; the bed creaked.

The object was not to think any more of the past. It could spoil her present. She had to look ahead. She and Alejandro would be working together, each doing for the other what had to be done to make one splendid performance. Someday they would perform in a movie house that had a real stage show, and later in a theater with real velvet curtains and an orchestra. She remembered the dining room of the hotel in Tres Lomas. It had once been a theater and still had its high ceiling, its darkness, and long faded red curtains that separated the dining room from the front desk. As a child, every time she went into that dining room, she had dreamed of being a performer. Marrying Alejandro had been the right choice, after all. She wanted to wake him in order to talk about projects, make plans for the future. She couldn't help moving, and each time she did the bedsprings creaked louder. Alejandro grumbled, "Are you sick or something?" "I feel fine." Now she had a new element for the building of her happiness: he was concerned about her health. Nobody had ever asked her how she felt, except for Don Mario, who had been somewhat paternal.

At dawn she was ready to jump out of bed and finish her box of mirrors, but Alejandro was still asleep, and she decided not to wake him.

You have to be careful with happiness, it's so fragile and precious. It can break just as you're getting close.

It was ten-thirty when Alejandro got up. Clara made coffee for him in the pot she always carried with them.

"Are we going to paint it?" she asked, pointing to the frame they had built the previous day.

"Yes, we'll finish it this afternoon."

"What color will you paint it? I'd like it to be red, but it could also be green or yellow."

"You can't help yourself, can you? Fantasy is so much a part of you. This clumsy thing is supposed to look like a table. It has to be brown. You'll see; when the mirrors are attached, the illusion will be perfect—a table with four thin legs and nothing between them."

"And my head will stay on the table?"

"Of course."

"How wonderful! I'll be able to smile at everybody and wink and even stick out my tongue if I feel like it; a head without a body doesn't know what it's doing."

"Sure, play games and see what happens. Now hurry up and hand me the can of paint that's under the bed. At noon I have to see the boss of that traveling show. After all, we still aren't sure they'll hire us."

"You won't have lunch with me?"

"No, I'll have lunch with him. For your own good. They don't have an Aztec Flower and I'm almost sure they'll hire you. And me too, I hope."

"Fantastic!" Clara shouted, flinging her arms around his neck.

Alejandro returned at three o'clock. Clara jumped out of bed in her petticoat and opened the door.

"What did he say?"

"Don't shout, don't shout! It's siesta time."

"Why so considerate? They didn't hire us, did they?" She was shaking him to get him to answer.

"Yes, but only you. They have two magicians already. They don't want me. But I can announce your act."

"What's the difference? As long as we're working together. I'm almost finished with the dragons on your jacket. You can wear it when you announce me. The secret pockets I sewed in won't be of any use now. But you could always do one or two magic tricks to distract the people from looking at me. So they won't see how we did it."

"Now you see it, now you don't."

Clara didn't pay any attention to him. "You can announce me with a lot of blather, like Marcovecchio used to do. Remember how well he talked? Wasn't he a genius at announcing you? Are we going to work in a theater or a circus? How pretty a circus must be inside, with wild animals and horses and wise monkeys. I've been to the circus four times."

"What circus are you talking about? This fair is the same as all the others we've been in; each performer has his own booth. You even have to get your own customers."

"You're so good at that kind of thing. You'll get millions of customers. And I'll be the queen of the fair. You'll see. A queen without a body, but a queen at last. Do you think it would be a good idea for me to wear a little crown?"

"I think it would be a good idea for you to shut up. Get me a beer; I'm dying of thirst."

Clara put on a dress and a pair of sneakers and went to the hotel dining room. When she returned with the beer, Alejandro was sprawled across the bed, naked and asleep.

She sat at the edge admiring his body: it had the grace of a sleeping tiger's. Then she looked at the box that was already taking shape. The only thing that remained to be done was to attach the mirrors that now were propped against the wall, returning the image of her feet swinging a few inches from the floor.

They'll cover me completely. It's a shame—after all, I'm not in bad shape. But no. No regrets. It's a blessing that at last I can work with my head alone and not with this body that always gets me in trouble.

She knelt in front of the mirror and smiled.

"Why didn't you wake me up sooner?" Alejandro said the minute he opened his eyes. "It's very late, and we have to finish this piece of junk tonight. Shit! This beer is warm." He put on his undershorts and touched the painted table, grumbling, "It's so damn humid, nothing is going to dry."

You're going to spoil my happiness. You'll get into the habit of complaining, and then you won't be able to stop yourself.

"When do we start?" Clara asked.

The Head

"Start, start. As if I haven't been working all my life."

"But I haven't, and I want to start so we can always be to-gether, always." She kissed him on the back of his head.

"Oh, leave me alone. You're tickling me." But he laughed. She kissed him on the cheek.

"You're worse than a mosquito."

"But a mosquito that loves you a lot."

Alejandro took her in his arms gruffly and kissed her on the mouth, leaving her lips wet and stinging.

"That isn't the kiss of a mosquito," she said. "It's big, like a hippopotamus."

When you're happy, everything is easy. A few kisses and Ale-jandro is calm again.

Perhaps it was her fault he was so surly and discontent; all he needed was a bit of tenderness.

Alejandro put his hands around her neck. "Do you have a tape measure? Let's measure you so I can saw the hole in the cover of the box."

She handed him the tape measure and he put it around her neck. Then he whistled admiringly.

"Fifteen inches. A pretty neck to choke. I can do it with one hand."

"Just try. I'll bite you and scratch you and kick you."

"We'll try that tonight. Now hand me the saw and hold the cover for me. We can't waste any more time; we have to leave for Entre Rios at dawn."

"In one of those trailers?"

"Of course not. By train, like good and happy bourgeoisie. They take over one or two cars and pay for all of us."

"Is it a long trip?"

"I have no idea. We change at the capital; Entre Rios is far away. We're going to a city called Urdinarrain."

"A city! A much more important place than all these miserable little towns. We're getting ahead. Oh, Alejandro, be careful with the saw!"

With precision, Alejandro sawed a semicircle in each cover and then screwed the hinges to the borders of the table. The covers lifted up, and in the center was an opening like a trap.

Clara was full of admiration. She had the most skilled husband in the world, capable of building unique and magic things.

"You're a genius. You do everything so well."

"I'm an architect who's only good for handyman work." Clara wondered why he became sad when all she had done was praised him.

"Let's get the mirrors on," she said to put an end to his sadness. "Will my head be reflected in each of them?"

"Your head, thank God, won't be reflected at all. But hurry, we have to be at the station at three in the morning."

He took one of the mirrors and put it against a board that was diagonal to the legs of the table.

"Why are you putting it that way, inside? I won't fit."

"You'll have to shrink a bit, my dear. And don't talk so much. The delicate part of the job begins now. Give me another mirror. Fast, otherwise this one will move out of place."

"Fool!" The cry remained floating in the air and Clara didn't dare raise her eyes; she could only look at her hands, astonished, as if they didn't belong to the rest of her body. At her feet, the pieces of the broken mirror glittered. She didn't remember the crashing sound of the glass when it had fallen a moment ago. She could see only her sweaty, treacherous hands. It had slipped away from her without any effort, without a warning, but with a certain grace. Clara began to cry; her sobbing made her whole body shake while Alejandro squinted at her accusingly.

Fool, fool, fool, she repeated to herself with each spasm, as Alejandro insulted her without words.

The Head

After a long silence, he finally spoke. "You had to ruin everything. You keep bringing bad luck. What if we can't find a glass dealer in Urdinarrain who can cut a mirror for us? The best thing we can do is hang ourselves."

He dismantled the table boards angrily, wrapped everything carelessly in an old blanket, and tied the package with a rope. Clara blew her nose and asked, "Aren't we going to try the table?"

He didn't bother to answer.

3   The train trip was like so many Clara had taken through La Pampa Province with Alejandro. The other passengers were happy as they passed a bottle around. Some of them were singing. They were all her fellow workers, but she was unable to speak a word to them, because from the corner of her eye, she could see Alejandro, sullen and withdrawn, his arms folded across his chest. A fat woman opposite them kept opening her wicker basket to take out something to eat. When she chewed, her cheeks became deformed, and Clara watched this in fascination. Finally, the fat woman noticed her persistent gaze and offered her a sandwich. Clara answered, "No, thank you," in a faint voice.

"Why not?" the woman insisted. "Try one, they're fresh. I wrap them in a damp napkin so they won't dry out."

"No, thank you; I have no appetite," although she was dying of hunger. The last food she had had was lunch the day before. "That way, at least, you'll pay for the mirror," Alejandro had told her. She really did want to pay for it and, as an act of contrition, refused whatever was offered to her.

The fat woman stopped worrying about Clara and continued to dispose of the pile of sandwiches.

In the morning haze, Clara looked at the landscape of endless fields. The low horizon was occasionally broken by groups of trees that marked the entrance to a hacienda. Tres Lomas was probably not far off, but for too many years she had not thought much about her town, and now she could no longer depend on her memories. Alejandro had fallen asleep, and Clara knew that even in his dreams he was sorry he had married her. He wasn't the only one; she, too, was sorry sometimes that she had taken that step without thinking much about it. As if it were a game.

The fat woman spoke to her again, startling her.

"What did you say?"

"Do you have a newspaper? We have to cover everything and close the windows. The dust is getting to be hell. It even gets in your teeth."

Clara didn't have a newspaper. She was surprised to see that the tall stack of sandwiches had disappeared. To hide her feelings, she casually ran her fingers through her hair, as if to fix a rebel lock; it was dry and brittle. If only she could go to a beauty parlor to have her hair done up in a style suitable for her debut.

But Alejandro won't give me a penny; I'll have to wash it myself and roll it in rag curlers as soon as we get to the hotel.

"Who can give me a newspaper," the fat woman shouted suddenly. "I've got to shut the window because of this damn dust!"

"Stick your ass out of the window and there'll only be one crack to cover," someone yelled from the back of the car. Everyone laughed, everyone except the fat woman, of course, and Clara, who was not in the mood for jokes.

At last a newspaper was passed to the woman. She went to the toilet at the end of the car and returned with the paper wet and rolled up. Carefully, she tucked it around the edges of the window to cover any opening. When the job was finished, she fell back onto the hard wooden seat with a sigh of relief.

"Now we'll be more comfortable, you'll see." She turned to Clara. "You're new here, aren't you? We're all good people. Once the tents are up, we get along very well. I have a shooting gallery. I make a pyramid of cans and people throw cloth balls at them. We have good prizes and it's a lot of fun. The kind of young people I like always come. I used to have rifles, but they give me the creeps. I prefer the balls. What do you do?"

"Me? The Aztec Flower."

"The Aztec Flower? It's been a long time since we've had one in our group. The last one left a year and three months ago, to be exact. One day she said she was sick and tired of spending her life shut in a box and she decided to stay in Bragado with a plumber. She was a very good girl. My name is Chola, Chola Pedrazzi. What's yours?"

Clara was listening with such intensity that for a moment she couldn't answer. Finally she managed to articulate, "Clara."

"Have you been working as an Aztec Flower for a long time?"

"No, I'm just starting. This is the first time I'll have to use my head in my work. I'm very happy."

"It sure doesn't show."

A vendor went by with a basket of drinks, and Chola Pedrazzi bought a beer. Clara had to tell her she didn't want anything, but her throat was so dry it felt as if it would crack at any moment. Alejandro was still asleep, his head against the wall of the train. Better that way. He couldn't look at her with accusing eyes.

After hours of traveling, they arrived at Once, the terminal Clara would have preferred to forget. They had to go to Lacroce terminal to take the train for Entre Rios. The tents and other material had gone by truck with the boss. Alejandro found out when the train was scheduled to leave and decided they would take a bus to the terminal.

As they crossed the square, Clara remembered that other square, with the grass and the clock tower. Her waiting post.

I want to tear myself away from Alejandro. I want to run, to return to the side entrance of Parque Retiro, where I could lose myself in memories of that brief happiness I once knew. I want to run away, but the heat is unbearable. Always a situation I don't want, always being held or pushed around.

Angry but meek, she got in line for the hateful bus that would take her to the next train and Alejandro's hateful silence.

When they got off the bus at Lacroce, Alejandro told her to wait for him. Handing her a wad of one-peso bills, he disappeared behind the swinging doors of a bar where a long table had been set up for the members of the fair. To placate her stomach and everything else inside her that was complaining, Clara bought herself a cheese sandwich and an orangeade. She didn't leave a tip, and she carefully wrapped the change in her handkerchief; every penny counted toward payment for the broken mirror.

On the train to Entre Rios, Alejandro chose the last seat of the car, where nobody could spy on them and where there was no fat woman to chat with Clara. Her weariness overcame her, and she fell asleep.

When she woke up, she was surprised to find the train floating on the Paraná River. She couldn't resist getting off the train to explore the ferryboat and to go up onto the bridge, where a few passengers were huddled together. Below, the river ran slowly and heavily; it made her want to close her eyes. She would have enjoyed sitting on the floor, holding on to one of the rails and letting her legs dangle over the side, but there are many things a woman cannot allow herself to do when she is alone.

Loneliness is like that; it's not so much the lack of company, it's the impossibility of doing a thousand little things you'd like to do but that are only justifiable in a group. Like playing on a swing in a square at night, or watching a billiard game, or sitting with your legs swinging in the breeze. Perhaps, instead of running after men, it would have been better if I'd gotten myself a few girl friends, friendly types, the kind you can have a good time with.

She stood there, her elbows on the rail, her mind drifting, trying to imagine that the green color of the islands was caressing her cheeks.

I'd be happy there, without dust or heat or trains, my feet in the water all day and my head under the shady trees.

The crossing lasted two hours. When she was told to return to the train, she said to Alejandro, "I have a headache."

"Good. That's what you get for staying out in the hot sun."

He knew, however, that he didn't have the right to treat her like that. She had gone a whole day with almost no food, very little sleep, and no complaining. Deep inside, he admired her. He wanted to possess and humiliate her, but at the same time he admired her. It was a pain. That trusting head resting on his shoulder made him nervous. She was good; he was forcing her to lead a dog's life, and instead of apologizing, he battered her with reproaches. It was unfair, very unfair, but he couldn't help it. Others had to pay for what he could have been and wasn't. His need for revenge was fierce and demanding, and he forgave no one, least of all Clara, who was, despite her courage and generosity, a whore he had found on the street. He hated her; he hated her and he had married her exactly for that reason.

Clara wasn't able to fall asleep on Alejandro's shoulder. She felt an intense current radiating from his body, which shook her, agitated her, ruined anything good that came her way. When she was near him her blood stirred in mysterious ways. Alejandro was powerful in his hatred, he was contaminating her. I hate him, she said to herself, I hate him.

Alejandro felt like the master of the truth, and he was astonished. I married her because I hate her, he kept telling himself, and the constant thought of how horrible it must be to be married to him made him want to laugh. And he vomited a hearty laugh. Clara didn't hear him. She slept until they reached Urdinarrain.

4   "Put everything up carefully, boys. We're staying fifteen days," the boss shouted, strutting around the empty lot where the fair was being mounted. "Put everything up carefully."

There were sighs of relief, there were complaints. There were those who thought of taking a rest and those who wished they could leave this place as soon as possible.

Clara and Alejandro were indifferent. Fifteen days in one place or another were all the same to them. The day before, their day off, they had had to work: they looked for a glass dealer, had the mirror cut to exact measure, and worked late into the night putting the table together. When they finally went to bed, Alejandro left the light on, to annoy Clara.

The next morning she was exhausted. She helped Alejandro put up the tent. She felt sick to her stomach, her temples were pounding, she was unable to coordinate her movements.

In spite of everything, the tent is pretty, with those green and yellow stripes and overhead the sign saying "Aztec Flower" in different-colored letters. I should be proud. It's going up little by little; first the frame made of pipes, then one wall of canvas, then another, and finally the roof with an overhang of yellow fringe, like blond bangs.

As the tent got closer to completion, her enthusiasm increased, and she told herself that the previous Aztec Flower had been a fool to leave this life to live with a plumber.

I'll never leave this tent, even if Alejandro beats me and yells at me.

Her affection also grew as the tent went up. Her affection grew for the structure that would, in a sense, be her home.

Alejandro, on the other hand, didn't forget so easily. He wallowed in his hatred. "Stop singing like a fool and work," he would grumble, or "Don't you see this rope is loose? You're good for nothing." She would act as if she had heard nothing, concentrating instead on a banner that had just been unfurled or a stage curtain with its dazzling print of forest and flowers, a little faded perhaps, but so real.

Voices were echoing on all sides, shouting greetings or orders. Clara, too, wanted to shout and sing, even to applaud and run, but Alejandro's frown curtailed her impulses. Some distance away, she spotted the fat woman from the train, loaded down with boards. She waved enthusiastically and was pleased when the fat woman gave her a friendly nod in return. Later, she decided to rest a bit in the shade, and she walked some twenty steps to the nearest tree. When she got there she did an about-face, and she couldn't suppress a cry of amazement when she saw that all around their beautiful tent a city of canvas and metal had grown, drenched in color, with wheels and planes just like the ones in Parque Retiro. She wanted to run through the tents, to jump from place to place, to laugh and sing, but Alejandro scolded her.

"Get right back here and finish this thing if you don't want to have to work straight through lunch."

She rushed to lay out the canvas mat on the stony ground before Alejandro started hurling more insults.

Half an hour later, they went back to the hotel for lunch. Alejandro refused to go to the dining room with her and locked himself in their room. Clara found herself in front of the long table where everybody had already congregated, and she wished she were tiny so that nobody could see her. Everyone looked at her with curiosity, until the fat woman signaled to Clara to join her. Clara grabbed that signal as if it were a lifeline.

"Thank you, madam. Thank you."

"Call me Chola. We all get to know each other here, for better or worse. How do you like your tent?"

"It's pretty," she answered, taking a napkin.

"Not bad for a tent," Chola said. "Wear light clothes, though, or you'll die of the heat inside," and she turned her back to Clara to talk to her neighbor on the other side. She forgot about Clara for the rest of the meal.

Clara felt awkward. She didn't know where to look or how to start a conversation. A man asked her to pass the salt, but unfortunately she didn't hear him. When the coffee was brought in, the boss shouted, "I want to see everybody at the square at two-thirty sharp. We open at three; whoever's late doesn't work."

He got up and walked around the table, chatting, giving a pat on the back here, a reproach there. When he came to Clara, he asked, "Didn't your husband come to lunch?"

"No, he stayed in the room to rest."

"Don't forget to tell him he has to be at the square at two-thirty. Are you looking forward to your debut?"

"Yes, I can't wait."

"That's good," he said with a brief smile.

At two-thirty, when they arrived at the square, a lot of young people were already lined up, waiting. Clara walked past them with her head high, feeling their envious looks: now she belonged to that world on the other side of the ticket box. Begrudgingly, Alejandro had agreed to wear his silly jacket with the dragons, and he looked more handsome than ever. She wore a light dress and had fixed her hair as best she could, with curls that fell to her shoulders, or rather to the table.

There was a platform in her tent, and, on the platform, her table. Alejandro helped her up and lifted the two covers so she could get into the box. She installed herself there as best she could, with her knees against her chest, and he closed the covers that pressed lightly against her neck. The illusion was perfect, the dividing line down the center of the box invisible, and the two mirrors, placed at a forty-five-degree angle, gave the illusion that there was nothing between the table legs. Alejandro whistled in approval of his work and went to look for the boss.

"Great. Your living head is a thing of beauty"—he pinched Clara's cheek—"a thing of beauty. Well, here's your book of tickets. Try to speak effectively and attract a lot of people. All right, get ready. There's the bell. They're opening the gates."

Clara wanted to tell Alejandro that the edge of the two mirrors was sticking in her back and to ask him to please find a board she could lean on, but he had already disappeared. She also wanted to ask him for a kiss, at least, but she heard the voices and the shouts of children arriving.

Suddenly, Alejandro's voice rose above all others, like a storm, swooping up his audience. Then his voice lowered, softened, and spoke caressing, musical words filled with lures and promises. While he talked, she was able to forget the pain and remember the night she had met him, how imposing he had been on his pedestal. Now she was the one on a pedestal, or rather her head was. "A thing of beauty," the boss had said, and she felt happy.

Without warning, the curtains opened, and about ten people silently filed into the tent. Alejandro turned the lights on, and the ten people cried out at once in amazement. "Please don't touch," Alejandro kept saying, and the people moved around the platform, looking at her with a mixture of skepticism and astonishment. Clara smiled and stretched her neck languidly, while Alejandro explained that the formula for preserving a beheaded woman had been created by the Egyptian Pharaohs, the same ones who had built the pyramids and mummified the dead. They had kept the formula a jealously guarded secret for thousands of years, but the Aztec Indians had discovered it with the help of the magic juices of a plant found only in three places in the world. He had inherited the formula from his father, who had learned it from his grandfather, who was a descendant of the great Quetzalcoatl, the White God.

Clara watched Alejandro with the same fascinated look the public gave him, and she forgot to smile.

What he's saying can't be too far from the truth. After all, he has an Indian face, with that aquiline nose and dark skin.

When he finished his speech, Alejandro turned the lights on and ushered the people out, carefully making certain that no one outside could peek in. When the last spectator had disappeared, he approached Clara and whispered between his teeth, "Don't forget to smile."

When the next group came in, she remembered to smile, because there were two children who wanted to give her cotton candy to see if the head was able to eat. Clara, who loved cotton candy, would have taken a bit with pleasure, but Alejandro kept the people at a distance, saying, "Please don't touch, please don't touch."

The groups grew smaller as the afternoon grew older. Clara felt the drops of perspiration running along her forehead and slipping through her eyelashes, but her hands were locked in and she couldn't dry herself. When she closed her eyes, she saw only vast darkness. The air inside the tent was becoming unbearable. She wanted to talk to Alejandro, but he ran off whenever he had a chance.

After a long wait, a woman with five children came in, and Clara purposely didn't open her mouth.

"That head must be sad, loose like that, huh, Ma?" asked one of the children.

When they left, Alejandro came over to Clara and said angrily, "I told you to keep smiling."

"Let me out of here. I'm hot and I have a backache and cramps in my legs. Let me out.'

"No way. I have people waiting outside. I'm hot, too, in this damned jacket. You wanted to do this—now you've got to take it."

He turned and left without drying her sweat-soaked temples.

"Good," the boss said. "You had a good day yesterday. If you do the same today, we can sign a contract."

It was Sunday, and they had three sessions. Clara persuaded Alejandro to put a backboard in the box so she could get out when no one was around. She also managed to get a bucket of water, a soda, and a glass. At least she could wash her face, quench her thirst, and take an aspirin if she needed it.

She was more relaxed and in a better mood than she had been the day before. There were more people, and everyone was astonished and admiring. When blasts of heat seemed to suffocate her, when some edge in the box seemed to stick into her hips, when her legs grew numb, she would think of that red destiny. It was coming true, deliberately and neatly. That day they signed a two-year contract.

On Monday, the day off, the hotel was silent. The boss had loaded half the troupe into a big truck to go to neighboring towns and create a little publicity. Those left behind were trying to soak up the silence. Alejandro was napping, and Clara was beside him on the bed. She crossed her arms under her head and studied the disfiguring strains that years of humidity had left on the ceiling; she was looking for familiar shapes, as one does with clouds. But looking for familiar shapes was a bad sign. She was depressed.

That morning, on an enthusiastic impulse, she had gone out for a walk. Alejandro had given her a portion of the money she had earned the day before, and she decided to buy him a wedding gift at last, to make him realize that she loved him in spite of everything. A good belt, perhaps, or a striped shirt. But there wasn't a men's store worthy of Alejandro in Urdinarrain; there were only a few general stores and a gunsmith's shop. Although she hated weapons, she stopped to look in the window of the gunsmith's shop on the chance that there might be something appealing. She discovered a straight razor with a mother-of-pearl handle, like the one her father had. Exactly what Alejandro needed.

She left the gunsmith's shop with the razor wrapped in silky paper and a wide smile across her face. She decided to see the town. It was like all the other towns she'd seen—more people, perhaps, but they were spread out in houses built at the edge of dusty streets. She pressed the gift close to her heart, until she turned a corner where two old ladies were sitting in a doorway. In a friendly voice, one of them asked her, "Out for a walk?" Clara thought they had recognized her and that they would accuse her of cheating. She turned abruptly and ran to the hotel: an Aztec Flower must never show her whole body.

Alejandro accepted the gift with no show of pleasure. "I don't need presents," he told her as he unwrapped it. "It's pretty, thank you, but I won't be able to use it. I cut myself with those old-fashioned things."

No gesture of gratitude. Nothing. The indifference she had so admired was beginning to get her down. She felt encircled by a suffocating loneliness—Alejandro awake on the bed was the same as Alejandro asleep, the only difference was that awake,

The Head

his eyes glistened as they watched the fine trail of cigarette smoke rise and disappear in the wet stains on the ceiling. At least in the old days she had been surrounded by men. Some were disgusting, true, but some knew how to chat and be kind and entertain her. She had had to give up everything except her loneliness; it was overwhelming. She felt she was being choked by loneliness. Asphyxiated.

A sudden inspiration gave her hope. She sat down on the bed, and looking straight into Alejandro's eyes, she said, "Alejandro, we should have a baby." A child to keep me company, she said to herself.

He went on smoking, indifferent, watching the smoke rise, as if he hadn't heard her.

"I want to have a baby," she insisted. "A baby."

He answereed without looking at her, without even taking the cigarette out of his mouth. "You've just begun to work and already you want to get out of it, right?"

"I don't want to get out of anything. I just want to have a baby. It won't be a bother to you at all, I promise."

"You don't think you'll have to stop working, eh? Do you think I should build a billiard table so your big belly can fit?"

Clara bit her lower lip. She had wanted to use her head so much, but she hadn't realized it meant forgetting the rest of her body. She wondered if being an Aztec Flower really was her destiny, or if she had been mistaken once again. She wished she could read her little red paper, but to avoid temptation she had burned it a month ago. Too bad. It might have explained everything.

The next day they started to work at six in the evening. Although the temperature in the tent was pleasant, Clara felt oppressed and couldn't make the slightest effort to do well. "Smile, smile, you ingrate. Keep smiling," he whispered to her between threats, but she could only manage a weak grin and think of her child.

The weekday nights were empty and sad. Few customers, little money, little joy. For three nights Clara could only manage a weak grin, which she wore the following morning and afternoon as well. Several days passed this way, until one midnight, when they were returning to the hotel and Alejandro condescended to talk to her.

"We can't go on like this; each day we get fewer customers. We're going from bad to worse, and next weekend we'll really hit bottom. The same people come to the fair. Nobody pays twice to see the Aztec Flower. It's not like the shooting gallery or the ferris wheel. We have to think of something new. Think."

Clara didn't feel like thinking. She felt like forgetting, and she went to sleep as soon as her head hit the pillow. Alejandro didn't turn off the light, however, and he woke her up two hours later.

"I've got it," he said, shaking her. "I know what we'll do. Be glad you've got me—you couldn't think up anything new yourself. Look, we'll put your box outside the tent every so often, and we'll make people pay to see how the trick is done. A great idea, right? The same ones that paid before will pay again, out of curiosity. First I'll put you in the box and charge as usual. Then I'll take the mirrors away to show how it's done, and I'll charge them again. The only ones who get burned are the suckers who come to see the Aztec Flower thinking it's a marvel."

"But that's like undressing in public," Clara protested, still half asleep.

"Oh? You're shy now? You were a whore in your youth! What the hell do you care? Don't be a fool; don't go looking for trouble. Now I'll have to get a table with wheels to put your box on. Something that's strong but easy to push outside the tent."

She was confused. Did she or didn't she work with her head? Now that beast wanted everyone to see her as she truly was, with a miserable body she no longer wished to show all hunched up inside a box, with her legs parted by mirrors set at an angle. Alejandro was becoming more and more loathsome.

On Friday night, they presented the trick as usual, but Alejandro had already prepared for the following day. He made the preparations with the same kind of care with which a hangman readies the gallows. The boss agreed to the plan, and he even wanted Clara to wear a white satin bathing suit he had in storage, but she refused emphatically. With the sequins that were left over from Alejandro's jacket, she embroidered the edge of a wide green skirt that would cover her legs.

Perhaps the weekend would turn out to be marvelous. Actually, it was much better to be outside the tent, beneath the canopy, than to be inside, dying of heat. Besides, she could see the life of the fair, the colors and the activity. She looked everywhere, fascinated with the balloons and the merry-go-round loaded with children. It wasn't hard for her to smile: she was surrounded by people, and many of them were happy to pay, even knowing they had been deceived. Then Alejandro would roll her into the tent, lift the covers, and dismantle one of the mirrors. She would get out of the box in a few graceful moves and ask the people inside the tent to be kind enough not to reveal the secret to the people outside. She enjoyed talking to the public—it made her feel like an actress.

It was during the high point of that Sunday, when happiness had reached its climax, that Clara discovered the blond girl. She was standing apart from the crowd, under a tree opposite the Aztec Flower's tent. She had been there a long time, Clara realized, and she had no intention of leaving. All day, Alejandro rolled the table inside and out again, and the blond girl stood there, always under the same tree, her long hair loose in the wind, her heavy breasts rising and falling as she breathed.

Alejandro talked nonstop, and he never took his eyes off the girl. As soon as he had sold a fair number of tickets, he pushed Clara inside the tent. The fourth time around, he helped Clara back into the box, but instead of pushing it outside, he left her there, imprisoned in the tent. He came back almost immediately, but Clara already felt a hatred so intense she was afraid it would shatter the mirrors.

"Smile, stupid. Keep smiling," Alejandro insisted.

5   Monotony was the sound of a train with rain slapping against its windows. They had been traveling like that for many hours, but Clara still couldn't contain the realization that at last she was going to see the ocean.

The day before, Wednesday, at lunchtime, the boss had announced, "That's it, boys. Tomorrow we go to Mar del Plata."

"Bah," somebody had said. "First we have to put up with the heat, and now that summer has ended, they hit us with Mar de Plata so we can freeze to death."

Although she was struggling against her own skepticism, Clara had also told herself "bah." For the last three nights, Alejandro had gotten up silently and had not returned until morning. Accustomed to living with men who were not hers, Clara didn't know how to claim the one who was hers. Through half-closed eyes she watched him leave and come back. What a nasty business! He was her legal husband and had no right to betray her like that; it was an easy and mean way to avoid having a child.

That isn't going to stop me from having a child with another man. I'll choose one who's healthy and strong and handsome. It's too bad I signed one contract to be faithful forever to Alejandro and another to play the Aztec Flower for two years. I wish I'd never learned to write. I'm tied, feet, hands, and head. This is not my destiny! I'll fight to change everything one more time.

The train cut across the plain and the fine rain followed it. The landscape was much greener, with more trees, but it no longer interested her. She no longer cared whether or not she went to the sea. She leaned her head on the back of the wooden seat and half closed her eyes. Alejandro looked to see if she was asleep, and she thought again how much she hated him. He was thinking the same thing—the body of the girl from Entre Rios had been soft and ample and deep, and he had had to leave her and wander through the world saying, "Ladies and gentlemen, I have the great honor of presenting the marvel of all time, the mystery of ancient Indians that even now, in this mechanical age, astonishes and disturbs us," and then to open the curtains of the tent to see Clara's tired, worn-out head that didn't even smile.

The train entered the terminal and they got off. They were near the sea; if she breathed deeply, perhaps she could smell it. But she only felt the cold creeping inside her, and she wrapped herself tightly in her thin coat. Her winter coat had been left behind in Alejandro's room, and now she missed it. She missed many things; she felt forsaken. The black coat she wore now had only two buttons, and they opened at every step because the buttonholes were too big; besides, the back was worn out and the fabric no longer had its nappy finish. With her left hand, she raised the collar to keep her neck warm, and with her right she picked up the suitcase. She walked behind Alejandro toward still another hotel.

When they finished supper, she asked him to go with her to see the ocean.

"Ridiculous. Don't you see it's dark and raining?"

She wanted to tell him that the rain didn't matter, that she had dreamed of seeing the ocean for too long to let that stop her now.

"If you don't come with me, I'll go alone," she protested.

"I don't care. You can go to hell alone. But then you'll catch a cold and want me to wipe your runny nose when you're in the box."

Clara went to their room obediently, but when Alejandro went to the bathroom, she sneaked out and tiptoed down the stairs.

She ran two or three blocks. The deserted and dark streets were hostile, the cobblestones were destroying her shoes. Finally, the cold defeated her and she stopped under a street lamp to catch her breath. Her lungs hurt, and every time she inhaled, she felt as if a thousand icy needles were pricking her insides. But she kept moving ahead, straining to hear the sound of waves. She imagined the designs made by the foam at the edge of the beach, and that gave her the strength to go on. Once or twice she thought she heard steps behind her, and she tried to hurry: Alejandro might be coming after her, to force her to return to that sordid hotel.

Another sordid hotel, like all the others. I can't run any more. Alejandro will catch me and my destiny will be to live forever inside the hotel, and inside the tent, and inside the box, and inside all those things. Me, shut in by boxes and tents and hotels. Because I signed.

Darkness, loneliness, cold. Darkness, loneliness, cold. Each

The Head

step was a painful echo. The rain had soaked through her clothes and was trickling down her back. The only warmth came from the tears flowing from her eyes, until they too turned against her and froze, tracing icy furrows on her cheeks.

She stopped. It wasn't worth getting to the sea in the state she was in. It no longer mattered how beautiful the sea might be. She had to change her situation first, shake off everything bad in her life, everything that imprisoned her. When she faced the sea she had to be free as the sea itself, able to feel one with it.

She lost her way returning to the hotel. She wandered through the deserted, badly lit streets. At last she found the faded sign. She was soaked and exhausted, but she had made a decision, and that decision kept her on her feet.

Alejandro was sleeping, as if nothing had happened. Her hatred was stifling: he hadn't even taken the trouble to look for her.

Good. That way I'll have no regrets.

Her first impulse was to smash Alejandro with some heavy object, in the kind of rage he himself had taught her.

Fury is more contagious than love, or anxiety, or desire.

From the mirror, her own reflection looked at her with bitterness. She felt like breaking it, but she closed her fists tightly and drove her nails into the palms of her hands. That slight pain helped her to regain control. Breaking a mirror wasn't what she had to do in order to free herself from him forever, from her terrible and wandering imprisonment, from that wooden box squeezing her on all sides.

She tiptoed to her suitcase and opened it. With systematic care, she took out her nightgown, a jacket, and a towel. She undressed, dried her hair, and put on the nightgown and jacket.

At the bottom of the suitcase she found the razor. She had kept it out of pity, unable to leave it abandoned on the night table where Alejandro had left it. Now it wasn't exactly pity that moved her to look for it.

Alejandro was stretched out in bed. She took a close look at him. Neither the dim light of the lamp nor her movements had awakened him.

Clara went to bed with the razor hidden up her sleeve, like a cheating gambler. She was determined to play fair, however; only blood, lots of blood, and then freedom.

I have to be careful. First of all, I mustn't tremble.

Softly, she slipped the razor under the pillow to wait there for the right moment, when Alejandro was in his deepest dream, when the light of sunrise would illuminate the most delicate part of his throat, the part that throbbed when he breathed. The razor, thank God, was sharp. It would cut a hair in the air, and it would cut the veins without touching the throat. So easy.

Everyone knew Alejandro liked to sleep late. No one would look for him until lunchtime. Maybe, if she asked them not to disturb him, they would leave him lying there until the day they had to take their tents down. By then she would be far away, without contracts or signatures. If she destroyed all their documents, how would anyone know who she was? Free, like the sea. In the meantime, just a little effort to remain calm. Calm.

A persistent ray of sun made her ear warm and woke her up. Desperately, she discovered it was already full daylight. Too late to do anything. Her first thought was of the razor. She had to hide it. She slipped her hand under the pillow but she couldn't find the slippery surface of the mother-of-pearl handle. Nothing. She searched further behind the pillow and then behind the bed. The razor was no longer there.

Her blood froze when she realized that she was alone in the bed, that Alejandro had deserted his place, leaving only the indentation of his body. She buried her head under the pillow

The Head

and wanted to disappear, but his voice brought her back to reality.

"Were you looking for this?"

She turned around, startled, and saw him there, at the far end of the room, with the razor open in his hand. He looked like Asmodeo about to jump, and her terror wouldn't let her guess the great magic trick Alejandro was envisioning.

Suddenly, he was the Juggler, the first card of the Tarot, symbol of the living god playing with life and death. He was the Juggler and he licked his lips as he approached the Aztec Flower with dancing steps.

Clara saw the gleam in his eyes, and she knew that much more than her throat was threatened.

It's my destiny. It's useless to try to escape now, to scream or try to defend myself. I'll be the head without a body. Done without tricks or mirrors. My head will be on a real table, under which Alejandro will crawl, carrying Asmodeo's black, furry body.

At last Alejandro had her at his mercy, as he had wanted to have her from the start. She would never slip through his fingers again. Clara raised her eyes meekly and stared into his.

"Keep smiling," she said. "You must keep smiling."